By Isabelle Holland

A Fatal Advent

A Fatal Advent

ISABELLE HOLLAND

DOUBLEDAY

NEW YORK
LONDON
TORONTO
SYDNEY
AUCKLAND

M

Holland

Oct. 20, 1989

PUBLISHED BY DOUBLEDAY

a division of Bantam Doubleday Dell Publishing Group, Inc.,
666 Fifth Avenue, New York, New York 10103

DOUBLEDAY and the portrayal of an anchor with a dolphin are
trademarks of Doubleday, a division of Bantam Doubleday
Dell Publishing Group, Inc.

Library of Congress Cataloging-in-Publication Data
Holland, Isabelle.
     A fatal advent / Isabelle Holland. —1st ed.
        p.   cm.
     ISBN 0-385-24815-6 :
     I. Title.
   PS3558.O3485F3   1989
813'.54—dc20   89-11797
                                                        CIP

ISBN 0-385-24815-6

I would like to offer my sincere thanks for their help and encouragement to
The Reverend Robert Stafford,
Curate,
and to
Dr. Gerre Hancock, Mus. Doc.,
Organist and Master of Choristers
of
St. Thomas Church, Fifth Avenue
New York City
and to
Mr. Gordon Clem, Headmaster,
The Choir School, St. Thomas Church.

A Fatal Advent

PROLOGUE

As the body fell, the man's surprised eyes seemed to stare back at the killer, as though wondering how such a thing could have happened in such a place. The killer looked down at the limbs spread out, the blind, demonic rage of a few minutes past receding.

If the old man had just kept his mouth shut, the killer thought, none of this would have occurred! But he kept going on and on, the Church at its most moralistic: Why did you do this? How on earth could you have done that? Don't you know right from wrong? The attitude and tone condescending and patronizing, generations of authority behind it.

Well, it was done now. The old man was silenced.

1

he trouble with Christmas, the Reverend Claire Aldington reflected, as she walked rapidly down the hall to the rector's study, was that it combined two powerful but frequently opposing forces in the same event: the high religious feast and the orgy of spending. She knew it was far from an original thought. She had, in fact, only that morning made a small bet with her husband, Brett Cunningham, that seventy-five percent of the Episcopal churches throughout the country would feature a sermon by the rector noting, deploring and/or castigating that very fact.

Her husband, wisely, refused to take it. "It's too easy," he said, handing her the C section of the New York *Times*. "How are you going to prove or disprove it?"

"You're probably right," she grumbled, taking the paper.

"In fact, you obviously are. Still, it's a pain! The post Christmas hangovers are frequently more financial than alcoholic!"

"Which becomes your department. Never mind, darling. You're better at binding up wounds than most!"

Brett had disappeared behind the business section of the paper, so he didn't see Claire's quick flush of pleasure. There had been amusement in his tone, but also another note that still had the power to move her in odd ways. They had been married almost a year. Brett, the cool, rather reserved banker, had turned out to be a tender and passionate lover, which had not surprised her at all. What still did, was her own reaction to his voice which managed to convey so much while saying something so totally ordinary.

Now, approaching the rector's study, she forced her attention back to whatever it was he wanted to talk to her about.

The Reverend Mark Hastings (Harvard, B.A.; Cambridge, M.A.; Union Theological Seminary, D.D.) had been rector of St. Anselm's only a month. After the stormy tenure of one rector and the brief office of the next, who had departed thankfully, glad to be called as dean to a small cathedral on the West Coast after only a few months, Mr. Hastings had set himself to bring peace and stability to the diverse and angry elements of the St. Anselm's congregation.

It was not proving easy. There was the old guard, the old-old guard, the yuppies and everyone else. The old guard, and the old-old guard, mostly comprised the well-to-do WASPs who had once made up one hundred percent of the congregation: the men who headed up corporations, law firms and investment banking houses and their wives. The difference between them was that, while both groups were fundamentally conservative, the old guard recognized the inexorable changes brought by the passage of time and was willing to spend money to aid social causes, whereas the old-old guard kept its feet firmly cemented in the 1950s. The yuppies came from a variety of ethnic backgrounds and, considering their poor reputation, were surprisingly generous.

Everyone else was made up of a few couples, a fair number

of single people in medium- to low-level jobs, and the very poor, both black and Hispanic, once members of St. Matthew's, St. Anselm's chapel, in the West Forties.

Built a century before by the wealthy St. Anselm's communicants to accommodate their immigrant servants, St. Matthew's Chapel, whose congregation had fallen to a handful, was now being phased out, the victim of changing populations and West Side gentrification. Sitting in what was originally a meadow, it was also placed strategically on a bedrock that would form the foundation of a huge luxury development and St. Anselm's was being offered top dollars for the site. Resistant at first, the previous rector, the vestry and the business manager of St. Anselm's finally counseled selling. To keep the dying church going was a severe strain on the diminishing fund that had been set up for it. In plain words, as the business manager pointed out, St. Anselm's could not afford to keep St. Matthew's going as well as continuing to pay the increasing sums for its outreach programs, which included shelter for the homeless, a hospice for the sick and halfway houses for addicts and teenage pregnant girls. The sum being offered would help finance these services, and a new vestry, made up from members of both St. Anselm's and St. Matthew's, had voted in favor of the sale.

The one holdout was the Reverend Joseph Martinez, vicar of St. Matthew's, an activist who felt, and did not mind saying loudly at every opportunity, that this was another example of the rich swallowing the poor out of sheer greed.

And then there were the homeless, who nightly used the basement of the parish house as shelter. Sixteen beds had been set up there, and a kitchen off the basement hall provided coffee, juice and buns early in the morning before the occupants were dispatched for the day. The previous rector had lobbied hard to have the city increase their allotment of beds, but the city laws were inexorable: only so many beds to so many bathroom facilities.

In addition there were the daily feedings of more homeless —usually around one hundred—in the basement. Those who occupied the beds and those who came to the feedings were not strictly speaking members, but they were a more or less continual presence. Volunteers from the church cooked and served the food, and other volunteers, usually two at a time, stayed overnight for the sake of the safety of the homeless themselves and, incidentally, of the church property.

The big basement room being now fully occupied both day and night, the church staff and volunteers had to shift for themselves in other—and frequently less convenient—of the parish house rooms.

As Maude Butler, the rector's secretary, when pushed too far, had been heard to exposulate, "If we are given one more activity which requires one more room, I, for one, will have hysterics! Between the homeless wandering in and out and up and down the stairs, and the choir boys racing around, it's like bedlam."

Claire knew that, while Maude, no great activist, was luke-warm—to say the least—about the mission to the homeless, she adored the boys, aged nine to thirteen, who made up St. Anselm's justly famous men and boys' choir and who spilled from the choir school across the street into some of the parish house rooms for extra classes, as well as into the choir practice room at the back of the first floor.

Everybody enjoyed the boys who could sometimes be wild and noisy, but on the whole were remarkably well behaved. The organist and choir master, Eric Fullerton, a sardonic man, was given to saying, "Thank God forty is all the school and choir will hold. Any more, and it wouldn't be bedlam, it would be World War III!"

As Claire was well aware how fond he and his wife were of the young choristers, she always grinned when she heard him muttering about the "little monsters."

She bumped into him now outside the rector's door. "Hello, Eric. How are the cherubs?"

"Far from cherubic. We're having to put in an extra hour's rehearsal beginning tomorrow morning," he said. "We can't let those English boys outshine us. It wouldn't be patriotic."

Claire glanced at him. "The Norwich choir. That's right. They're due about now, aren't they?"

"How can you be so blasé? For us, it's the big event of the year."

"Sorry. I know, and I'm looking forward to it. Besides the usual seasonal carols and hymns and the Festival of Carols, what else are you going to sing?"

Eric was about to answer when the Reverend Lawrence Swade rumbled up, looking, as he often did, somewhat disheveled. Like Claire, he was an Assistant Rector at St. Anselm's.

"Hello, Claire, hello Eric," he said. "Have you been summoned to the presence, too?"

"We have," Claire replied. "There was a message waiting for me that Mark wanted to see me at nine-thirty. I take it you got one."

"I did indeed. As usual, I was a little late, and there were not one but two messages stuck on my desk to that effect. I like Mark. I really do. But there are times when I wish he weren't so bloody prompt. He must get here at six in the morning, even on mornings when he doesn't take the early Eucharist. It probably comes from being single."

"Widowed," Claire corrected.

"All right," Larry said, "be pedantic."

"There are larks and there are nightingales," Claire said philosophically. "I've always thought of myself as a lark," she said. But lately—" And to her intense annoyance she blushed.

Eric grinned. "Ah, the joys of a new marriage! I—"

But at that moment the door swung open to reveal the rector. "I thought I heard you out here. Come in!"

The Reverend Mark Hastings was tall, lean and remarkably handsome. Fair-haired and blue-eyed, he was an American who looked and sometimes sounded like an Englishman. The son of a diplomat who had been stationed in London, he had gone to an English public school, as well as an American prep school, and had returned to England after Harvard to study Economics at Cambridge. He had seemed destined for a brilliant, scholarly career when he astonished everyone by being ordained as an Episcopal priest. Now forty-five, he had served as rector at large churches in Boston and Philadelphia before being called to St. Anselm's.

"Sorry for the early summons," he said. "But I have three bits of news, all connected with Advent and Christmas, and I thought the sooner the better, in view of the fact that Christmas is only three weeks off. Please—sit down!"

He moved quickly behind his desk and Eric, Claire and Larry seated themselves in the chairs in front of it.

"You alarm me," Claire said. "We're already short one staff member and—"

"Yes, well, that's my first piece of news. Relief is in sight sooner than we thought. As you know, the sale of St. Matthew's has finally gone through and the church closed down. So I've asked Joe Martinez to come help us out as a third assistant rector. The bishop's given his approval, and Joe's just about finished with the last of the mopping up involved." Hastings added, almost defiantly. "Our own Hispanic and black congregation is growing, thanks to the merging of the two parishes, and when I saw Joe last week, he was feeling pretty angry at the Church's losing the only mostly Hispanic Episcopal church in the midtown area." He paused again, then grinned. "He's promised to keep his fires banked at least through New Year's, although I must say I think the more we pay attention to the 'least of these' so to speak, the more we are carrying out what our Lord commanded."

"I've never met him," Larry said. "But I think you're right. I'm glad he's coming."

"Claire?" Hastings said, turning to her.

"I have met him," she said, "and I agree with you and Larry. It's not his activist principles I quarrel with. It's just—" She hesitated, unable to find the right word.

"Because he's so angry?" Hastings asked her. "Can you blame him? He sees the richest city in the world ignoring the growing thousands of homeless."

Claire's heart sank. "I don't blame him for what he feels," she said. "Plenty of others feel—and preach—about the same."

"Then what is it?" Hastings sat back. The morning sun, slanting through the side window, picked up the usually invisible gray streaks in his hair and threw the strong, straight nose and chin into outline.

"I don't know," Claire finally said. "Probably nothing. But he reminds me of that cartoon character who always goes around with the cloud raining down on his head. Only in Joe's case, there's thunder and lightning as well."

"Maybe we can throw a little sunshine his way," Hastings said. "Now to my second item. I've just heard that my old professor at Cambridge, Alec Maitland, is coming over to spend Christmas with us. I've asked him to honor us by preaching at one or two of the services and it will be a rare treat for the congregation. He's close to eighty, but he has all the vigor of a man twenty years younger. When he was dean of St. Paul's in London he didn't half pack them in!" Suddenly Hastings sounded, as he did from time to time, totally English. "The only problem is, as you know, the rectory chose just this time to spring a leak in the ceilings of both of the spare bedrooms, and I'm not yet sure where we're going to put him up. But that's a relatively small problem. If worse comes to worst, the seminary would be delighted to give him a room. Unfortunately, it's not the most comfortable of places. But we shall see. I'll offer every kind of bribery to the contractor if he'll get my ceilings mended within the next day or two because Maitland's arriving Thursday, which is only three days away, but, since we spent several weeks dithering about the contract, I'm not sure how accommodating he'll be. Anyway, Larry, you're in charge of the schedules, so do put Alec in for some of the noon services where the public can hear him between bouts of shopping, as well as at least one Sunday. Who knows? It might swell the coffers for some of our homeless feedings."

"Is this an official visit, I mean, from Canterbury to New York, so to speak?" Larry asked.

"No, it's just a private visit to me. He's been threatening it for years. And then there's the Norwich choir. They've been here before, of course, and are old friends. I know you're looking forward to greeting them, Eric. They'll stay in the school, of course. The boys down't mind doubling up and I believe their choir master—" He glanced down at the paper on his desk.

"Christopher Porritt," Eric finished for him. "He's staying with us. I'd like to go over some of our own music plans with you. Next Sunday I thought we'd do the Veni Emanuel, the Warlock carol and perhaps the Cleobury carol. The first two we do every year, of course, but the other one is new."

Hastings smiled. "Do you mean new to St. Anselm's or altogether new?"

"Both, really. It's a traditional carol but a recent arrangement."

"Not too dissonant and atonal, I hope," Hastings said.

"No. I wouldn't want it if it were."

Both men were smiling, but Claire, listening, caught a faint tension between them.

"Speaking of our own excellent choir," Hastings said, "do you think we could put in one or two boys who sang in the St. Matthew's choir?"

"I can certainly audition any that anyone thinks would have the voice and the musical capacity. It's too late for this year, but there may be vacancies for next year, although you'd have to talk to the headmaster about that."

"Yes. I already have. He seemed doubtful, since there are far more applicants than there are places to fill. Still, I think any boy from St. Matthew's should have a special claim on us."

"If he has the voice, I'd be delighted to audition him." Eric paused. "If it's minority representation, as you know we already have two young black boys and one Hispanic—all excellent singers."

"I see you're not an ardent affirmative action candidate on principle," Hastings said.

"In a small boys' choir, with an international reputation, no. I'm perfectly happy to audition any boy with him on one side of a curtain and me on the other, so that I can't tell what racial or ethnic background he comes from. But he has to be top calibre."

"I see," the rector said.

Eric went on, "While we have an excellent academic standard, the heart of the school really is the music. Those boys practice and study music for four hours a day, they rehearse the music to be sung in the choir for an hour every single morning before school and then, spread out, three other hours during the day. No boy with a mediocre talent would have the motivation to do all that. It's very tiring."

"All the boys, I take it," Hastings put in, "board in the school? Aren't there any whose families actually live in New York?"

"Yes, but—"

"Because then, if they lived at home, their beds might be available for other boys who live elsewhere."

"The headmaster would never hear of it. For some of the boys to live at home and others in the school would destroy the unity of the school, and they would not be available at odd hours for extra work and rehearsal. I had to give extra time for three of the boys to rehearse their solos for next Sunday."

There was a silence.

"By the way," Hastings said, "who is the fair-haired boy who sings like an angel?"

Eric smiled. "That's a good description. He's Timothy Bentham."

Cut of curiosity, Claire asked, "What would happen if his voice broke tomorrow?"

Eric put his hand out, as though to ward off the idea. "Don't even suggest it might happen. It would be disaster, nothing less. My other good soloist cracked his voice about a month ago, and of course that's the end. It can happen any time, and I must admit Timothy, who is tall and mature for his age, is just on the brink."

"Ah well," Hastings said. "Obviously we have to wait. But if any of the present choristers cracks his voice, would you at least consider listening to one of the boys from St. Matthew's?"

"Of course."

"The choir'll make a nice back up for Dr. Maitland," Larry said pacifically.

"He'll outshine them all," Hastings said, getting to his feet. "I was thinking there might even be some special music to mark the occasion, Eric."

"That's a good idea. I'll pick something especially English."

The rector smiled briefly. "Good." He paused. "I don't suppose anybody has any new light on our ongoing problem."

"The petty thefts?" Larry asked. "No. It's hard to catch up with that kind of thing with so many people running in and out."

"And it's not as though they were valuables."

"Well," Claire said, "money is valuable."

"Have you missed much?" the rector asked.

"Not money, a Japanese propelling pencil I was rather fond of."

"Actually," Larry said, "as I'm sure you know, Mark, it was Maude, your secretary, who lost money."

"It was all of a dollar and change," the rector said. "Not liable to drive her into the poverty line."

"Still," Larry pointed out, "if it's the dollar and change you've planned to use to go home with, it's inconvenient. But I'm still not sure what we can do about it."

"We're certainly not going to hire any more security guards," the rector said sharply. "Besides, as you know, Maude isn't that sympathetic to our feeding and sheltering work and may be enjoying making a fuss about her loss."

"However she feels about it," Claire said, "she certainly puts her time in volunteering in the kitchen."

"Maybe that's when she lost the money," Eric said.

"Why do we automatically feel it has to be one of the homeless," the rector asked irritably. "Other people come in and out all day. Your clients, for example," he said to Claire.

"Very true. Still I'd be surprised if it were one of them."

There was a short silence. The rector stood up. "Thanks, Larry, Eric. Claire, if you'd wait behind a moment?"

What does he want me for that he doesn't want discussed in front of Larry and Eric, Claire wondered. The man behind the desk was still a relatively unknown quantity, and, while he was extremely agreeable to everyone, there was a curious distant quality about him that made him difficult to know.

"I was looking over the records—the income and the outgo, so to speak—for your department," Hastings said, sitting down again, "and a couple of questions occurred to me. For instance, what do we charge for therapy here?"

The question took her by surprise. "The fee is on a sliding scale. The highest figure is a hundred dollars per hour, the lowest is ten."

"And how do you arrive at who pays what?"

"I hand a new client a list of fees scaled according to salary and/or income and ask which is applicable to him or her."

A brief smile flickered over Hastings's face. "That's pretty trusting, isn't it? I mean, you don't get a report from the—er —client's employer?"

"Or husband, or portfolio custodian," Claire finished drily. "No. Since the whole relationship is built on trust, that's the best way to start out."

"You mention portfolio custodian. Surely anyone who is in the happy possession of a portfolio would probably go to a psychiatrist at considerably more than your top fee?"

He's not trying to be offensive, Claire told herself firmly as she felt her irritation rise. "It's really not a question of the rich going to a psychiatrist with an M.D. at a staggering fee while the poor have to put up with a psychotherapist with only a degree in clinical psychology. A pastoral counselor—"

"If that sounded condescending, I apologize," Hastings said quickly. "I certainly didn't mean it that way."

"No offense taken. Most of the people who come to me or to any pastoral counselor want the tie of the spiritual with the psychological and prefer therapy to formal psychoanalysis. But there's no question, some clients do come to us because they can't afford most psychiatrists, although I know at least three doctors who also have sliding scales and are particularly generous with patients who can't afford to pay much."

"You call them clients—just like a lawyer?" He was smiling, but Claire felt another surge of irritation.

"I'm not an M.D. so I don't refer to them as patients. I think customer would sound as though I were a department store."

"Probably. I notice a Manuela Valdez who is a—er—client of yours. If her husband is the one I'm thinking of, he seems to spend a great deal of time in jail, and she has several children, so any fee at all must be a strain for her. I hope the church pays that for her."

"Actually, her fee is five dollars, and, no, the church doesn't pay it, because an important part of successful therapy is for the client to feel she or he contributes something, however small. And Manuela is employed. By the way, how did you get that file? One of the basic rules of therapy of any kind is total confidentiality. Not only what passes between the client and the therapist is under the seal, so to speak, but even the fact that she is having therapy is. There are those who, for whatever reason, don't want others to know."

"I see." Hastings closed the file. "I certainly did not mean to intrude. But when I went in this morning this file was on your secretary's desk. I assumed, obviously wrongly, that it was therefore not highly confidential. It is, after all, only a list of your clients, not any confidential information about them."

Claire silently cursed the fact that she had trusted her

brand new secretary to close up the files, lock them and lock the door when Claire left early to make a hospital visit the previous afternoon. Joanna was well meaning, but a little skittery. Claire was fast discovering that not all of her instructions went into Joanna's memory bank. But Joanna's aunt was employed by the church in the cafeteria kitchen, and Claire had rather reluctantly promised the woman she'd give her niece a try. The more Claire thought now about files lying loosely around the office for anyone to pick up and read, the worse she felt. Joanna would either have to change radically, or go.

"I'm afraid Joanna, who is new, is not turning out to be as reliable as I—and her aunt—hoped. I can't have files lying about. Obviously, the office was also unlocked. What time were you there?"

"I'm rather an early bird. About seven-thirty."

So the door had been unlocked and the file on the desk all night, Claire thought. "Well," she said, "I am responsible for what goes on in the pastoral counseling department, so it's my fault. I'm sorry." She paused, both mortified and angry. "What was it you wanted to know about the department?" she asked as pleasantly as she could.

"Only just the day-to-day running of the department." There was a small pause. "I, personally, have always questioned whether therapy—of any kind and however well-intentioned—belonged under the aegis of a church. This is the first parish I've been connected with where the—er—service is given."

"I see. Your feeling is unusual—at least in today's world." Suddenly she felt like one-half of a staged Russian–U.S. diplomatic dialogue, with both sides uttering polite, meaningless civilities. "Psychiatry and the church certainly started out as enemies or at least mutually suspicious. In the last few years, though, both psychologists and clergy have seen they're dealing with different aspects of the same troubles. Now there are many priests who are also therapists."

"Yes. That's certainly true." He paused. "I must apologize.

I hadn't realized I was reading, so to speak, highly classified material. But since I was, I also noticed that Hope Meredith is one of your clients." Hastings gave a rueful smile. "It's perhaps unworthy of me, but I do hope she pays a fat fee. She could certainly afford the most expensive Park Avenue psychiatrist."

"As a matter of fact," Claire said, getting to her feet, "she had one of those expensive Park Avenue psychiatrists and left him after several years of getting nowhere. Money and its consequences are among her chief problems. But just as death is universal, whether one is rich or poor, so is pain. And poor Hope has had her share of it."

Hastings also rose. "I'm sorry if I've been looking into areas I shouldn't, but I was going on the theory that any service given in the church is the business of the rector and the church as a whole." He paused for a minute, then continued. "By the way, when your fee is paid, do you keep it or does it go to the church. I don't know the etiquette on this, I'm afraid."

"Of course I keep it," Claire said. "Being a therapist is my profession, along with being an ordained priest."

As she walked down the hall she came on Larry Swade, tenderly holding some coffee from the deli across the street from the parish house. It was generally thought to be the best coffee in town, second only to the brewed coffee in a deli up on Broadway not far from the Cathedral.

"I don't suppose you brought me any," Claire grumbled to him, but smiling as she did so.

"It's yours," he said, holding it out, but with such a bereft look that she broke out laughing.

"I wouldn't dream of taking it. I notice that you snooted the cafeteria coffee."

"Who would take Episcopal coffee when you can get the deli variety?" He glanced at her. "You look mad. What happened?"

"Do you know what Mark asked me after you left? How

much I charged and whether or not I kept the fees from therapy."

"Ye-es. When we heard Mark was coming here somebody commented that he has some odd prejudices. Maybe Freud and his works is among them. Reverence for the great father of psychiatry used to be common among intellectual snobs, but the moment the middle classes rushed into therapy it became infra dig."

"Like doing anything for money."

"My dear, only yuppies admit to that. To show our freedom from material values we drive Hondas; they go stalking around in Cadillacs."

"I thought that was the mafia."

"Now, now." Larry looked at her. "He did get under your skin, didn't he? Was it just his clubfootedness about therapy?"

"I don't know. Why didn't I become a Methodist?"

"Don't let the social guilt of our clergy get you down. We're still trying to make up for being called the silk-stocking church."

"He's also something of a sexist. I'll bet anything he doesn't put the same question to Joe Martinez, who's a social worker, or to Eric."

"You sound as though you gave as good as you got." Larry had taken the top off his coffee container and now took a sip. "Ah, ambrosia! Hang in there, Claire. There are all kinds of rumors that Mark might become a bishop before too long. The diocese of our nation's capital has been casting him wooing looks, and you know John Price is about to retire."

"Then I wish they'd hurry up, although I'm bound to say I'm also tired of St. Anselm's being some kind of way station to higher glory."

"Training ground, training ground. Look upon it as a compliment. But I shan't be sorry to see him go to loftier realms." His round face was as kind as it was intelligent, more intelligent than those prejudiced against his girth, could see. "You're a good therapist, Claire, and a wonderful parent. If you left this place, I think I'd hand in my papers, too."

"It's stupid to be as sensitive as I am. But he was—I found him . . . well, demeaning."

"He comes from the academic world. Their values can sometimes be downright weird!"

"One moment he sounds like a radical, ready for the barricades, the next like a member of the ancien régime."

"I've observed they frequently spring from the same root."

Squashing down her grumpiness, Claire proceeded to her office.

"Joanna," she said, as she walked into the reception area, "do you know you not only left the office unlocked last night when you went home, you also left this file of schedules on your desk!" She was angry and for once didn't mind showing it. Kindness and the permissive approach obviously didn't work.

"I didn't leave the door unlocked," Joanna said indignantly, her blonde ponytail bobbing. "You've told me about it again and again, and I specially remember checking the door after I'd closed it. It was locked!"

"It couldn't have been," Claire said more mildly. "How would the rector have gotten in if it was locked?"

"I don't know!" It was almost a wail, and Claire realized she could go only so far with the twenty-year-old Joanna and no further. It wasn't the girl's fault that she wasn't the kind of person Claire needed. But it was her fault if she were lying.

While Claire was debating how to deal with this thorny problem, which included also dealing with Joanna's highly valuable aunt who supervised the kitchen, Claire's client, none other than Hope Meredith, walked in.

With the rector's recent comments about Hope on her mind, Claire smiled and said, "Good morning!"

"Good morning," Hope said. But it was flat and uninflected and Claire recognized the signs of Hope's recurring depression. "Come on in," she said more gently.

Underneath the fur coat that Hope dropped casually on a chair in the reception area, she had on the expensive, casual, not-too-well-fitting tweed jacket and skirt that was the hall-mark of someone born to the Social Register. Her shoes were low-heeled plain pumps, her fingernails were buffed but uncolored, and her straight brown hair hung limply. She was not fat, but she seemed to bulge rather than curve. Blessed or unblessed, Claire thought, picking up the fur coat and taking it into the study with her, Hope had a considerable fortune and had therefore never needed to work. In Claire's opinion, she would have been far better off if the goad of economic need had been in her back. Instead, Hope had laden herself down with rounds of voluntary work that seemed to give her little satisfaction.

"Let's not leave this coat out there," Claire said, putting it on a hanger on the back of her door.

"All right," Hope said indifferently. And then, with no change of inflection, "Don't you trust Joanna?"

"Even Joanna has to go to the bathroom sometimes, and the door doesn't always lock the way it should. And, as you know, we have many people of—er—all kinds wandering in and around the parish house."

"Mummy's always saying that the church isn't the way it used to be when she was first married here."

"New York isn't the same as when your mother was first married. I thought your mother was English, by the way. She didn't grow up here, did she?"

"Oh, no. She came over for a holiday with her uncle once and met Daddy."

"Was it a happy marriage?" As Claire knew, Samuel Meredith had died ten years previously when Hope was around twenty-one or -two.

Hope slumped down in the sofa opposite the chair Claire had placed for herself. "I'm not sure what happy is anymore. They used to have terrific arguments. That is, Daddy would argue and Mummy would freeze up."

As the product of a transatlantic marriage, everything about Hope proclaimed the divided traditions. Brought up partly in English and partly in American private schools, she seemed to fit in nowhere. Her accent and way of speaking slipped back and forth, and, instead of seeming rich in her two origins, she appeared unhappy in both.

"Did you ever think of living in France?" Claire asked with a smile.

"No. Why?" Anxiety, even alarm, filled her voice.

"It was just a frivolous question, Hope," Claire said. "In a totally foreign country like France you might just accept that it is that—totally foreign—and not worry constantly about whether you were being too English in the States or too American in England, the way you do now. You know a lot of people would consider it an added attraction—being a little of both!"

"I'm not other people," she said, with unusual directness for her.

"True." Claire stopped there and waited. It was a difficult thing to do, but Claire had arrived at the point where she was willing to sit out the entire session, forcing Hope to bring up a subject, rather than making it easy for her by introducing one. What Hope needed, Claire thought, as much as she needed anything, was initiative. With her frozen, controlling mother, and her fierce father, she had long yielded up any attempt at her own initiative, and a disastrous marriage, lasting only a year, and ending in an annulment, had only cemented that fact.

•   •   •

At the end of a rather exhausting day, Claire locked up first her files and then her office and went home.

Fourteen-year-old Jamie, who was now considerably taller than she was, and almost as tall as Brett, was returning from a walk in the park with Motley, his beloved dog, as Claire approached her apartment. Motley was part shepherd, part retriever and part who knew what, and he adored Jamie with the same fierce possessiveness that Jamie had for him.

"Hi," Claire called, and waved.

For so many years Jamie had been short and stocky, so it

was almost unsettlingly unfamiliar to see walking towards her this tall, pleasantly lean fourteen-year-old. That he would remain that thin she sometimes doubted. His late father, also an Episcopal clergyman, was tall but inclined to squareness, and Claire thought Jamie might very well broaden out.

"How was the walk?" she asked.

"Okay. Actually, we ran around the reservoir."

"I thought I'd seen signs on the fence there saying 'No dogs' or some such."

"But it didn't say 'Absolutely no dogs,' did it, Mot?"

Motley obligingly barked.

Claire thought of pursuing the point but decided not to. Instead she said, "Homework?"

"Done."

The trouble was, he was almost certainly telling the truth. Jamie had developed an unnerving habit of getting straight A's. This had followed a conversation between Jamie and Brett just before she and Brett were married in which Jamie had confided that he wanted to be a vet. Brett had pointed out that studying veterinary medicine was no different from any other kind of medicine. It, too, rested on a strong base of good grades in science and mathematics, in neither of which Jamie had shown the faintest interest or ability.

That exchange had had a revolutionary effect. Jamie had begun to study and his grades had soared. Claire found herself wishing that an equally dynamic experience would change Jamie's current attitude of being a male chauvinist. But she was afraid that that was a more complicated issue that would respond only to more complicated treatment. In the meantime, whenever Jamie was being particularly obnoxious she reverted to a name she had once invented for him, Much Macho.

"We got a card saying that Motley's due for his shots. I thought I'd take him in Saturday."

"You might take Patsy, too," Claire said, referring to her stepdaughter's cat. "She's probably due, too."

"Martha should take her own pet," Jamie grumbled.

"Yes, Much Macho," Claire replied. "That might be a little difficult, since she's in Massachusetts."

"Well, she'll be home for Christmas, won't she? I mean her college gets a break, doesn't it?"

"Yes, of course it does. But I don't know why you should be so unobliging. After all, when you've been sick, she's taken Motley out."

"Not as much as he's used to. He's used to running and all she did—"

"Jamie—why do you go on like this?"

"I just don't see why just because she's a girl she gets let off—"

"Okay, forget it. I'll take Patsy myself."

"Well, I didn't say I wouldn't . . ."

Claire had the apartment key out and the door open before Jamie had got himself and Motley out of the elevator. Putting her coat into the hall closet, Claire walked into the living room, having a faint hope that Brett might be home a little earlier than usual.

But he wasn't there. Feeling disappointed, Claire was heading towards her own study when a head popped out of a bedroom down the hall. "Martha!" Claire said delightedly. "What are you doing back this early?"

Martha, the daughter of Claire's first husband and his first wife, came towards her, her tall, leggy body looking unusually lissom in black slacks and a green sweater. Martha had survived the anorexia that had bedeviled her middle teens, but she had not put on weight, as she had so feared she would.

"Sometimes," Claire said, sighing, "I wonder how you could have been your father's daughter. He was unquestionably lovable, but he was also unquestionably roly-poly. I think Jamie might end up in the same direction. You're not back on any crazy diet, are you?" She finished up anxiously.

Martha came and put her arms around Claire and gave her a hug. "Relax, I'm eating like the pig I basically am."

"It's wonderful to see you, but isn't this rather early for the Christmas break?"

"Well . . ."

"Well, what?" Years of mother and stepmotherhood produced what Claire called, to herself, an early distant-warning twinge. "Are you in trouble of some kind?"

"We didn't really mean to break up the lab. It just happened—not by me," she added hastily. "I didn't even know it was on. But, it happened. The dean went into orbit and the disciplinary action went into high gear—"

"What disciplinary action? Which lab? Martha, what are you talking about?"

"Ho, ho, ho!" Jamie said, sauntering in. "So Ms. Perfect is being punished—sorry, disciplined—who'd have—"

"Jamie, shut up! Martha, come into the living room and for heaven's sake, begin at the beginning."

"Well," Martha said, trailing after Claire. "I know you and Brett are not going to be pleased after all the effort to get me in after my not-so-good grades—"

"You mean your rotten grades," Jamie's voice sounded positively jubilant.

"Jamie!" Claire turned. Jamie slumped down in a chair and lowered his gaze to Motley, who was sitting up and staring at the dog biscuit in Jamie's hand.

Claire turned back. "Now, what happened?"

"Well the group decided to take action—"

"What group, Martha?"

"Oh, I thought I'd written to you that I'd become active in an animal rights group that is opposing the use of living, feeling creatures in medical labs—" Her voice had taken on heat and indignation.

"Of all the half-assed notions," Jamie muttered.

"How would you like your Motley to be stolen and sold to some creeps who'd wire up his head and start doing experiments on his brain!"

"I'd take bloody care that nobody would get a chance to steal Motley," Jamie said, getting heated himself. "But, if you believe in science, just remember that some of the experiments benefit the animals, too. And it's just like some stupid female nerds to—"

Martha gave a small shriek of rage, and at that moment Claire heard the sound of a key in the front door. With a feeling of incredible relief, she realized Brett was home. Somehow, he could always handle these squalls better than she could.

But, when she turned, she saw he was not alone. An elderly clergyman with round collar and a dark purple rabat were in the front hall.

"My dear," Brett said cheerfully, "I've brought an old friend to stay. Martha, I see you're back, have you graduated early?"

"They suspended me till next semester," Martha said, running up and kissing his cheek. "I was just telling Mother about it."

"Well, I want to hear, too, but in the meantime, Claire, I want you to meet the former dean of St. Paul's in London, Alec Maitland."

2

"How very nice," Claire said, going forward, her hand out and her mind working furiously. "I think it was you our rector, Mark Hastings, was mentioning today."

"Yes. I'm afraid I pulled a fast one on Mark, as I believe they say over here. He wasn't expecting me until Thursday but I got this opportunity to come over with one of my former parishioners—a free ticket on the Concorde, what a treat!—so I jumped at it. It was very sudden so I didn't have a chance to alert anyone before I left London. When I arrived, I rang Mark, who offered me a room at the seminary, which did not sound terribly attractive. So I decided to call Brett instead and he most kindly invited me to stay here. But I accepted only on the understanding that it would be convenient for you. So, please, be candid."

With one part of her mind Claire was registering that there seemed to be more going on here than met the eye. With her mouth she was busy reassuring the old priest that it would be in no way inconvenient.

"There are times when I'm almost ashamed of the size of this apartment," she said. "But Brett insisted and almost had us signed up before I even saw it. Now I'm delighted. We have loads of room. Let me introduce my stepdaughter, Martha Aldington, and my son, Jamie Aldington."

The dean wasn't tall and probably seemed shorter than he actually was because of his stoop. He also seemed frail, though his face and eyes were lively. As he gently joked with Jamie and Martha, Claire reflected that at some time he might have been a schoolmaster. That ease with the younger generation did not always come naturally.

Behind his head she looked at Brett and gently raised one eyebrow. He grinned back, then went over and kissed her. "What was all this I was hearing as we came in? Martha, have you been involved in political action of some kind?"

"Yes, Brett, I have. And I'm quite resigned to the fact that you wouldn't approve, but it's the way I feel and I remember you once telling me that people ought to stick up for their beliefs."

"Quite right," the former dean said, smiling. Then he added, "As long as it is within reasonable limits and doesn't hurt someone else."

Brett took off his coat and hung it in the hall closet. "Did I say that? How rash? Are you planning to blow up my bank?"

Martha forgot her twenty years and broke into a giggle. "Of course not. We weren't going to blow up anything—just sit in, but it got out of hand, sort of. At least—well, one or two started to . . . to trash the place."

"What place?" Brett asked.

"Some lab," Jamie said indignantly. "I told her what the lab did benefitted animals as well as people."

"But you should see what they do to the animals," Martha

said. "They stick electric wires in the heads of baby monkeys—"

"Well," Dr. Maitland said, "I suppose it has to be done in the name of the god, science, but I agree it sounds horrible."

"And that's not all!" Martha warmed to her subject. They—"

"Spare us the details," Claire said. "I'll take your word for it."

"Yes, but that's what people, well-intentioned people, say all the time," Martha said tearfully. "They—"

"Nevertheless," Brett said firmly, "I don't think we need to have a blow-by-blow description here and now."

"That's what people always—"

"No, Martha!" Claire said firmly.

"Oh, all right. But that's why I'm home."

By this time Brett had led Dr. Maitland into the living room, and was putting a sherry in his hands when Claire came in.

"As I said, Dr. Maitland, Mark Hastings, our rector, was mentioning you only this morning. We're all looking forward to your visit here, and I know Mark hopes to inveigle you into preaching at some of our pre-Christmas noon services."

"That would indeed be a pleasure," the old dean said, and sipped his sherry.

Claire turned to her husband. "You never mentioned you knew Dr. Maitland," she said with mild malice, knowing she was putting him on the spot. But, after all, he had not exactly prepared her for this visit either.

"I know. I suppose I hadn't got around to it. We met—er —how long ago was it?"—he turned to Dr. Maitland—"fourteen, fifteen years ago? When I was over on that banking business."

At that moment Claire's attention was diverted by the appearance of Martha's cat, Patsy. Since Motley had placed himself in command of the hearth rug, Claire knew from previous experience it could mean a mild declaration of war.

"Motley," she said warningly, and turned her attention back to the dean.

"—a difficult time, and that other affair. Too distressing!" the dean was saying. "But my pleasure in being here is because of that, so I mustn't complain, must I?"

At that point Patsy wandered over to the rug. Motley got up and barked. The cat hissed and they both rushed into the hall.

"Not entirely a quiet household," Brett said.

Claire excused herself to see about dinner.

She went first into their bedroom to take off her round collar and change her blouse. Then she went into the kitchen. She was busy chopping some vegetables for a casserole when her husband wandered in and closed the door. "Sorry about that, but I had no time to warn you, and when I tried to call here, the line was busy."

"Martha," Claire said philosophically. "Now she's home we might have to install a second phone again. Sorry. Where is he now?"

"Settling into his room and bath down the hall. He may be very holy, but he's not unaware of physical comforts."

Claire grinned at her husband. "I must say, you don't sound totally enchanted. Don't you like him?"

"I like him, although I may say he's one of the most pigheaded negotiators I have ever met—in or out of a round collar. He's the kind of cleric who manages to convey that his way—it goes without saying—is God's way."

"You have my sympathy, retroactively speaking. I've known a few of those myself. But I'm sort of surprised that I hadn't heard you mention him before. After all, a dean of St. Paul's is something of a VIP. Was he dean when you met him?"

"Yes, but my visit was purely business."

"What was the business?"

"It concerned the charitable and mission funds coming through the bank from the London and New York dioceses."

"But I thought the two churches—the Episcopal in the

States and the Church of England, for all their fond references to one another and our polite deference towards Canterbury—were quite separate."

"They are, but they occasionally come together over the funding of a worthy common cause—as the famine in Africa, the flooding in India, more often than not crises in the Third World."

"Speaking of the Third World, that was your specialty in Army Intelligence, wasn't it?"

"You make it sound ominous. I was in Intelligence during the Vietnam War, and am on reserve. Occasionally they call me back in and give me an errand. Nothing James Bondish."

Claire was about to question this modest and somewhat vague statement when she made the mistake of glancing at her tall, good-looking husband. As her heart quickened she felt her attention diverted. Brett was not as movie-star handsome as Mark Hastings—his nose was aquiline rather than straight and his hair black with gray streaks—but she found him almost unbearably attractive, and loved the long, narrow gray eyes above the high cheekbones.

Smiling, he bent his head and kissed her again. Then he glanced down at her hand. "Careful," he said, "don't add your fingers to the casserole."

Claire looked down herself and laughed. The knife, held in her right hand, was posed over the fingers of her left. She put it down.

"Are you angry at me?" he asked, picking up a slice of carrot and putting it in his mouth. "I wouldn't blame you, but my back was to the wall, and when I couldn't get you on the phone I weakly gave in and brought him home."

"No, of course not. It's just—" She frowned and put the casserole in the oven.

"It's just what?"

"I don't know. Surprising, I suppose, but that doesn't feel like the right word."

. . .

Dinner was pleasant. The former dean was quick, amusing and had a formidable intelligence. Jamie's interests were questioned and discussed. "My first cousin is a vet in Lincolnshire," Dr. Maitland said. "Perhaps you could do an exchange student stint with him."

Jamie, who could be stonily unenthusiastic about any kind of clergy warmed up and much of the rest of the meal was spent talking of the ins and outs of a vet's life.

Towards the end of dinner, the dean turned his attention to Martha and her protest activities. "I'm bound to say that, despite the fact that I know the medical laboratories do good work, I'm on your side about using animals for experimentation, especially when, as I understand, often some other methods would be just as good if a bit more expensive."

It was Martha's turn to warm up. I'll give him this, Claire thought to herself. He knows how to charm people. But between Brett and the dean, for all their politeness, she sensed an odd tension.

. . .

That night, as she was preparing for bed after her shower, Claire brushed the red-brown curly hair that had been her despair when she was younger and long straight hair was considered chic.

"It's hard to believe I used to have my hair straightened and then would iron it. That was when I was in high school."

"You have beautiful hair," Brett said. "As well as other seductive features."

"Someone once told me I had the legs of a chorus girl."

"A person of rare perception," Brett said. "Except that in my experience, such as it is, chorus girls' legs occasionally can be surprisingly lumpy. Yours are lissom."

"Thank you. You sound very knowledgable. I wonder if I should be jealous."

"Yes, do! I'd find that greatly satisfying!"

She laughed and put her brush down.

Later, in bed, half asleep, she said drowsily, "For once I'll be able to get the march on the rector. I'll announce casually that his great good buddy is staying with us."

"Do you think that'll put you in favor or out?"

Claire gave a sleepy giggle. "Who knows?"

■ ■ ■

It was Martha who made the suggestion about Bloomingdale's. They were all at breakfast and the dean was talking about Christmas in London—the festivals, the church choir concerts, the madness of Piccadilly and Oxford Street. "I hope that I'll be able to enjoy the same kind of thing here, although that will depend, of course, on what Mark has in mind for me to do."

"You must come downtown to my area and go to Trinity one day," Brett said. "They do an impressive job over Christmas. If I don't have to have lunch with somebody, I often drop in there for the noon service. I'll be happy to take you there one midday."

"That's a splendid idea," the dean said.

"You can't, quote, experience, close quote, Christmas in New York without at least seeing Bloomingdale's," Martha said. "It's off the wall at Christmas, I mean awesome."

The dean looked puzzled. "Off the wall?"

"Pandemonium," Brett explained. "The marketplace in full cry. I agree it's something to see, although I wish sometimes the gift-giving and the religious festival could be separated. Not exactly an original thought. Get Claire on the subject of the variations on that theme that will be delivered from a variety of pulpits in the next week and a half."

"Speaking of Christmas," Jamie said. "Ma, what would you like to have as a present?"

Claire looked with amusement at her son. Given his almost permanent state of being broke, to think up something that would (a) be affordable, but (b) not so affordable as to insult him, would be a challenge. "I'll give it some thought and let you know," she said.

"Well, don't wait too long," he said. "I was hoping to get my shopping done in the next few days."

"Why the hurry?" Brett asked.

"I have other things to do," Jamie said loftily.

"I still think the dean should see Bloomingdale's," Martha said.

"As a matter of fact," Brett said, pushing away his boiled egg, "so do I. Mammon at its glitziest!"

"I must admit," the dean said. "Even in the East End of London we have heard of Bloomingdale's."

"I'll take you there after breakfast," Claire said. "I don't have a client until after lunch, so it'll be a good day to do it."

An hour and a half later, as they entered Bloomingdale's ground floor, the roar of successful commerce hit them. Beneath the wreaths, the ribbons, the lights, the sprigs of pine and holly, crowds, mostly but not entirely of women, stormed the counters, credit cards and purchases in hand. Behind the counters embattled clerks, some with rather desperate expressions, tried to listen to whatever shoppers they were waiting on while at the same time shutting out the shouts and cries of others trying to get their attention.

"I am waiting on someone, Madam," one clerk, tried beyond her patience, shrieked. "You *must* wait your turn."

Over the public address system, a syrupy "Silent Night" assured the shoppers that all was calm, all was bright.

"No, Clarence," a female voice from the middle of the surging huddle near Claire and the dean bellowed at her companion, a rather haunted-looking man. "That's not the kind of watch she wants at all!"

"Merry Christmas," cooed a young woman with a perfume spray in front of Claire and the dean, as she launched a missile of drops at Claire.

"Fuff!" Claire said, wiping her face. She didn't much like perfume. She glanced at the dean and saw him also wiping his face. "Sorry about that!" she said.

"Bless my soul!" the dean commented, putting away his handkerchief.

Using the escalator Claire guided the dean from floor to floor. He didn't say much, but his gloom seemed to deepen with each level of abundant material goods. He brightened only with the toy section and with the household appliances. Among the latter, looking to Claire like a denizen of some remote and deprived savannah, he happily examined devices that whirled, mixed, heated, cooled and blew with a smile that grew broader. "How my wife would have loved this," he once said wistfully.

Two hours later he was obviously glad to leave this temple of Mammon. "It does make one think," he said.

Claire decided not to ask him the nature of his thoughts. Then she put him in a taxi and gave the driver the address of Brett's club, where he and Brett were due to have lunch.

"Splendid," Mark said that afternoon, when she told him at the regular staff meeting about their evening and morning. "How nice of you and Brett! He's a bit early in arriving, as you know, but I have been busy finding him a reasonably comfort-able place. There's no reason why you should carry the whole burden."

Claire felt a surge of relief, even as she knew she should make some vague protest. "Of course we're delighted to have him," she said insincerely.

"But not for the entire two weeks of his visit, I feel sure. Anyway, I've been on the phone to Adam at the choir school, and he assures me there'll be a room and bath there by tomor-row. The current occupant, some VIP in the choir school will be leaving then." Mark was clearly pleased with himself for having thought of the headmaster as a solution to the dean's housing problem.

"The dean seems like an amiable person," Claire said. "He got on like a house afire with Jamie and Martha. Was he once a schoolmaster?"

"Indeed, yes. Mine, when I was at public school. Then he went on to take a chair at Cambridge, which was one reason I went there. Great luck for me!"

Was his enthusiasm real or faked, Claire wondered? And why could she never tell with him?

Mark went on, "I hope you told him how much we want him to preach at some of the noon services."

"Certainly I did."

He glanced at Larry Swade. "Well, I'm sure Larry has your telephone number and can reach him there when he wants to. Twist his arm, Larry!"

"Will do."

"Better still," Claire said as they got up, "you and Wendy come to dinner tonight." Courteously she turned to Mark. "And you, too," she said, "if you can."

"I'd love to, but I can't. I'm afraid I'm stuck with a vestry meeting that will probably go on and on."

· · ·

Claire was sitting in her office that afternoon, between therapy sessions, when she looked up and saw the Reverend Joseph Martinez standing in her doorway.

She took in the tall young man, with his black hair, fiery blue eyes and square, short-nosed face, and smiled. "Where is your harp, Joe?" she said.

He frowned. "What harp are you talking about?"

She wondered if she were straining his not-too-evident sense of humor. "I know your name is Martinez, but were any of your ancestors ever mixed up with the Irish? There are times when I look at you, especially when you're in full battlecry, when you remind me of the song, 'The minstrel boy to the wars has gone . . . with his wild harp flung behind him.' "

He grinned. "All right. Yes, you might say I come by my rebellion on both sides. My mother's maiden name was O'Connell, and her grandfather was an ardent member of the Sinn Fein."

"Ah! Yes indeed. By the way. I've often wondered. What exactly does Sinn Fein mean?"

"Ourselves alone!" He said it with such ringing defiance she was startled, then they both laughed.

"What can I do for you?" she said.

"Maybe you can add your voice to my current project."

"Which is—?"

"Have some of the notices around here in Spanish."

"I don't want to arouse your ire," Claire replied, "but don't you think that since this is an English-speaking place it's good for those who can't speak English to take every opportunity to learn?" She saw his nostrils flare and said resignedly, "I guess I should have known that argument wouldn't have appealed to you."

"Why don't you tell that to the companies that put Spanish ads in the subways. On some of the lines there are more ads in Spanish than in English. Or is it all right if there's a profit motive behind it?"

"Come on, Joe. I'm not the enemy."

"Aren't you? Aren't you and most of the others of the white middle- and upper-class majority in this church against everything that would make the Hispanic minority feel more as though it belonged?"

"Since you seem determined to do battle, then why do we have to do for the Spanish what nobody did for the Polish, Russian, Yugoslavian, Scandinavian and Italian speaking immigrants who came over?"

"They were white and didn't have to cope with racial bigotry!"

Claire felt herself getting annoyed, which happened regrettably often with Joe. Unfortunately, he had a tendency to make her combative in return. "There are other kinds of bigotry, Joe, as well as racial. The Italian-Americans could tell you about that some time, or your mother about the anti-Irish prejudice, which was ferocious."

"My mother is the worst bigot of all!"

"But she married your father!" Which, of course, meant nothing, Claire realized. In fact, it would make her sound worse.

"That made it worse," Joe said, as though he were reading her mind.

Claire sighed. "I approve of signs in Spanish under certain conditions. I notice now that the bank machines ask you whether you want to go on in Spanish or in Japanese, and I think that's fine, and it's not just because they're motivated by profit! But, Joe, I've met a lot of our Hispanic congregation and they all seem to me to speak English quite adequately!"

"That's hardly the point—"

"But it is the point!"

"What is the point?"

Joe turned around and revealed Eric's lean, narrow form hovering behind. "Are you foaming off at the mouth again, Joe?" Eric asked.

Joe visibly relaxed. Eric was one of the few staff members he never seemed to resent. "Oh, hi," he said. "I was just trying to talk Claire into backing me to put Spanish signs around the church for the Hispanic congregation."

"But they speak perfectly good English, and their children —certainly those who are in Sunday school—and/or are interested in the choir—speak, if anything, better than the kids who come from other parts of the country."

"That's not the point," Joe started, but some of the steam had gone out of his protest.

"You mean you were just trying it on?" Eric asked innocently.

Joe gave a rather sheepish grin. "Can't blame a guy for trying!"

"Yes I can," Claire said vigorously. "Haven't you ever heard of the boy who cried 'wolf' once too often!"

"Well, of course with your rich banker-husband—"

He stopped as Claire turned suddenly in her chair. "What was that?"

"For God's sake, cool it, Joe!" Eric said, gripping Joe's arm and shaking it. "There's nobody who's done for this church as much as Brett has. And what's more you know it! Because I've told you. What's got into you?"

Joe's black brows were closing over his nose when his face suddenly relaxed. "Yes, you're right, Eric. Sorry, Claire! That was out of line!"

"Yes," she said. "It was. Just ask some of your Hispanic friends in the congregation!"

Eric shook his head. "You're a fathead, Joe! Surely you know that Brett spent a lot of time with the Spanish banks helping get extra funds allocated for some of the young people's activities here!"

"All right, all right, I'm sorry!" He glanced at Claire's face. "I mean that!" He waved and disappeared down the hall.

"What on earth gets into him?" Claire said. "It's as though another personality comes over him sometimes and flips him out of all reality!"

"That's more your department than mine," Eric said. "But I know what you mean. The funny part is, when he's out on a social occasion, he can behave in a perfectly rational fashion. Couldn't be nicer, and wows any girls who are around. My wife says they all think he's devastating!"

Claire sighed. "I seem to bring out the worst in him."

"Maybe you remind him of his mother," Eric said.

"From the way he described her, that would justify anything up to if not including murder." Claire made a face. "Well, anyway, he seems to like you, Eric, even though you're the very personification of all the upper-crust Anglos he detests."

Eric smiled wryly. "I refuse to take him seriously or to fight with him."

. . .

Claire ran into Dr. Maitland as she was coming out of a therapy session later that afternoon.

"Ah, there you are," he said. "I bear instructions from Brett that I'm to bring you home with me in a cab."

Claire hesitated. "I'd love that, and with the Swades coming to dinner, that would be a great help. But . . ." she paused. "I'm going to have to turn you down. There's a client of mine who left a message that she particularly wants to talk to me before the end of the day, and I said I'd be here. You take the taxi home and tell Brett I promise I'll get another one."

"He did say that you wouldn't come quietly. But he also made the point that to try to get a taxi at your usual going home hour would be next to impossible."

Claire grinned. "I'll send up a prayer. The guests aren't coming till seven-thirty, so it won't be quite as hair-raising as I think Brett is afraid it will be. And I have managed to get someone to help in the kitchen. So go along with a free conscience."

"Very well," he sighed. "But I'm afraid he's not going to be pleased with me, or perhaps I should say, even less pleased with me."

"Don't tell me you quarreled at lunch," Claire said, thinking she was making a joke. "I don't believe it!"

"Not quarreled, exactly," the dean said cautiously. "We had a—er—disagreement. Quite sharp, I'm afraid." For a moment the dean's pleasantly smiling mouth narrowed and Claire had a sudden glimpse of him as a formidable opponent. Then the smile appeared again. "But it's nothing that should distress you. Our friendship—your husband's and mine—has been fairly littered with verbal joustings over the years."

Feeling a little as though she had been told not to worry her pretty head, Claire was about to comment when Eric and a choir student, Timothy Bentham, turned into the hall, sheets of music in their hands.

"Eric!" Claire said. They were obviously in a hurry, but Claire thought the more people connected with the church and choir school the dean could meet, the better. "Eric, I'd like you to meet Dr. Alec Maitland, former dean of St. Paul's. He's visiting the church and will be staying in the choir school in the next day or so." She said to the dean, "Eric Fullerton is the choir director, and Tim is in the choir."

"Ah!" The dean said to Eric. "You're responsible for that wonderful boys' choir that is so justly famous."

"We try. Timothy here is one of our leading soloists."

With his fair, wavy hair Timothy was almost a stained-glass version of a choir boy. He smiled now, showing slightly crooked teeth under braces.

"Do you like music, Timothy?" the dean asked.

"Yes. I like it a lot."

"I know you have to work hard."

"Right on!" Timothy said with fervor.

The dean looked slightly startled. Eric and Claire laughed.

"He means 'yes, very,'" Eric explained. "We can't let the Norwich choir outshine us."

"From what I've heard, they'd have to go a long way to do that."

Eric looked gratified, then took a furtive glance at his watch. "Please excuse us," he said. "I have an appointment and Timothy's due back in school."

"Of course. Don't let us hold you up!"

As Claire and the dean watched Eric and Timothy walk down the hall, the dean said thoughtfully, "The boy's voice should break before too long, although you can never be sure exactly when, but I expect Mr. Fullerton's well aware of that."

"He is indeed. And that's probably the reason he's been giving Tim so many solos lately—to use him as much as he can before the curtain comes down."

"How young is the youngest in the choir?"

"I think Eric once said ten, although there are nine-year-olds in the school being groomed, so to speak."

"And they all attend the choir school?"

"Yes."

"Lucky youngsters!

"Now," the dean went on, when Eric and Tim had disappeared, "I found my way here after about three people guided me up one staircase and down another, but I seem at the moment to be totally lost. How do I get downstairs to the main entrance?"

"It's a bit labyrinthine, I'm afraid. The whole parish house was adapted from a few old townhouses and people are known to get lost. Here." Putting her hand on Maitland's arm, she turned him gently. "You go down this way to the end of the passage and turn left. After that you take the first turning to the right, then go left again and you'll find yourself standing in front of the elevators. After that it's easy. Get in, punch L for lobby and you will, God willing, be delivered to the ground floor facing the Lexington Avenue entrance to the parish house." She glanced at the sharp, intellectual face. "Are you sure you'll be all right?"

"Of course, my dear. It's quite clear. And don't let me hold you."

Claire watched him as he set briskly off in the direction she had indicated. Something in her felt she should follow and get him to the first floor, phone call or no phone call. But Deborah had seemed frantic.

When she saw him turn, Claire flew back to her offices just in time to hear the phone ring and her secretary say, "I'm afraid she's out, Deborah, but I'll—no here she is. Hang on!"

As Claire plunged for the phone she dismissed the last of her worry about her houseguest.

"Deborah, what's happened?"

"I'm afraid, Claire, he—Carl—" at that point Claire heard Deborah start to cry and her words were lost.

Claire listened as Deborah at the other end took a breath and started to explain. Her words were jumbled and sometimes ununderstandable. She was not too coherent. But it was clear Carl had physically assaulted her.

"My God!" Claire said. "That's horrible. You can't stay there tonight." An automated voice asking for more coins interrupted. "Are you where I can call back?"

"If you do," Deborah said, "I'll be the most unpopular person in New York. The other two phones don't work and there's a line behind me."

"Then come here to the parish house now."

"I'll be there in about ten minutes," Deborah said.

When Deborah rang off, Claire dialed Brett's office. He

picked up his own phone, which in Claire's experience of senior executives and CEOs was charming and unusual.

"I'm so glad you pick up your own phone, Brett," she said, "and I don't have to plow through an array of haughty secretaries."

"When I know it's you," Brett said, "I always pick it up."

"I take it your ESP is in fine working order."

"The best. What crisis are you about to unfold?"

"More ESP, I suppose," Claire grumbled.

"No, the teaching of experience. Since we're both due to be home in less than an hour and are expecting dinner guests after that, I have to assume that some portion of the sky may be falling. Am I right?"

"I'm afraid so. A client of mine, one who hasn't been with me too long, has just been beaten up by her husband. She obviously couldn't go home tonight and didn't seem to have too many ideas of where she could go, so I told her to come to the parish house and I'll try and arrange something here."

"Poor girl! Anything I can do in the meantime?"

"Call Annie, if you would, and see if she can come an hour earlier. Most of the dinner is done. I made beef Stroganoff over the weekend for just such an emergency. It was in the freezer but I changed it to the lower part of the refrigerator this morning.

"All Annie has to do is set the table for seven—if Martha and Jamie intend to honor us and I hope they do—heat up the soup, which is also in the refrigerator, and warm the rolls. I'll get there as soon as I can."

. . .

Claire gave a passing thought to the dean as she hung up and felt again a twinge of conscience that she hadn't seen him all the way to the elevator. Again she told herself that he was far from decrepit, mentally or physically, and Deborah's crisis seemed more urgent.

At that point reception buzzed her and told her that Deborah Quinn was on the way up.

While she waited for Deborah, Claire reviewed in her mind what she knew about Deborah and her marriage.

Curiously, she had met Deborah's husband, Carl, before she had met Deborah. Carl was working in a small equipment repair shop not far from the church where they occasionally fixed broken typewriters and Claire had taken her own portable from home there. When she left a deposit with her home and office address, the good-looking young man waiting on her said, "St. Anselm's? My wife seems to think we ought to go there some Sunday morning. She's into this church business." His tone was both surly and sarcastic.

Claire said easily, "Come along then, both of you, some Sunday morning. We have wonderful music. You might like it."

"This'll be ready in a week," he said, suddenly withdrawing his interest.

But the next Sunday, as she looked out over the congregation while reading the First Lesson, she saw him sitting in a pew halfway back beside a young woman. Afterwards, seeing them at the coffee hour standing together, Claire walked up to welcome them. She received a swift impression of a young woman not quite as well endowed with good looks as her tall young husband with his thick, curly hair and coinlike profile. She also seemed very anxious for her husband to be pleased. After chatting with them for a while Claire had another impression: that Carl's social and educational background should have guaranteed a better job than working in a typewriter repair shop.

When Deborah called to make an appointment a few weeks later, Claire was not totally surprised.

Claire was expecting a tearful and possibly near hysterical young woman. What she was not prepared for were the bruises that flowed over the left side of Deborah's face and across her nose, nor for the blood that showed at one nostril and at the side of her head.

"My God!" Claire stood up and went over to her. Deborah was neither small nor helpless-looking. Claire herself was five six, and Deborah was taller than that and, though far from fat, she was sturdily built. But she had been no match for the man who had beaten her up.

"I'm sorry," Claire said, and thought how inadequate the words were. There was something so truly obscene about the evidence of what had happened that, for a moment, Claire didn't know what to say. Then she took a breath.

"No human being, male or female, child or adult, or an animal, for that matter, should have to put up with that. Has it happened before?"

Deborah hesitated. "Yes, but only a few times."

"But you never mentioned it in therapy. Why?"

"Because . . . I know it's crazy, but I . . . I thought it was probably my fault. I'd . . . I'd gotten angry and said some nasty things."

"Nothing you could have said would justify physical assault—you must know that!"

"Yes. I guess."

Claire had not often had to cope with abused wives so far in her career, but she had read a great deal about the subject and had been to workshops and seminars where the matter was discussed and former abused wives tried to explain what led them to put up with the battering for so long. She decided that the need now was for some practical questions. "Do you have anyone you can stay with?"

Deborah thought for a moment, started to shake her head, stopped and said, "No." She put her hand up to the side of her face, as though it hurt.

"You work at a magazine, don't you?"

"Yes."

"Do you have any friends from there you could stay with?"

Again a pause. Then, "No."

Claire reflected for a moment what she knew about Deborah: not a great deal, because the young woman had been in therapy only a short time and was not given to talking about her life outside her marriage or her job.

"When did this happen? Those bruises seem fresh."

"Three hours ago."

"You weren't at work today?"

Deborah started to shake her head again, and again stopped, since it obviously gave her pain. Again she put her hand up to the side of her head. "I was this morning. But . . . Carl isn't working right now. He called me and seemed angry and upset and wanted me to come home. So I said . . . I told my boss he was sick and I had to go home and I did. When I got in he yelled that there wasn't any food."

Claire took a not-too-wild guess. "Had he been drinking?"

"Yes. But he'd finished all we had, and didn't have any money. That was what he was mad about. He accused me of drinking it. But I hardly drink at all—" She started to cry again.

Claire said, "Was that when he hit you?"

"No. I said I'd go out and get him some more whiskey."

"Oh Deborah! Why didn't you just walk out?"

Deborah didn't reply. She kept her eyes on the floor. Claire had known it was a stupid question before the words were out. If Deborah had been able to just walk out, she wouldn't be sitting here now. "When did he hit you?"

"He asked me what excuse I'd given for taking the time off, and I told him I'd said he was sick and I needed to nurse him. It was dumb of me. Dumb!"

"Why? It was the truth."

"Because it makes him furious for anybody—especially me —to say he needs anything from anybody. I should have re-membered that."

"And that's when he hit you."

Once again she tried to nod and once again stopped and put her hand to her face. "Yes," she said.

Claire glanced at the clock on her desk. It was now past five. But no matter what the time she had to find a place for Deborah to spend the night. There were various hot lines for abused wives to call, and there was a residence in the city where sometimes a bed was available in an emergency.

Claire got out her own telephone directory, riffled through the pages and dialed a number.

"I'm sorry," the woman at the other end of the line said, when Claire briefly explained Deborah's need for a place to stay, "but we are full up to the top, and that includes various sofas and sleeping bags. Have you tried—" and she read out another number.

"Thanks." Claire hung up for a moment, then dialed the number she was just given. It was busy.

Deborah stood up. "Look, I know Carl, he's probably sobered up and will be filled with remorse. I can go back safely now. I—"

"No!" Claire said.

"But he'll be even angrier if I spend the night out and he's worried."

"Tough!" Claire said, dialing the number again. "Maybe it would do him good to know you have other options."

"You don't understand. He's had such rotten luck! He—"

"Sit down, Deborah," Claire said firmly. "You're not going back tonight." At that point the receiver at the other end was picked up. But that place, too, was full up. "Try the House of the Saviour," the tired woman at the other end of the phone said. "It's not a residence for battered wives, it's an Anglican retreat house. But they might have a bed."

"Thanks," Claire said, and hung up, wondering why she hadn't thought of that herself. She had often spoken at retreats at the old house on East Ninety-fourth Street and was fond of Mother Mary Margaret who was in charge. As Claire looked up the number and dialed, she watched Deborah who had risen once again and was walking around the room. The phone was answered on the second ring. "House of Our Saviour," a light high voice said, one that Claire did not recognize. She asked to speak to Mother Mary Margaret. When the older nun came on Claire explained Deborah's need and asked whether or not there was a spare bed.

"Of course," Mother Mary Margaret said. "She'll be quite safe here."

Claire heaved a sigh of relief. "I've found a bed for you. It's a little on the spartan side, because it is a retreat house, but it will certainly serve for the moment. Do you have any night things?"

Deborah once again started to shake her head, then said, "No."

"Well, you can sleep in your slip and something tells me Mother Mary Margaret will most likely have a toothbrush. Come along, I'll drop you there in a taxi."

"Are you sure this is the right thing? Carl gets so angry when he's worried about me. I'm sure it would be all right now, because he's bound to be much soberer."

"What makes you think that?"

"Because he didn't have any money to buy any more booze."

"That doesn't impress me as much as it might. From what I know of alcoholics, they show all kinds of ingenuity in getting liquor."

"But—"

"Do you want to be hit again? He might really injure you this time!" She'd never really grasped before, Claire thought, that women who weren't certifiably insane would go back for more. But she knew that what she was hearing from the battered wife in front of her was far from unusual.

By the time they got to the sidewalk it was nearly six o'clock and a few taxis were coming by with their lights on. Pushing Deborah into a cab ahead of her, Claire gave the address of the retreat house. They traveled up first Park and then Madison Avenue in silence. When they arrived Claire told the taxi to wait, then took Deborah in and introduced her to Mother Mary Margaret. When Deborah disappeared down a corridor escorted by the young nun who had first answered the phone, Claire said to Mother Mary Margaret, "It sounds absolutely unbelievable, but I had to persuade her not to go back to her apartment and drunken husband tonight. I'm telling you this, because she might try the same arguments with you."

"If she does, I'll certainly do my best to persuade her not to go, but, of course, this isn't a prison. If she insists, I won't bar the door."

"You don't sound as surprised and horrified as I am."

"Oh, no. I started out life as a social worker, you know, and all of us who worked in the settlement houses learned that the abused wives were just as much of a problem as the abusing husbands." She said it so placidly that Claire was once again astonished.

"I know that theoretically from books and lectures. But this is the first time I've come up against it. I'm beginning to appreciate again the distance between theory and experience."

"Also remember," the older nun said, "that it's her problem, not yours. Go on home, Claire. You've done all you can. And speaking of husbands—nice ones—how's yours?"

"Wonderful!" Claire said with so much feeling they both laughed.

· · ·

She was thinking of this with a smile and a warm glow as the taxi took her down Fifth Avenue and turned into Eighty-second Street. It was now a quarter to seven, but there was nothing Claire could do about the dinner and the guests except hope that Annie and Brett had been carrying on her own job.

She paid off the cab and almost ran up to the front door, getting out her key. It was one of the older New York apartment houses, the tenth floor of which she and Brett occupied. "I'm home," she said cheerfully as she pushed open the front door.

But there was no equally cheerful voice to greet her. Brett appeared in the door of the living room. "Claire, have you any idea whether Maitland had decided to run other errands before he came back here?"

"He was supposed to come straight back. He isn't here?"

"No. He hasn't come back."

3

"I tried calling you," Brett said. "But first your line was busy, busy, then the switchboard closed. All I got was a tape giving numbers to call for various crises. I tried Hastings but he wasn't in. Then I rang Swade, but he didn't have any idea what Maitland's plans might have been."

The feeling that had been a twinge of conscience—that she should have seen the old dean into a taxi—rushed back. "I knew I should have put him into a cab myself," she said. "What on earth could have happened to him?"

Brett came over and helped her off with her coat. "We don't have to fear the worst immediately. He might just have decided to go shopping or go to a museum or see an old friend, or half a dozen other things."

"Yes, for an hour, maybe. But he knew we were having dinner tonight."

"He might have forgotten for the moment. After all, he's not that young."

"But did he seem—well, senile, to you?"

"No. But a little vague maybe. That can come with age, and it doesn't come all of a sudden necessarily. A person can be perfectly alert and a few minutes later lose track of the time or what he's supposed to be doing."

"I'm the psychologist, you're the banker. How come you know this so well and I don't?"

"Because I lived through it with my father."

Claire went up to him and put her arms around his neck and kissed him. "I'm sorry, of course. But I still feel awful because I didn't take him down and see him off in a taxi."

"You had what seemed like a more immediate crisis. Under those circumstances I'd have done the same."

"But, Brett, what are we going to do? Should I cancel the dinner? Larry and Wendy will be here in less than half an hour."

"No. I don't see why we should. Alec might still come wandering in." He looked with concern at Claire. "It's not that late yet. When—if—it gets later and there's no Alec, we can figure out then what to do."

"All right. Let me go into the kitchen and see what's going on. Are Martha and Jamie here?"

Brett grinned. "See for yourself!" and he wandered back into the living room.

Claire went into the kitchen. Annie, a small gray-haired woman wearing a gray dress mostly covered by an apron, was standing at the stove, Martha was arranging the salad in an artful way, and Jamie was serving as umpire between Motley and Patsy, both of whom seemed interested in Patsy's dish.

"Hello, Mom," Martha said. "Did you know that Dr. Maitland hasn't shown yet?"

"Yes, darling, I know. I don't suppose he said anything to you about what he might be doing?"

"No. We did have a talk this morning, but it was on vegetarianism."

"Hello, Jamie."

"You know, I think Patsy's trying to push Motley around."

Annie scraped her vegetables into a bowl. "I'd say it's the other way around. Good evening, Mrs. Cunningham." Annie was one of the few people who called Claire Mrs. Cunningham. Professionally, she was still known as Ms. Aldington.

"Hello, Annie. Thank you for coming early and pitching in. Is everything where it ought to be?"

"If you can overlook the fact that the cat almost got into the beef Stroganoff." Annie had been in New York forty years, but her voice still echoed with the sounds of her native County Kerry.

Claire glanced into the dining room and was relieved to see the table set and the wine glasses in their places.

"I wish Dr. Maitland would show up. I feel awful."

"Why should you feel awful?"

"Because I should have seen him into the cab."

"He's not senile," Jamie said indignantly. "We had a long talk about the place of animals in creation."

"Yes, we had one, too," Martha put in, "but sometimes his mind seems to go off in the middle of a sentence. It happened once or twice while we were talking."

■ ■ ■

By eight-thirty they were sitting with the Swades at the dinner table and Claire was trying to conduct rational conversation to cover her anxiety about Dr. Maitland.

They had just launched on the beef Stroganoff when the phone rang.

By mutual consent there was silence as everyone heard Annie answer the phone.

"Just a minute," she was heard to say.

Brett was already standing when Annie came into the room. "It's for you, Mrs. Cunningham. Mother Margaret . . . Mother Mary Margaret wants to talk to you."

With an unpleasant premonition Claire went to the phone. "Yes, Mother Mary Margaret."

"I'm sorry to tell you that Deborah has just left. We tried to stop her but we couldn't."

"Thank you. I was afraid this might happen. But if she wants to go back, there is nothing either one of us can do." She took a breath. "Please don't feel bad. I'm sorry and I fear for Deborah, but I am certainly not flagellating myself. And don't you, either."

As Claire put down the phone Brett appeared from the dining room. "I take it that wasn't about Dr. Maitland?"

Claire shook her head. "Deborah, the girl I was telling you about, left the House of Our Saviours where I had taken her for safety tonight. She just walked out."

"To go home?"

"Almost certainly. Brett, I simply do not understand how she—or any woman—could do that. Intellectually, I know. I've read a ton of books about the psychology of extreme dependence, but you should have seen her! She was bruised and battered and bleeding—but she still wanted to go back. Said her husband would probably be sober by now and sorry, and that he would get furious if she spent the night out." She looked up at him. "Did you ever know anyone like that?"

"Yes, to everyone's shock and horror it seems one of banking's better known senior vice presidents had a custom of knocking his wife about, and when it finally came out, thanks to her children, she refused to leave him and also refused to testify against him."

"What was she like—I mean to meet, to talk to?"

"As normal seeming as anybody except, well, once or twice when we were out on some kind of outing—several families together—I saw a flash of rage from him when some minor thing went wrong, and I expected her to reply in kind, or at least freeze up. But she just bent her head and went on. It only lasted a second or two, but I remember finding it chilling." He paused. "There's nothing more you can do, is there?"

"About Deborah, no, but is there anybody else we can call about Dr. Maitland?"

"We could try Mark Hastings again and if he's in get from him a list of people the dean might know."

Claire was already dialing. "He was only going to a vestry meeting, so I don't see why he shouldn't be in, unless of course he was invited to dinner somewhere."

But there was no answer. Claire went back into the dining room. "Larry, is there anybody you can think of that the dean might know whom we could call? It's now nine, not a horrendous hour, but he was supposed to be here for dinner and, according to Brett and Martha, could have moments of vagueness. I hadn't seen that, but I do wish I'd put him in a taxi!"

"Stop fashing yourself, as my Scots cousin would say," Larry said. "But I do agree it's worrying." He paused, a ruminative look on his round face. "I'm sure there are people up at the Cathedral who know him." He looked at Claire and Brett. "Are you at the point when we want to admit that we've mislaid him and haven't a clue as to where he might be. If he does come wandering in during the next half hour he might well be furious if the entire diocese had been informed that he was too senile to know where he was supposed to be when."

"Probably," Brett said. "But I think that's less and less important."

At the end of half an hour Claire or Brett had talked to the suffragan bishop and an assortment of priests. None knew where Dr. Maitland might be.

Claire and Brett and Larry, now all standing in the hall, looked at one another.

"I'm going to call Lieutenant O'Neill," Claire said, mentioning the police officer with whom she had struggled over one or two cases in the past.

Dialing the number she had hoped never again to have to use, she heard the phone picked up. "Homicide."

"Is Lieutenant O'Neill there, or is he off duty?"

"No, he's here. Who's calling?"

"Claire Aldington."

In three seconds O'Neill's voice came over the phone. "Surely to God St. Anselm's doesn't have another murder," he said jokingly.

"Don't joke, Lieutenant. No, thank God. But we do have a missing person. An English dean to be precise. Or former dean, once of St. Paul's Cathedral in London, no less."

"And you've lost him?"

"Yes. He was staying with us last night. He was at the parish house this afternoon to see the rector, Mark Hastings, who is, strictly speaking, his host, and I was supposed to see him into a taxi, but I had another crisis breaking and simply told him how to get to the elevator. He was going to come back here immediately because we were planning a small dinner party. But it's nine and he's still not here. I can't reach the rector, and nobody at the cathedral seems to know anybody he might know. Lieutenant, he's seventy-eight and while I didn't see any—er—signs of senility, Brett and Martha said he could be vague. We're worried stiff about him. I know you're not missing persons, but maybe you could have some suggestions."

After a short pause the lieutenant said, "You know, I guess, that an adult is not considered to be missing until he or she's been gone for twenty-four hours."

"Yes, I know. Still . . ."

"What does he look like?"

"Not tall, frail, gray hair, a beaky sort of face."

"Wearing clericals?"

"Oh, yes, the English style, round collar, purple rabat, but gray suit."

"You say you saw him in the parish house. What time was that?"

"Around a quarter to five. He'd had his session with the rector—at least I assume he did, that was what he was there for. I saw him in the hall later and he said he was a little confused about how to get downstairs to the front door. I gave him the instructions and watched him trundle off in the right direction."

"And nobody's seen him since?"

"Not that anybody knows."

"I can ask missing persons to keep an extra eye out for him, but beyond that, at this early stage, there isn't much more I can do."

"I suppose not."

"I'm sorry!"

When she hung up Brett said, "Let's try Mark again." They did, and there was still no answer.

"I wish he were married. I wish he weren't a widower," Claire said irritably.

"Why?" Brett asked. "What possible difference could that make. If his wife were alive she'd almost certainly be out to dinner with him."

Claire knew she sounded unreasonable but it didn't stop her grumbling. "A woman wouldn't just leave a house like that with no answering tape, no sit-in person no nothing." Then she sighed. "We'd better get back to Larry and Wendy. What a party for them this turned out to be!"

But both Swades were of that happy breed who were not easily discomfitted. "It's been lovely seeing you, anyway," Wendy Swade said. She was as slight as her husband was tubby. She adored Larry and, as Claire was fond of reminding him, spoiled him rotten. They both, Claire reflected, had that rare talent—a capacity for happiness.

By eleven-fifteen they had left, the dining room had been cleared and the silver, glasses and dishes put in the dishwasher. Martha and Jamie were in their rooms and Brett and Claire were sitting in the living room, watching the television news. Claire had taken off her shoes and was sitting cross-legged in the middle of a huge arm chair brought from Brett's apartment when they were married.

And then they both sprang up as the young anchor woman said, "This is just in. The body of a man was found in St. Anselm's parish house this evening by a security guard.

The rector of St. Anselm's has been informed and is at the precinct now. He identified that dead man as—'' and the young woman glanced at a paper and read, "Dr. Alexander Maitland, former dean of St. Paul's Cathedral in London."

At that moment their phone rang. Claire reached it first.

"O'Neill," the lieutenant said briefly.

"We just heard on the news."

"Yes, I wanted to phone you before, but couldn't. Things were happening too fast."

"But—Oh my God, this is awful!—what happened to him? Where exactly in the parish house was he found? How long had he been there?"

"According to what we know now, which isn't a lot, he died somewhere between five and eight. The guard found him at the bottom of one of the staircases in the parish house. He fell—or was pushed—and struck his head. He must have been dead in a second."

"Oh, that poor old man! I wish I had gone with him to the elevator and taken him down."

"I'm sure your husband doesn't wish that. You might be dead, too."

"But who would want to kill such a harmless old man?"

"It's our job to find the answer to that. Are you okay?"

"Yes. Yes, I'm okay."

"I know it's late, but the sooner we get to this the better. Would it be possible for you to come down here now? The rector has been here, we're trying to organize the investigation and it would be a big help if you could. I need a detailed account of the last time you saw him, what you talked about and so on."

"All right." She turned to Brett. "Did you hear enough of that to know what it was about?"

"I believe so."

A sense of impending evil suddenly went through Claire. She shivered. Brett went to her and put his arms around her.

∎ ∎ ∎

Half an hour later they were in the crowded, depressing-look-
ing police station with its dark-green walls, its peeling paint
and people sitting around being questioned at various desks,
or simply on seats at the side of the walls.

Claire and Brett were shown into O'Neill's office immediately, a section cut out of the general room, its walls mainly of
glass.

O'Neill rose to his feet. "Thanks for getting down here so
fast. Here, please sit." And he placed two chairs in front of his
desk.

Claire and Brett sat down, and Claire slipped off her raincoat. She was still in the silk dress she had put on just before
her guests had arrived.

O'Neill sat down again behind his desk. He was a man of
medium height and stocky build, with sandy hair and blue
eyes. "Now, Reverend," he said, "begin at the beginning.
When did the dean arrive?"

"You'd better ask Brett that," Claire said. "I only came
into the picture after he'd talked to Brett and Brett had invited him to stay with us until other quarters could be
found."

O'Neill turned in his seat. "Mr. Cunningham?"

"He arrived at Kennedy Airport sometime yesterday
morning, having come over on the Concorde with an old
friend. He called me from the airport and said that, as he had
come two or three days before he was expected, the rector
couldn't put him up because the rectory roof was leaking."

"Tut," O'Neill said, "I thought you Episcopalians kept
your clergy and rectories in better condition than that. It
almost sounds as though it were a Catholic rectory up in the
Bronx somewhere." His tone was joking, his eyes watchful.

"As I am sure you have already done, you can check this
with Mark Hastings. He will confirm it."

"I did, and he has. The dean, Dr. Maitland, called you
from the airport." O'Neill, who had been looking down, suddenly looked up. "As the reverend here said to me when she
first called about his being missing, the former dean of St.

Paul's Cathedral in London can certainly be considered a
VIP. Why would he call you, Mr. Cunningham, when he
could have called anyone from the bishop down. He must
have a lot of friends in the Episcopal diocese here."

Claire opened her mouth, but glanced first at Brett. The
question may have had to do with clerical matters, but it had
been thrown to Brett.

"In a minute, Mrs. Cunningham," O'Neill said, and
Claire noticed that he was now addressing her as Brett's wife.

Brett said, "We called the Cathedral, to see who Maitland
might have known. He knows the bishop, but the bishop is in
Chicago, he hadn't met the suffragon bishop or any of the
younger clergy—it's been some years since he was dean—and
the elderly canon whom he does know, was unavailable. His
phone didn't answer."

"But why did he call you, Mr. Cunningham. I mean, I
know you've been an active member of St. Anselm's for some
time and have served on the vestry and have done various
jobs for the church, but I'm sure that could be said of others.
Did you know him before?"

"I met him in London on a matter concerning aid or
mission money being put together from the New York diocese
and Westminster."

"And you were sent over by the diocese to handle that?
Not some priest from the Cathedral, or from the diocesan
office."

"The Church needed an experienced banker. I had been
involved with the diocese for some years and had met a lot of
the people in Westminster, that's when I met Maitland."

"So he called you from the airport and said there was no
room at the inn, so to speak—how topical, by the way, it
being now the first week in Advent, if I have my Church
calendar right."

"You do," Claire said, smiling a little.

"So he called you, Mr. Cunningham."

"He reminded me in his exquisitely polite way that I had

once issued that well-known invitation, 'If you're ever in New York,' etcetera, etcetera."

"Were you surprised?" O'Neill asked sharply.

"Very. But when he explained, and I realized that he hadn't been really active in several years and mightn't therefore know as many people here as he once did, it seemed less surprising."

"Did he say why he was here?"

"He said the rector had asked him to come for part of Advent to preach, and so on, but that he had been given an unexpected treat to come on the Concorde with an old friend and that he was earlier than the rector was expecting."

"Of course Mark Hastings verified that," Claire said. She had noted before that she could be more defensive when Brett was up for questioning than when she herself was.

"He did," O'Neill replied. "Apparently the dean had taught him at school and then later at Cambridge and he thought the dean's well-known sermons would add to the Christmas festivities."

For the first time it occurred to Claire what a terrible blight this would put on the whole of St. Anselm's planned events for Christmas. How appropriate would it be to go on with how much of the carefully planned schedule? Then she reminded herself that schedules were pale considerations beside this horrible death.

O'Neill stared down at his notes. "So, the dean calls Mr. Cunningham and asks for a bed." He glanced quickly up at Claire. "Did you know he was going to be your guest?"

"No. Brett didn't have time to tell me. He tried to call me but was unable to reach me," she added.

"So your husband just turned up with the dean. He stayed the night?"

"Yes."

"And today?"

"Well, I took him to Bloomingdale's this morning so he could see the secular part of the Christmas season in New York at its most—er—secular."

"That must have been an eye-opener! Whose idea was that?"

"Martha's. Among other things, a young saleswoman squirted perfume on him."

"Good God! Where did you go from Bloomingdale's?"

Claire hesitated half a second. "I went on to St. Anselm's."

Brett put in, "She sent the dean off to my club where we were having lunch."

O'Neill stared at his notes a minute and then at Brett. "And was it an amicable lunch?"

Again there was a barely discernible pause. "On the whole, yes."

"But there was some disagreement?"

"Yes."

"What about?"

There was a longer pause. "I'm afraid that is confidential."

"Oh? Confidential Church business?"

"Yes."

"I see. How strong was your disagreement?"

As though he were there, Claire could see the dean's narrowing mouth and hear his words, "Quite sharp!"

"Fairly strong," Brett said.

O'Neill leaned back a minute. "Who won?"

Brett smiled a little. "We achieved a negotiated settlement."

O'Neill turned to Claire.

"When did you next see the dean?"

"Around four forty-five this afternoon. He came looking for me in the pastoral counseling office, saying Brett had suggested that we share a taxi home." Claire hesitated, as once again she felt the sharp needle of conscience.

"But you didn't. Any particular reason?"

"Yes. A client had called frantically when I was busy in a session saying she had to talk to me. I was waiting for her call when Dr. Maitland showed up inviting me to take a taxi home with him. I told him about the crisis and said I'd have to come later. As I told you, he was a little confused as to how to find the elevator, so I gave him detailed instructions and watched him go down the hall."

Brett reached out his hand and clasped hers. "It is not your fault. I repeat, not your fault. You had a greater obligation to this client."

"What's wrong with this client?"

Claire hesitated, but she hadn't, after all, identified Deborah. "She arrived bruised and battered after being beaten by her husband, but planning, nevertheless, to go back to the man because he'd be upset if she spent the night out."

O'Neill looked up at her. "Yeah, it's pretty incredible, isn't it? We see that a lot here. So she went back home?"

"No. Not then. I talked her into going to a retreat house in the East Nineties and I took her up there in a taxi and left her with Mother Mary Margaret. Tonight, while we were having dinner—the Swades were there because I'd asked them in honor of the dean, who, of course, was not there. Anyway, Mother Mary Margaret called and said she'd just walked out."

"Gone back home?"

Claire was about to say yes when she hesitated. "I haven't checked. I assume so."

"Okay. Then what happened?"

"I called you and told you the dean was missing."

"So that brings us up until his body was discovered."

"Where did you say he was found in the parish house?" Brett asked.

"At the bottom of a flight of stairs between the second and third floors."

"But, if Claire pointed him to the elevator, I wonder why he was using the stairs," Brett said.

"That's what we have to find out." O'Neill stared at his notes. "According to the rector, the dean didn't know anyone at St. Anselm's except himself, and, of course, Mr. Cunningham. Was that your impression?"

"I didn't ask him," Claire said. "There was no particular reason to."

O'Neill studied his notes again. Then he looked up at Brett. "In London, when you met the dean. Was he involved in this business of the charitable funds?"

"As dean of St. Paul's at the time, considerably."

"Was he—er—in agreement with what you did? I mean, was there any friction between you?"

Brett hesitated. "He had some very definite views about where the money should go and how it should be spent and in whose name."

"Did you agree or disagree?"

"Technically, it really wasn't my place to do either. I was there to do the banking work, once they'd decided what they wanted to do with the funds.

"And you had no opinion?"

"Yes, I had an opinion, but I didn't express it."

"What was your opinion?"

Brett sighed. "The dean wanted the funds coming from either side of the Atlantic to be sent separately, as separate gifts. But because of the way the thing was originally set up, that would have been more time-consuming and more expensive."

"Did the dean know you disagreed with him?"

"Probably. He was a sharp old man, and although I studiously tried to avoid stepping out of my neutral role, he knew what I thought."

"Was it a nasty fight?"

Brett smiled wryly. "In its own stately, Anglican, elaborately polite way, yes."

"And the dean lost."

"Yes."

"Had you been in touch him or he with you since?"

"No."

"Do you think that he might have still held a grudge against you?"

Claire expected Brett to say no immediately. When he paused for a second or two, she broke in. "Lieutenant, I can't see where these questions are going. That was fifteen years ago!"

"It's all right, darling," Brett said.

"What I'm doing, Mrs. Cunningham,"—O'Neill managed to sound both patient and irritated—"is to find out where the dean might have gone, who he might have seen—"

"But what's that got to do with whether or not he dis-agreed with Brett?"

"I don't know. But you know as well as I do that I have to explore every avenue that occurs to me. What's the matter, are you afraid he had a fight with the dean and bumped him off?"

As Claire stood up angrily, O'Neill passed a hand over his forehead and said, "I'm sorry, I apologize. It's been a long day and I can see even longer days coming up. But can you imag-ine the pressure on this office by everybody from the mayor and the bishop down? Not just a distinguished Englishman gets killed on my turf, but a dean of one of the world's great cathedrals."

"He's only doing his job, Claire." Brett reached up to his wife, pulled her back into her seat.

"Was the dean upset when he left you after lunch, after your—er—" O'Neill looked down at his notes—"negotiated settlement? By the way, how did he get to the church?"

"I wanted to put him into a taxi, but he would have none of it. He insisted on taking the bus."

"Was he upset?" O'Neill persisted.

"I'm not certain. It's hard to say."

"You can't give me an idea?"

Brett shook his head. "No. The English—at least the En-glish of his generation and class—don't splatt out their feel-ings the way we're inclined to."

"Only when they have the Irish in front of them," O'Neill said unexpectedly.

"I didn't realize you were an Irish activist," Claire said, "although I suppose I should have guessed, given your name."

"The other half of me is German from Yorkville, so I'm

not the ardent Irish patriot that my wife—my former wife—is."

"Ourselves alone!" Claire said, without thinking.

O'Neill looked surprised. "Who's been talking to you about the Sinn Fein?"

"The what?" Brett said.

"The Irish rebels during the throubles," O'Neill said, putting on a brogue. "The political wing of the IRA."

"Joe Martinez," Claire said, smiling. "St. Anselm's own radical priest. I was talking to him this afternoon. His father's Spanish, but his mother was Irish. He was the one who told me that Sinn Fein means 'ourselves alone.' "

"Interesting," O'Neill said.

"What do you mean?" Brett asked.

"A Church of England dean is killed in the same parish house where a young radical priest talks about the Irish rebels. I can't help wondering if Father Martinez says Sinn Fein when he means IRA?"

4

"I wish I'd never mentioned Joe Martinez," Claire said vehemently as they went home in a taxi. "I don't like him, but I certainly don't think he's been out murdering the English Protestant clergy."

"I doubt if O'Neill does either. But it's as plausible as anything they've come up with. Other, of course, than thinking I did it."

"Don't joke, Brett."

"All right."

"You were joking, weren't you?" Claire sat up. "Weren't you?"

"Yes. Darling, sit back, or the way this man is driving, you'll be thrown back. You've worked with O'Neill before. You know he can't leave any possibility, however remote, out of consideration."

"I wasn't married to you before."

"I'd hate to think that means you've lost your wonderful ability to look at facts and add them up to a reasonable answer."

"Love isn't famous for taking the long, neutral view," Claire said.

Brett put his arm around her and pulled her to him. The driver, glancing in the rear view mirror, saw a man in his forties passionately kissing a pretty red-haired woman in her thirties. It makes the world go round, he told himself philosophically, and wondered how well they knew each other or if this were a first encounter. When it came to sex, he was a cynic.

▪ ▪ ▪

As Claire approached the parish house the next morning, she saw, with a sinking heart, police cars, reporters with cameras and a noisy crowd milling around the parish house steps.

"Damn!" she muttered. If she'd thought ahead she could have entered through the church and avoided this. Now it was too late. A young woman with a microphone had seen her and was running over. Claire walked slowly forward.

"Are you Reverend Aldington?" the reporter asked. She was in her late twenties, had black hair, dark eyes and a probing expression.

Claire tried not to wince at the unAnglican form of address. In writing, she was The Reverend Claire Aldington. In speech she was Ms. Aldington. But she despaired of getting this across. "Yes," she said, "I'm Ms. Aldington."

"How well did you know Dean Maitland? Wasn't he staying with you and your husband?"

"Yes, he spent a night with us."

"How do you feel now, knowing that was his last night?"

It was questions like this that made Claire, from time to time, intensely dislike the press. "I feel dreadful," she said sharply. "As anyone would. He was a delightful man."

"Did you think when you last saw him that—"

But Claire had had enough of this public milking. "I'm sorry, I have an appointment and I must go inside."

"Just a few more questions."

"No. Not now." And she pushed past the mike up to the steps, ignoring the other mikes aimed at her and the reporters asking varieties of the same question.

"Oof!" she said as she got inside and leaned against the door.

"They're like sharks," Jenny, the receptionist, said. She was a bright, pretty girl who planned to study theology and was getting what she called an insider's view of the church while she went to night school. "It's funny when I think that before I decided to take theology I thought I might want to be a television reporter."

"I wish they'd think of some question other than a variation of 'Now that you see your husband lying at the bottom of the pool, how do you feel?' "

"It's greed," Jenny said. As Claire looked blank, she added, by way of explanation, "Ratings!"

Claire started toward the elevator.

"By the way—"

Claire turned. "Yes?"

Jenny was studying a piece of paper. "I'm not sure whether this is really for you. According to the security guard on duty —Jeff, I think—the man was too drunk to be able even to talk properly. Anyway, according to Jeff, some crazy showed up last night yelling something and Jeff thought one of the things he yelled was your name." Jenny frowned. "I've seen clearer handwriting—"

At that point the elevator door slid open and Mark Hastings got out. "Hello, Claire," he said. "This is a sad day."

"It is. I'm terribly sorry about the dean." Mark, she reflected, had blue shadows under his eyes and a strained look around his mouth. "It's particularly hard on you," she went on. "You'd known him such a long time."

"Since I was a boy. He was a grand chap."

"Have you talked to people in London?"

"Yes. His nephew's flying over and I got a call from the Archbishop of Canterbury. He's sending his personal chaplain, Canon Roberts, over. Of course, we don't know when the police will let us have the body to be returned."

"I was at the precinct last night—" Claire started.

"So the lieutenant told me this morning. Sorry you and Brett had to go down."

Though Claire felt the rector was reluctant to talk, and on this occasion she couldn't blame him, she blurted out, "Did O'Neill say whether they had arrived at any definite theory about what happened?" She was suddenly aware of how much she still hoped it would turn out to be an accident.

"No, they're still at the guessing part. Jeff, the security guard, is down there now. Also Jim Seldon. I'm afraid I promised the press outside some sort of statement. I'd better get on with it." He pushed past Claire, and she watched his tall figure go down the steps.

•   ■   ■

Clients kept Claire busy the rest of the morning, and, since there was a cafeteria in the parish house, she was grateful not to have to venture out for lunch. Her office window overlooked Lexington Avenue and from time to time, when she checked, she saw the number of reporters and cameras had not diminished much.

She was just turning her attention away from the window and back to the desk when she heard Joanna give a cry. "It's gone," the girl wailed.

Claire's patience with Joanna had been sorely tried when Joanna had denied forgetting to lock not only the confidential files but also the door to the pastoral counseling offices. Joanna still swore she had not forgotten, that someone else had unlocked the door, unlocked the files and removed the scheduling folder, leaving it on her desk for the rector to find. To Claire, this explanation was ludicrous, and convinced her, if she needed convincing, that Joanna was inadequate for a job that required tact and reliability. In the twenty-four hours

since, Claire had been trying to think of a way to transfer
Joanna to another less sensitive department without offending
her aunt. If her aunt left, St. Anselm's would find itself with a
huge daily feeding program and no one adequate to take it
over. So far, Claire had had no inspiration, which possibly,
along with lost sleep, accounted for her grumpiness.

"What's gone?" she asked now without interest.

"My fountain pen. Jimmy, my boyfriend, gave it to me. It's
one of those expensive, imported ones. Jimmy works at a sta-
tioners and he got this for me from there."

Claire had met Jimmy and was not impressed. But she also
knew she was, at this point, biased. "Maybe you left it at
home," she said with a marked lack of sympathy.

"I did not! I was using it early this morning! I went out to
get the loose-leaf paper you asked for yesterday, and left it in
my desk drawer. When I came back it was gone."

"If anybody had been in I'd have known," Claire said. "I
haven't budged from this chair since I came in."

Joanna was quiet for a moment. Then she said piously, "I
got in early this morning, a long time before you, and I went
to the ladies room after I'd opened up *and* to the store closet
for the paper. I bet it got stolen then."

Claire didn't believe it for a moment. But it was true that
after an exhausting night of little sleep she had taken advantage of the fact that her first client had cancelled to come in
later than usual.

"Maybe you've just put it somewhere you've forgotten and
it'll turn up later."

"No I haven't," Joanna said.

· · ·

Several clients later Claire was preparing to do some much
needed paperwork when her door was flung open and Joe
Martinez stood there, his face flushed.

"I told him he couldn't go in," Joanna said from the desk.
"But he ignored me."

"It's all right," Claire told her. "What is it, Joe?"

"I suppose it's you I have to thank for that going-over by the police."

"What do you mean?"

"I guess you thought that because I made the mistake of telling you about my Sinn Fein grandfather that made me a member of the IRA! I should have known better than to trust somebody like you!"

Light broke. "You've been talking to Lieutenant O'Neill."

"Surprise, surprise! Didn't you tell him I probably knocked off the old dean?"

Claire took a breath. "We were talking about Sinn Fein because of his own name and because he made some Irish put-down of the English. I told him you had told me what it meant. That's all. And if he accused you of having anything to do with the death of the dean, then I'll be astonished. Did he?"

Joe's color had faded a little. He strolled in. "No. Not really. He just wanted to know about my radical politics. But I don't like the police. They have one standard for the white middle class and another for the blacks and Hispanics. Are you going to deny that?"

Claire hesitated. "Not entirely. But the police, like the clergy—and the activists—are made up of individuals. Some are fair, some aren't. I've worked with O'Neill before. He strikes me as being eminently fair—a lot fairer to you than you are being to him."

"I'm not in a position of power. He is."

"That doesn't automatically make him the oppressor."

"That's the kind of thing you *would* say, of course. I hope you don't brainwash Jamie with those ideas."

"I didn't know you knew Jamie."

"He used to come over to St. Matthew's for ball games with the youth group from St. Anselm's."

"So he did," Claire said. "I'd forgotten that. Anyway, Jamie's entirely capable of forming his own ideas."

"That's good." Joe sat down without being asked. "Did you know they're also grilling poor Jim Seldon?"

"The homeless man who sleeps here?"

"Yes."

"But why him and not any of the others who sleep here?"

"Something to do with a previous record, or so they said."

"That's not unreasonable."

"I just hope Jamie's ideas shape up as different from yours."

Claire could feel her temper slipping. "One, as far as Jim Seldon is concerned, the police are almost certainly going to question anyone who was in the parish house yesterday. Two, if it's any interest to you, my husband and I were summoned to the precinct last night. Three, my own husband was questioned more closely than I appreciated since he had only met the dean once fifteen years ago. Four, don't ever come into my office again like that without knocking. It's only by accident that I didn't have a client here."

Joe got up. "Maybe the fact that your husband was here in the parish house yesterday afternoon might also have something to do with the fact that the police wanted to talk to him. But did they hold him? No. They're holding Jim Seldon, one of our homeless, because years ago he had a prison record. Hold a banker? Not on your gold credit card!"

"What do you mean Brett was here yesterday afternoon?"

Joe turned at the outer door. "Why don't you ask him?"

• • •

Claire was dialing the phone before Martinez's footsteps had faded down the hall. But it was Brett's secretary who answered. "I'm sorry, Mrs. Cunningham, Mr. Cunningham has left for the day."

Had Brett said anything about leaving his office early? It was true he had left the apartment before Claire had had her first cup of coffee, so it was entirely possible he could have murmured something while she was half-asleep. But she was quite sure she would have remembered anything to do with his coming home early.

"Joe's lying," she said aloud.

"Why would he do that?" Joanna asked, licking the envelope of a letter that Claire had dictated. "I mean, do you think everybody's not telling the truth because you're a therapist?"

"No, Joanna, I don't have a complex that makes me think people lie."

"You practically accused me of lying."

"I didn't—I just said I thought you might have left your pen somewhere without realizing it. I do that all the time."

Joanna, rather pointedly, didn't say anything.

Claire dialed her home. Martha answered. "Is Brett home?" Claire asked.

"No. Were you expecting him to be? It's only four-fifteen."

"If he gets in before five, ask him—no, I think I'll come on home myself now."

After she'd hung up Joanna said, "Do you want me to see if I can get hold of Manuela Valdez and cancel her appointment? She changed her usual time to five, but I guess you forgot!"

Claire had a sudden overwhelming urge to go over and shake Joanna, who was getting her own back and obviously enjoying it. But she took a deep breath and counted slowly to ten, a tactic she hadn't had to use for a long time. At one period in her life, her quick temper had fulfilled all the expectations that went with her red hair. But only rarely since her training had it got the better of her.

Reaching the count of ten she said carefully, "No, don't. What with one thing and another I had forgotten about Manuela changing." If Joe were here, she added to herself, he would assume, of course, that I had forgotten Manuela because she's Hispanic. For a brief, unsettling moment, Claire wondered if Joe could be right. But she knew he was wrong. She liked Manuela, whereas if she was given to forgetting clients she found difficult, she would have forgotten Hope Meredith long before.

At that moment the phone rang.

"Pastoral counseling," Joanna said, with now a slight lilt

in her voice, causing Claire to reflect on how invigorating a little getting-back-at-the-boss could be.

Joanna turned to Claire. "It's Deborah. She wants to talk to you."

Claire glanced at her watch. Manuela was not due for another fifteen minutes. "All right. But let me know when Manuela arrives. Hello, Deborah, how are you?"

"Much, much better," Deborah said. "I'm sorry to have made such a fuss. Carl was terribly worried about me when I got home. And worried that I might think he didn't love me."

Marveling at the human capacity for believing what it wants to believe, Claire said, "I take it he didn't strike you again when you arrived home."

"Oh no. Carl was asleep."

Passed out, more likely, Claire thought.

"But when he woke up we had a long talk. Everything's going to be all right."

"I'm glad!"

"But—I'm sorry, Claire, about this—but Carl feels that I should not . . . not be in therapy. He thinks—"

"He thinks I'm having a bad influence on you, no doubt, encouraging you to stick up for youself."

"Yes," Deborah said. "Well, not exactly, but we don't have that much money and . . ." Her voice trailed off for a minute and then, as though she'd had an injection of courage, "And he really feels if I have to have therapy it should be with a psychiatrist or a real psychotherapist, not . . . not just somebody in a church."

Claire could almost hear Carl Quinn's words being snarled out at his wife.

"I *am* a real psychotherapist," Claire said mildly, "and I practised as one before I was ordained. As for a psychiatrist— they usually cost a lot more money. Do you have any idea why Carl has these prejudices against the Church?"

"His mother was very religious and was always ramming it down his throat. And I think he's right in the way he thinks about the whole thing."

Knowing it was useless, Claire said, "But he said you were interested in going to church, and I feel that since you and Carl are having the . . . the kind of trouble you are, you need support all the more. I really think you should come at least one more time."

"No. Carl says that we ought to . . . to sort of draw a line and start fresh. Please don't think I'm not grateful, Claire, but . . ." Her voice faded as another voice—Carl's, Claire suspected—said something behind her.

"Thanks for everything, Claire," Deborah said, and hung up.

Claire replaced the receiver. This was not the end, she thought, and resolved to call Deborah the next day at work and talk further to her. At least she could suggest Alanon— the family branch of AA—or the National Council of Alcoholism. Putting the matter for the moment out of her mind, Claire turned her attention to Manuela, who had just come in.

Manuela was bright, hard working and a good mother, and Claire found it rewarding to work with her. "Everything all right, Manuela?" she asked her, as the attractive young woman sat down.

"Oh, yes. It looks like I'm even going to get a raise at work. Which is wonderful." She paused and added. "I'll have to wait until Peter gets a little older before I can apply to school, but I'm really eager to do it, and the extra money will help."

With Mark's comments fresh in her mind Claire said, "Is the money spent on therapy more than you can handle? I didn't think it was, or I'd have asked before." She hesitated, then decided to give credit where it was due. "But the rector asked that question. And if it's too big a burden, I know the church would take it on for you."

"No, Claire, it is not. And I prefer to do it myself. As I told you before."

"I know." Claire smiled. "I remembered that, which was

why I hadn't asked you before." And I shouldn't have let
Mark upset me about it, she told herself.

. . .

As soon as Manuela had left, Claire reached for the phone
and dialed home.

"Motley residence," Jamie's voice answered.

"Some frantic person calling me up in a crisis would never
guess it's where I live," Claire said.

"It's where Motley lives, and nobody but me thinks he's
important." Jamie's voice sounded aggrieved.

"That's not true, Jamie!" She hesitated. "You know about
the dean, don't you?"

The night before she and Brett had left the apartment for
the precinct with no more than a brief explanation to Martha
and Jamie. The following morning Claire had got up after
Jamie had left for school and she had no idea how much Brett
might have told him.

"After all the stuff on the tube, I should think everybody
in the city knows. It's too bad. He was a nice guy. Do they
know yet who did it?"

"No. I even have the hope he might have got muddled
and fallen."

"Not the way they're describing it now."

Claire could hear the sound of the television set in the
background. "What are they saying?"

"That it was, quote, a deep, savage wound and couldn't
have been done by accident, close quote."

Claire sighed. "Well, I guess I pretty much knew that. Jamie, is Brett there?"

"Nope."

"Did he leave any message?"

"No. Didn't he with you? It's after six."

"I know it's after six."

There was a slight pause. Then Jamie said, "Is he okay?"

"As far as I know." There was another pause. Then Claire
asked casually, "Any particular reason for asking that?"

"No," Jamie said, equally casually. "Anything else?"

"No. I'm coming home now."

Claire violated her basic rule of frugality and took a cab home. All the way, jouncing around in the back over Manhattan's potholes, she tried to think of a way she could ask her son what, if anything, he meant by that suspiciously casual question. She knew Jamie well enough to know when he was being evasive. But she also knew how stubborn he could be if asked a sudden, unwelcome question. Into this brew could be thrown the fact that Jamie, who had immediately taken to Brett when she and Brett first knew one another, had become oddly aloof since they were married. Whereas Martha, who was not initially wildly enthusiastic about Claire's new boyfriend, had warmed up a lot since he had joined the household.

And behind all those maunderings, she realized, was her growing anxiety about Brett in the light of Joe Martinez's casual statement that he had been in the parish house the previous afternoon.

But when, she wondered? She had called him at his office sometime after five. When she had arrived home about ten to seven he was there, telling her that the dean hadn't returned. Technically, Brett could have been at the parish house anywhere between the time she talked to him on the phone and —giving him time to come up from Wall Street—the time she saw him at home. And he had said nothing. . . . It was inexplicable.

And then there was the poor old dean himself, an honorable Briton, who had spent his life in service in the Church of England, murdered horribly on American soil. Claire was not a rampant flag-waver, but it bothered her.

· · ·

Martha and Jamie were in the living room watching television when Claire opened the front door.

"Hi?" she said. Then, "Brett not home?"

"Not yet," Jamie started, and at that point Claire heard a

key in the lock and her husband came in. Claire went back out into the hall. Before she could stop herself, she said, "You're late."

"I'm afraid so," he said, and shrugged off his heavy raincoat. His thick, straight hair was still far more black than gray, but for some reason he looked older to her. And then she decided, with a pang of conscience, that it was because he looked tired and drawn.

"You look exhausted," she said, and went up and kissed him. Usually his response was immediate. He could be surprisingly demonstrative. But now there was a hesitation, a pause before he put his arm around her and walked towards the living room.

"Hello, Motley," he said, as the dog, who had become quite attached to him, came up, tail wagging.

Claire felt brimming with unasked questions and unexpressed anxieties, but she said, "Jamie feels that nobody, but himself, of course, appreciates Motley sufficiently." She glanced with a smile at her son as she spoke, but he seemed aloof.

"What's the latest on the murder?" Jamie asked.

"You tell me. You've been watching television," Brett nodded towards the screen framing a familiar anchor person's face.

Jamie shrugged. "They're saying somebody did him in. The dean's nephew's here and was interviewed." Jamie held his fist out as though it were a microphone and said in a fake treble, " 'How do you feel, Mr. Maitland, about your uncle being killed in the States?' "

"If they stopped asking that question," Claire said, "half of television news would go dead!"

"Was Hastings at Kennedy to meet him?" Brett asked.

"Yeah. There was also another clergyman type along. Elderly. English. Roly-poly."

"Sounds like the Archbishop's chaplain." Brett glanced at Claire. "I take it they didn't come to the parish house."

"No. Or at least, if they did, I wasn't aware of it." She

glanced at Martha. "I don't suppose anybody's started dinner."

"Sorry," Martha said. "I meant to, but Jimmy called and I made a date to go out with him and Emily and Todd tonight. They'll be picking me up in half an hour."

"What are you all going to be doing?" Claire asked, and waited for the almost automatic withdrawal that such a question nearly always produced.

"Go to some pizza place, maybe. Hang out."

Which tells me nothing, Claire thought. But then she ought to be used to it by now. Twenty years ago what would she have told her father? The sixties version of the same, she decided. But for all the sexual revolution and the exploding campuses of her late teens, she was still relatively sheltered. She considered saying, "Try not to be too late." But abandoned the thought. Why shouldn't Martha, aged twenty, be as late as she wanted? In another year she would be legally an adult.

"I don't plan to be too late," Martha said.

Claire smiled at her. "What about you, Jamie, you'll be here for dinner with us?"

"Yeah, I've got homework."

"Leftover Stroganoff plus vegetables and salad be all right?" she called back to the dining room.

"Do we have a choice?" Jamie said.

"Maybe you'd rather open a can of dog food," Brett said aimiably.

"Is that meant to be funny?" Jamie snapped.

At that moment the phone rang. Brett went into the hall to answer it. The other three seemed to freeze as he spoke. "I've told you everything, Lieutenant. There's nothing I have to add," and Brett hung up.

Claire went from the hall into the kitchen. "Come talk to me," she said to Brett.

"In a minute. I'm going into my study for a while." And he walked away from her toward the other end of the apartment.

Ten minutes later Claire was stirring the warmed leftover Stroganoff into a casserole dish when he walked into the kitchen. Martha, who had also come in, was putting some frozen green peas into a steamer. She had already done the salad.

"Sorry about that," Brett said. "Need any help?"

"No thanks," Claire said, "Unless you'd like to set the table."

"Sure."

Martha turned up the flame beneath the hot water in the pot under the steamer, then left, saying, "Better watch them. They only need about a minute after the steam starts coming up."

Claire put a lid on the casserole dish and stuck it in the oven. As Brett went into the pantry and was taking silver out of the silver drawer, she said, "Brett, I was told you were in parish house yesterday afternoon. Is that true?"

Brett picked up a clutch of napkins. "Quite true. Right after you hung up, Mark called and asked me to drop by."

"That seems odd."

"Why? I'm a sort of permanent consulting treasurer for St. Anselm's, having done the job when I was on the vestry for quite a few years."

"Yes, but you resigned from the vestry before Mark Hastings ever came here."

"True, but whoever the rector is, he still occasionally consults me."

Claire knew his answer was both reasonable and probably true. Almost certainly true, since Brett had said so. Yet she felt as though . . . as though what?

"What was it about?" she asked, hating herself. She never queried the details of whatever business he did at the church. In fact, he usually told her, often with considerable irritation at the general looniness of church administrators.

"Nothing crucial. Just something about the church fund and its administration." Like most well-to-do, or once-well-to-do Episcopal churches, St. Anselm's had been left an assortment of trusts and funds that provided the much-needed foundation under the varying annual collections and donations.

Dinner was a quiet meal. Martha had gone, chattering cheerfully with her trio of friends. Jamie was silent, and Brett seemed withdrawn—more like the man she remembered from before their marriage.

After dinner she stacked the dishes in the dishwasher for Annie, who was due to come the next day, and then hesitated in the hall. Brett was back in his study, Jamie in his bedroom. Claire decided to talk first to Jamie, then paused for a moment, aware that a confrontation sometimes had the opposite effect from the one desired, but decided to go ahead with it.

She knocked on his door.

"Yeah," he said uninvitingly from the other side.

"Jamie, I'd like to talk to you."

"Ma, I've got homework for tomorrow and an exam at the end of the week."

"This won't take long," she said, opening the door.

He was still dressed, of course, since he had to take Motley out before bed. Motley was lying on the carpet. Patsy was curled around his stomach.

"They seem to be getting on all right," Claire said, looking down at them.

"Yeah, the lion and the lamb, whatever that means."

"It means the peaceable kingdom. Which is not exactly the way I'd describe this household right now."

"What's the matter? There's no battle raging."

"No, just a kind of packed silence, not to mention your less-than-polite comment to Brett." Claire paused. "Are you angry about something?"

"What have I got to be angry about?"

"I don't know. But if you are, I'd like you to tell me about it."

"Well, I'm not. And there's this essay I've got to write—"

"In a minute. Are you angry at me? Brett?"

"Why should I be angry—"

Claire suddenly exploded. "Don't always answer my question with another question, Jamie! Give me a direct reply!"

"All right. I'm being direct. No."

"I don't believe you!"

"That's your problem!"

"Don't give me that smartass answer!"

"What's wrong with it? I've heard you say it to other people. Anyway, it's true!"

"If it's true, why are you acting as though we were on opposite sides of the Berlin wall?"

There was a silence. Jamie was making curlicues on the paper he had been writing on. Suddenly he said, "I've been thinking, maybe it's time I went to prep school. Most boys my age are at Exeter or St. Paul's or somewhere."

"You've always loathed the idea of boarding school. Why the change?"

"I dunno. Sometimes people change their minds."

"You don't sound like yourself. Something's wrong. Jamie—!"

Suddenly he stood up. "Stop bugging me, Ma! Just stop. And let me get my homework done. If I don't get decent grades there's no chance of my getting a scholarship, and without that I know you can't afford to send me to a decent prep school."

"Brett can help pay—"

"I don't want him to," Jamie almost shouted.

"Hey, what's going on?" Brett said, coming in.

"Nothing!" Jamie almost shouted. "Now please just leave so I can get this essay done!"

"Jamie—?"

"Just leave me alone!"

"We'll leave you alone when—"

At that moment the phone rang.

Claire, who was nearest, went to it. "Hello?" she said sharply.

"Ms. Aldington?" Lieutenant O'Neill's voice sounded formal. "I want to report to you that the autopsy result is now in and there's no doubt that Dr. Maitland was murdered, his head beaten in by a heavy instrument."

"Oh, my God!" Claire said, although the news wasn't entirely surprising.

"Is Mr. Cunningham there?"

"Yes. Why?"

"I want to speak to him."

Fear clutched at her. "Why?"

"Please let me speak to him."

The phone was taken out of her hand. "This is Brett Cunningham, Lieutenant." There was a pause. "All right." He put the phone down.

"What does he want?" Claire asked.

"He wants me to come down to the precinct."

"Why?"

"To question me again."

"But why—"

"He hasn't said so in so many words, but I'm pretty sure he thinks I had something to do with Maitland's death."

"'m going with you," Claire said.

"I'd rather you didn't."

"Brett—of course I'm going. So would you, in my place."

There was a short silence, then Brett said, "Please, I really would rather you wouldn't." He obviously meant it.

After a moment, Claire took a breath. "I'm sorry you feel that way. And it bothers me that you do—a lot. But I'm going anyway."

"As you wish," he said, and headed for the hall closet for his coat.

The ride down was silent, although Claire tried to get some sort of idea from him as to why O'Neill, who, she knew for a fact, wasn't an idiot, should be suspicious of Brett.

"Why does O'Neill think you're involved?"

"I'm sure he'll be happy to tell you that when we get there."

His reply was so uncharacteristic of their relationship Claire felt totally bewildered. It was as though, with no warning and for no reason, they were back to the time they first met, when he was an aloof, sometimes sarcastic, always removed figure in her life.

After that she didn't speak. When they arrived O'Neill greeted them. "I'm sorry about this," he said.

As Claire had reason in the past to know, a police precinct was a noisy place with voices shouting, telephones ringing, people talking, typewriters clacking. Yet it seemed oddly quiet. Many of the people present were staring, not at Brett, but at her. And then she realized she was still in her clerical garb: a suit, a black rabat and a round collar. How many women priests had they seen? She put her hand up at her collar and touched it, as though she weren't sure it was still there.

"Just for the record, Mr. Cunningham," O'Neill said. "Who was the woman you met at the parish house yesterday? We know you went there to meet her, and we'd like you to tell us who she is and why you chose to meet there." His glance slid sideways to Claire.

Before she could stop herself, Claire said indignantly, "He went to meet Mark—Mark Hastings, the rector."

"The rector was out of the office at that particular time. We know that because we know where he was."

Claire managed to prevent herself from turning and looking at Brett. Until that moment, she found herself thinking almost idly, she would have staked everything she owned, including her life and her son, that Brett would not lie to her, deceive her or go behind her back about anything. Of all men she had known, including Patrick, her late husband, Brett was the least shadowed. Her first love, a professor at her college, had never even told her of the wife he had left but was still married to. She found out about that wife in London when she was waiting, as they had both planned, for him to join her. And Patrick? Patrick had died in the same car as a woman with whom, Claire discovered afterwards, he was having an affair. Now Brett.

"I did not go to the parish house to meet a woman," Brett said. "I ran into her in the hallway when I was looking for the rector."

"Do you always greet women you don't know with a passionate kiss?" O'Neill asked.

"You're asking the wrong person," Brett said. "I was not so much kissing as kissed."

"It didn't look that way to our . . . our source."

"I can't help how it looked. That's the way it was."

"And you're not going to tell us who she was."

"As I've told you—"

"All right. Let's get on with it. You were also heard having a flaming row with the dean."

"We did have a disagreement. Yes," Brett said calmly.

A shockwave passed over Claire. A fight with the dean? Brett had said nothing about that, nor even about seeing the dean at the church.

"From what we were told it was a hell of a lot more than a disagreement. You were shouting."

"I was not. It's true, the dean did raise his voice." Behind the deliberate calm of Brett's words Claire could hear the strain. She wondered if O'Neill could.

"We were told—"

"By whom?" Claire asked.

"You know I can't answer that, Mrs. Cunningham," O'Neill said.

"An accused man has a right to know who his accusers are," Brett said.

"All in good time, Mr. Cunningham. I think it would be a very good idea if you started leveling with us. Admit it, you've had more contact with Maitland than anybody else the past twenty-four hours. You claim you only met him once, so here fifteen years later he is hardly off the plane when he calls you up and asks to stay with you. The next day you had lunch with him and then an hour or two later were overheard having a loud argument with him at the church. And I don't believe for a minute that it's all because of some gentlemanly disagreement about church funds. The man's dead, brutally murdered, and I want to know why."

Brett stood up. "Are you charging me, Lieutenant. Because, if you are, I'm entitled to call my lawyer."

For a moment the two men stood, facing one another, O'Neill looking dogged, Brett, Claire saw, almost without expression. On one level she couldn't believe what was happening, what she was hearing. On another—on another level something within her was screaming with pain.

O'Neill broke the gaze first. "No, I'm not charging you for the moment. But I must caution you officially not to leave town."

As he said the words Claire heard scrambling in the main part of the room. She glanced around and saw several people head for the door and knew they were reporters. Oh God! she thought.

She and Brett walked out of the police precinct. The street looked the same as it had when they had come here together —very much together—was it only the night before? There was the same pothole, the same gutter with scummy water in it—where did that come from, she wondered, it had not been raining —the same rather seedy row houses sporting the first Christmas wreaths Claire had seen, the men hanging about outside, the police cars with their headlights above. Brett had taken her hand and walked to the corner where they had flagged a cab. Together.

"There's something I have to do," Brett said now. "I'm going to put you in a taxi."

Her ability to protest had gone, along with her sense of trust and belief. "All right," she said.

He walked her to the corner and hailed a taxi, which obediently pulled up. Giving the driver more than enough money, Brett told him their address and ordered the driver to take her there. When he opened the door, Claire meekly and without looking at him got in. As she was driven uptown, Claire thought, he's probably going to see the woman. And then, I wonder where she lives.

. . .

The apartment was quiet—what else should it be? Claire stood in the hall, trying to make her brain function. She felt as though some drug had entered and half-paralyzed her. After a few minutes she remembered that Martha was out and that Jamie was writing his essay. She walked to his door with the idea of checking on him. But she couldn't make herself put her hand up and knock. She stood there for a moment trying to decide whether she was attempting to spare her son or herself and from what? But she still wasn't able to knock on the door. After a few minutes she went into the bedroom she and Brett shared.

The bed was large and covered with a green plaid quilt that served also as a counterpane. The lazy person's cover, she had called it. The bed did not strictly need to be turned down. All that was needed was to pull the quilt from the bottom and push back the flap on each side. Tonight, she found herself thinking carefully, she would only have to turn it back on one side. Tonight and forever?

Come off it, she told herself, trying to insert a little middle-aged sense—to say nothing of some backbone—into herself. You're not a romantic teenager!

No, she thought. She was a twice-married, thrice-betrayed woman in her late thirties. I must have a talent for picking men who'll do that, she jibed at herself, walking forward.

Patsy was in the middle of the bed. When Claire came up, she rolled onto her back, showing her fat dark-gray stomach with its white-bikini effect. She was neither particularly lively nor demonstrative, but this was one way in which she showed her devotion—total vulnerability.

Claire walked forward, dropped her coat on the end of the bed and scratched the top of Patsy's head. Patsy started to purr, a deep, rumbling, not-very-loud purr that she seldom allowed anyone to hear.

"Oh, Patsy!" Claire said, and started to cry.

It was as though a spiggot had been turned full on. The tears poured down. She couldn't stop them, and she couldn't stop the sobs, although she muffled them as well as she could, because she did not want Jamie to hear.

After what seemed like a long time she finally sobbed herself out. Vaguely she wondered what time it was and was astounded to see it was only ten-thirty.

She took a long hot shower, washing and drying her hair, then went to bed. Although nothing had been said, she knew Brett would not be back tonight. Resolutely she kept her mind off where he might be and with whom. She heard Jamie open his door, say "Come on, Motley" in a soft voice and leave the apartment, shutting the front door behind him. By the time she was in bed, he had come back. Martha, she knew, could not be expected to return for hours.

The bed felt enormous and empty and cold, but she wouldn't let herself think of that either. Nor could she go back over the past months in her mind, wondering what signs she had ignored in her idiotic happiness and confidence in her husband. Turning her face into the cool pillow, she went to sleep.

∎ ∎ ∎

It was still dark when she woke up. Claire had always hated the dark, going back to the days when her mother was dead and her father had to leave her at night with a sitter to work in his office as district attorney. She lay there for a moment, and felt her heart beat faster as she remembered everything.

Reaching around to the side, she pushed the ON button on her radio and turned the dial to a station that played nothing but classical music. They were now playing what she recognized as Mendelssohn.

Finally, painfully, she allowed herself to look at two important facts: the police—including Lieutenant O'Neill—were obviously convinced Brett had something to do with Dr. Maitland's death. And Brett had plainly been involved with a woman whom he had met in the parish house just prior to the murder.

The two were almost certainly connected, but for her were separate wounds and would have to be dealt with separately.

She found that to know that and to think about it rationally were two entirely different matters. She discovered, while lying there, that while her mind was unable to think clearly, it was also unable to leave the subject alone. Sleep had gone. She was wide awake. Where was Brett? Desperate and in trouble? In another woman's bed?

It was only a kiss. . . .

Brett did not kiss lightly. He did not kiss the wives of his friends, the way some men did, a peck on the cheek, and a "Hiya, darling?" And he rarely kissed her, Claire, in public. He was as old-fashioned as a Victorian about that, and she had always loved it. Affection from easily demonstrative people meant so much less. . . .

Or was she being a hopeless, outdated romantic even to think in those terms?

She heard herself say into the dark room, "I am a trained psychotherapist and an ordained priest. I help other people who have comparable problems. . . ."

But her mind, like an angry, stubborn child could not seem to move off its own misery.

"This is no good," she said and turned on her bedside light.

Putting on her robe, she went into the living room and turned on the television set. She never remembered afterwards what she watched, but it kept her mind from running around like a rat in a maze.

At some point she must have gone to sleep, because she awoke, stiff and chilled, as the first light struggled through the living room window. The set was still on. What she had been watching must have come through a seldom used cable, because there was nothing on the screen. But a tinny carol was coming through the audio. " 'Tis the season to be jolly," she said aloud. And then, in a conversational voice, "I hate carols."

"That's not very holy," Jamie said, coming into the room."

"I don't feel very holy." She glanced at her son. "How come you're up so early?"

"My essay. Remember?"

"I thought you were just using that as an excuse to throw me out."

Jamie didn't say anything, but walked to the window. "It's going to snow," he said. "Have you thought yet about what you want me to give you for Christmas?"

"Oh, Jamie, I'm sorry, no. But I will, I promise!" Claire stood up. She felt as though every bone in her body ached.

Jamie turned from the window and looked at her. "You don't look so great, Ma."

"I don't feel so great."

Life goes on, she said to herself, as she got into the shower and turned the water to hot.

．　．　．

She arrived at the church an hour before the early morning Eucharist, and spent the time listening to Eric rehearse the choir in its Christmas music. Usually he used the choir rehearsal room, but this morning he had the boys, about twenty of them and nine of the men, in the church. His assistant was playing the organ, as Eric stood in the chancel between the choir stalls and tried to persuade and/or harry the young singers into perfect delivery.

Listening, Claire could not have picked fault with them, but she noticed boys at various times raising their arms for a minute and knew from previous exposure that meant they knew they had made a mistake.

"If I don't make them do that," Eric said. "Then they'll think I didn't notice and will make the same mistake the next time—probably at the final performance."

Timothy Bentham, Claire noticed, never raised his arm, and she realized that he probably never made a mistake either. His clear, strong soprano soared above the others in the hymns where he sang the descant. Unlike Timothy, the small boy next to him often raised his arm. But to Claire, his voice, when not overpowered by Timothy's, sounded accurate and sweet.

Idly Claire tried to remember if she had ever met the Bentham parents. Most of the parents could usually be depended on to attend some portion of the Advent festivals, if nothing else. However far they had to travel and however much money it cost, even if it meant selling the family silver, those who took the trouble to send their sons for audition and fought to get them enrolled were nearly always to be found sitting in the pews listening proudly for at least part of Advent and Christmas.

And why not? Claire thought, and pushed back the traitorous thought that a more ordinary choir of men and women, and a children's choir of both boys and girls, would be just as good and be far less trouble. Then she reproached herself for even doubting the importance and efficacy of an old Anglican tradition. There was nothing quite like it. Rome put on pageants with color and flair, but there was something about the Anglicans that was unique.

"You all right?" A voice asked quietly. And then a familiar tubby shape slid into the pew beside her.

"Hi, Larry. Yes, why?"

"Because, my dear, you look like hell. It may not be kosher to say so here, but it's unmistakable."

She should have known she didn't have a prayer of putting anything past Larry. If she answered she was afraid she'd cry. "Don't ask me, Larry, there's a friend!"

"All right. But remember, that's what I am, a friend."

"Yes, I know you are." Briefly she touched his arm. "By the way, who's the small boy beside Timothy Bentham?"

"That's Malcolm Richardson. I think Eric has high hopes for him."

． ． ．

It was when Joanna was out of the room that she answered her phone herself and heard a voice say, "Mrs. Cunningham, I'm sure you've heard that your husband has been all but charged with the murder of the man who was your guest only two nights ago.

"Who is this?"

"The *New York Courier*. We'd like to get your statement—"

She interrupted. "I have no statement."

"And about the woman who was—" She hung up, and was sitting with clenched fists when Joanna came back.

"Did you get any telephone calls for me from members of the press, Joanna?"

"Oh, yes. But I didn't think you wanted to answer them. Did you?"

"No. And thank you."

She reflected she wouldn't have credited Joanna with that much tact and sensitivity. Possibly to make up, she said, "Did you find your pen when you went home?"

"No. I told you. I had it at the office yesterday morning. It was stolen—like your pencil!"

Claire sighed. "I'm sorry if I didn't seem to believe you. A number of things have disappeared mysteriously. Like my pencil! I hate to say it, but I can't help wondering if one of the homeless thought he could sell it for some booze or crack."

"That's what I think. And what's more, Maude agrees with me."

Claire wondered how the rather conservative, middle-aged Maude Butler would relish being referred to by Joanna by her first name.

"Of course," Claire said, forcing herself to be fair, "it could be somebody else."

"Like who?"

． ． ．

At five minutes to three, when Claire was enjoying a ten-minute break between clients, she watched her hand reach out to the phone as though it were someone else's and dial Brett's number. As she heard it ring she remembered a day or so ago—was it only that short a time?—that Brett had answered the phone himself and they had joked about his ESP where she was concerned. Well, she thought, if it were true, then he would undoubtedly not only not answer the phone but would instruct his secretary not to answer it. At that moment the receiver was picked up.

"Brett Cunningham," he said.

Claire took a breath and said shakily, "I have to talk to you, Brett. I can't go on like this."

"No. Neither can I. I'll be at home tonight. What time do Jamie and Martha generally get back?"

"I have no idea when Martha's in or out. Jamie—usually around five."

"Do you think you could make it home by four-thirty? We could maybe have a few moments alone."

"I'll be there."

Claire was gathering her things together at a quarter to four when Joe Martinez came in. "Jim Selden got let out of jail. It seems *he* was not guilty of killing the good dean after all."

A rare rage filled Claire. So, she thought, this tunnel-visioned radical had come to gloat.

"I'm sure you, for one, rejoiced to hear that my husband, the WASP banker—your synonym for the enemy of the people—was brought in instead and you've come to rub my nose in it! Please get out of my way. I'm in a hurry!" She almost ran down the hall to the elevator. When it didn't come right away, she took the stairs. They were old stairs with sharp, metal edges. As she ran, she reflected that it was at the bottom of the flight between the second and third floors that the dean was found. This made her think first of Brett, then of Joe Martinez upstairs, and at that point she almost tripped. Slow down, she told herself. Part of the problem was the darkness.

Now, within days of the shortest day of the year, it was almost totally dark at this hour, and the stairs were unlit. Putting her hand out, she felt along the wall, found a switch and flipped it. Garish light came on. It made the narrow stairs less hazardous, but it didn't improve the view, she thought dourly, taking in the graffiti on one side of the wall. Someone with a thick black pen had drawn some odd figures on the institution-green walls. Where had she seen those before? On other walls in the city elsewhere, probably. For all the efforts at scrubbing and cleaning, New York was still the graffiti capital of the world and, given the many people who came into the building every day, it was no surprise that St. Anselm's walls had not escaped. Which made her think again of Joe Martinez, and again her face flushed with anger and she could almost feel her blood pressure go up.

She didn't even bother trying to find a taxi, but plunged into the subway, where, of course, more graffiti greeted her eyes. But it was the fastest way home at this hour.

■ ■ ■

Both Motley and Patsy greeted her at the door, which indicated that their respective owners were not in. Slowly, she let her breath out. Why it had seemed so important that she and Brett have this few minutes alone, she didn't know. But it was. At that point she heard his key in the front door.

She was waiting in the living room when he came in, and turned, unsure for the first time since long before their marriage how he would greet her. For a second or two they stood there, then Claire went towards him and he opened his arms. He held her close to him, his face against hers, his arms wrapped around her. A long sigh from deep inside escaped her. "Brett," she said, "Brett darling." Anger and hurt were still there and would have to be reckoned with, but for the moment simply being in his arms was the only important thing.

"I swore to myself I would not do this," Brett said.

"Do what?"

"Hold you like this, until I had had a chance to speak a piece I have to speak. But your face when I came in was too much. I had forgotten the effect it sometimes has on me."

"What is it?"

He kissed her and pushed her gently away. "It's this. I realize that my actions over the last day must seem furtive and suspicious. I did meet the dean at the parish house and we did have a fight. But I did *not* kill him. Surely you believe that! And when I can I will explain it all, but until I have an opportunity to talk . . . to talk to someone else, I can't say more."

Claire could not stop her question. "And what about the woman?"

Color tinged his cheeks. "That was over a long time ago. For God's sake, don't worry about it! I must say I never expected to run into her again. Certainly not at St. Anselm's."

Claire heard the withdrawal in Brett's voice. Why? She thought. But at that moment he stepped back. The closeness was over.

She walked to the window and looked down on Eighty-second Street and, far to the right, to the imposing entrance to the Metropolitan Museum of Art. Oddly, she found herself remembering the Christmas tree that the museum always put up in the hall in the back. It was her favorite of all the many trees appearing at this season in multireligious New York. The figures placed on the tree were from the Baroque period, shepherds, shepherdesses, shapely but plump cupids with bows. And below the tree was the Nativity scene with the Christ Child, Mary, Joseph, more shepherds, sheep and a wonderful variety of animals. The tree soared up almost two storys. There were seats around, not too many, just a few, and the music played was Renaissance and Baroque Christmas music. It was a truly beautiful sight, and she must make a point of seeing it. At that moment, she became aware of her own tears. It was ridiculous, of course, that she should feel that way, but it was in moments like this that she was reminded that Brett had had a life of his own before they met. Knowing that, how silly it was for her to be jealous! But she was.

She turned. "Is there anything else you can tell me?"

"Just this: I love you with all my heart and soul and strength. Believe that and hang onto it!"

She looked at his face and noticed as though for the first time how weary he looked. When, for a second or two, she forgot about her questions and frightening doubts, she could see what he himself was going through.

"All right, darling. As you say."

He was holding her tightly when Motley gave a bark and there was the sound of a key in the front door.

Jamie, after one glance in their direction said, "Hi!" and disappeared into his room.

"I wish I knew what was the matter with him," Claire said.

Brett turned away. " 'Oh what can ail thee, knight at arms?' " he quoted casually.

"It's not that he's palely loitering," Claire finished the reference. "I can't imagine Jamie being or doing anything palely."

Brett gave a tired grin. "Neither can I."

"If I thought it would do the slightest good," Claire said, "I'd try to hammer out of him whatever's ailing him."

"But it wouldn't do the slightest good, and might do actual harm—like hardening his resistance."

■ ■ ■

Sunday was the second Sunday in Advent. Claire, sitting in the choir stalls near the lectern from which she would read the First Lesson, sent up a small prayer of thanks, as she did most Sundays, that she did not have to preach at the eleven o'clock Eucharist. She hated preaching at the main service, although she enjoyed preaching two Sundays out of the month at the nine-thirty family service, at which she addressed her comments to the children. Which actually meant, she reflected now, that she told them Bible stories and—if appropriate—drew small modern parallels at the end of each brief talk.

This morning she had talked about the Syrian general,

Naaman the Leper, winner of many battles and highly regarded by his king. Hearing of the Israelite prophet, Elisha, he had come to Israel to ask Elisha to heal him. Elisha hadn't even bothered to come downstairs. He had sent a curt message: "Go dip in the river Jordan seven times." Naaman had flown into a fine military rage and stormed that he had not come all this way to be told to wash in their miserable trickle of a river. His lieutenant let him rave and stamp and when he finally ran out of steam said, "If he had asked you to do something difficult, you would have done it. What's the problem with this?" So Naaman, swallowing humble pie every step of the way, got down from his chariot and dunked himself in the Jordan seven times. And was cured.

She elaborated on the point that her son, Jamie, she felt sure, would do anything he could to help her when she really needed it, especially during the many years she had spent as a widow. He had told her so often, and had meant every word of it. On the other hand, despite her almost tearful pleas, he would manage not to wash his hands before eating. . . .

For a moment she smiled to herself. Then she remembered that it was at that point in her sermonette that she felt something run across her feet. She looked down and saw a mouse disappearing among the choir stalls. If she had had any doubt, the squeaks, giggles and screams of various members of the mixed adult and children's choir would have corroborated it. "I wonder how that got in here," she said, with as much aplomb as she could muster. "We don't usually run to white mice, even though this is a church."

There was an appreciative chuckle from the adults of the congregation, mostly parents and a few single adults who wanted to have the rest of the day to themselves.

Jamie had had his three white mice (named Joseph, Mary and Poppins) before the advent of Motley. As a matter of fact, Claire had kept a few herself as a child and had never been afraid of them. Still, she wondered who had let the mouse loose at that moment, just as she was making her point. Afterwards, as the family's choir was marching sedately out, she had collected some of the children together and asked who had let loose the mouse. All swore total innocence. Claire looked at each little face carefully. Having brought up two children, and worked with many others, or she was a fairly good judge of when a child was lying. Almost always he or she gave himself/herself away: the too solemn look, the carefully arranged innocent expression and the eyes that looked back too steadily. But none of those looking at her was guilty of those mistakes.

Surely it couldn't have been one of the adults in the choir? The nine-thirty family service choir was not given to hubris. It hardly would have been possible when they were attached to the same church as the internationally famous boys' choir, which people from all over the world—to say nothing of from all over the country—journeyed to hear. Those who sang for the earlier service sang for the sheer pleasure of belting out popular hymns. And, although out of loyalty to St. Anselm's and to Eric the admission could not have been pulled from her, Claire found she enjoyed them more.

Why, she thought now, waiting to read the lesson? Was her appreciation of the pure Anglican tone of the boys' choir less than it should have been? Couldn't she hear now the beauty of the Venite, the ancient words sung in a Gregorian chant? She was able to pick out little Malcolm's light high voice, and of course Timothy's clear, sure and strong soprano. There was none of the female vibrato there—just the straight note, as unshadowed as a trumpet's.

She thought then about the old dean and his statement that Timothy was on the edge of having his voice break, and glanced now across the chancel space to where he stood in the front row of the choir stall, his fair head rising by almost a foot above Malcolm's.

At that moment Timothy caught her glance at him and gave a quick grin, hastily repressed, because Eric did not tolerate his boys' attention straying for even a second from watching his hands and face in the mirror above the organ, as he conducted as well as played.

Claire glanced at the smaller boy. Malcolm doesn't look too happy, she surprised herself by thinking as she rose to read the lesson.

· · ·

Advent or not, the rector devoted his sermon to the memory of Dean Maitland, talking movingly about his years as a student under the dean when the latter was his tutor at Cambridge.

"He was one of the kindest men I have ever known," the rector said in his clear, mid-Atlantic accent, "and one of the most profoundly Christian. And it was most deeply as a Christian that he could be—and often was—searingly honest. He had a capacity, not always comfortable for those around him, for seeing into the human heart and mind. You couldn't fool him, and all of those who spiritually and sometimes literally sat at his feet learned that."

Claire wondered how well that had sat with Mark, because it was hard to imagine him being humble and unhappily honest in front of anyone. And then she reproached herself. "You're getting to be a judgmental bitch," she told herself and wondered uneasily if that were a quality in herself that Brett had come across.

Glancing to where he usually sat, she saw him and Martha seated in their pew, and felt a surge of admiration for Brett for being there. She herself had had to come early, and had encountered the reporters grouped outside their apartment and at the Park Avenue entrance to the church. She also felt a gratitude to Martha for this show of loyalty. Martha was not an enthusiastic churchgoer, but she was extremely fond of Brett. She's growing up, Claire thought. Remembering the insecure, anorexic and unhappy adolescent Martha had been for a while, Claire reflected that her growth was as much due to Brett's kindness and interest as anything she herself had done. The generous and paternal attention of an intelligent and personable man could do a lot for a girl, as Claire well knew.

And, as was all too obvious, Jamie was not there. An irritation at her son took hold of Claire. She remembered Brett's words: trying to coerce Jamie would just make him dig his heels in more. But he could at least show the family flag! Once again Claire wondered what, if anything, was going on between Brett and Jamie. I could wring his stubborn neck, she thought!

"And now to God the Father, God the Son and God the Holy Ghost," the rector said, ending his sermon and turning towards the altar. Along with everyone else, Claire got to her feet, but a beat later than the rest.

■   ■   ■

"How do you think it sounded?" Eric said to her during the coffee hour.

"The choir?"

"Yes, Claire dear, the choir." Eric grinned. "What else do I worry about twenty-five hours a day?"

Claire smiled back. "All right. I just wondered—" At that point Larry rolled up. "Have a cookie," he said genially, holding out a plate of oatmeal delicacies.

Eric waved him away as Claire helped herself.

"You just wondered what?" Eric asked.

"I just wondered if little Malcolm is unhappy about anything."

"Possibly about the fact that he had not learned his solo this morning and got holy hell from me."

"But he didn't have to sing a solo today."

"That's no excuse. He has to sing at Evensong on Tuesday and should have been ready."

They were joined by Marguerite, Eric's wife. "We were talking about Malcolm," Eric said. "Claire thinks he looked unhappy during the service and I was explaining that I had given him what for for not knowing his solo for Tuesday.

"Lazy beggar," Marguerite, who was English, said. "Still, I know what Claire is talking about. I've thought lately that somebody might be bullying him."

"Like who?" Eric said.

"Like Timothy," Larry put in. "There's a lad who thinks there's no end to his influence and charm."

"Nonsense," Eric said. "You just pick on him because you resent anyone being that good."

"Now why should I do that?"

"It's a human tendency—throw stones at the model of perfection."

"You're surely not saying young Timothy is a model of anything, other than being an expert soprano soloist, which I grant you he is." Marguerite said.

"Hush," her husband said kindly. "I just want him to get through Advent and Christmas. His voice can go the day after Epiphany, if it needs to, which, of course, it does. By that time I think young Malcolm will be ready." He sighed. "If I could just pour the same amount of ambition in him that Tim's always had! Marguerite's right. He's sometimes a lazy little so-and-so."

Wendy Swade ambled up, a cup of coffee in her hand. "You shouldn't all be huddled together," she said reprovingly. "You ought to mingle."

"You're right," Claire said. "I'll be good and mingle, but first tell me who that stunner is over there. The one talking to Mark. I've never seen her here before, have you?"

Marguerite turned to look. "If we had, we'd surely remember."

"Somebody told me she's a new member from some prominent church in the South," Wendy said. "I think her name is Barton. Lavinia Barton. That's quite a getup, isn't it?"

"Now, now!" Larry said. He put his plate of cookies down on a nearby table.

"I hope," Claire said fervently, suddenly remembering Martha's newest crusade, "that Martha doesn't see her."

"Why?" Wendy and Eric asked together.

"Because in her new missionary zeal, she might go up and tear that indecently expensive-looking fur coat off her back."

"Ah!" Larry said. "Animals." He opened his mouth and then closed it again.

"Darling," Wendy said lovingly, "you look like a fish doing that. What were you going to say and why did you think better of it?" She hesitated. "Or am I being tactless?"

"I think I see one of the choir parents," Marguerite said. "Come on, Eric." They wandered off.

"Obviously I was," Wendy said. "Oh dear!"

"That's right," Claire said, "Marguerite was sporting a new fur coat last Sunday, wasn't she?"

"I rather sympathize with Martha," Larry said. "I'd hate for anyone to wear Dudley's coat."

"Darling, nobody would wear Dudley's coat. It's hardly a thing of beauty, even though he is the world's greatest dog."

"Jamie'd fight you on that one," Claire said, putting down her cup. "There is but one king and his name is Motley."

"Didn't see Jamie this morning. Is he okay?"

"Yes," Claire said briefly. If Larry had been alone she might have been tempted to confide her concerns about Jamie and Brett, but, much as she liked Wendy, she didn't know her as well and didn't feel as free around her.

Claire didn't see Brett anywhere, but Martha was having an earnest conversation with an intense-looking young man with a long nose and even longer hair. But before Claire could get to her one of the women of the church, a member of the altar guild and the Wednesday evening dinner and study group came up.

"Ms. Aldington," she said aggressively, and Claire's heart sank a little. Mrs. Winnicott was a good woman, a good Christian and an indispensable church worker. She could also, Claire thought to herself, be a royal pain. "Yes, Mrs. Winnicott?"

"I am truly horrified by the graffiti on our stairs," she said angrily. "I not only think it should be removed, but I think we should find out who is responsible for it."

"I certainly agree it should be removed, and I'll speak to the head of our custodians about it. Whether we can find who is responsible or not is something else. As you know, a church is not a closed domain. We have a lot of people in and out all during the day."

"And I think it's extremely unfortunate that it should automatically be blamed on the homeless, poor creatures. For one thing, as you know, I sleep with them once a week, and I can assure you that there is no way they could reach those particular stairs. Their beds are in the basement room, and both doors are locked."

Why, Claire wondered, did some of the most liberal and generous workers for the public good persist in thrusting their goodness in your face so often?

"If I sounded as though I were automatically blaming one of the homeless then I'm sorry. One certainly can't automatically blame anyone. But short of keeping a member of the cleaning staff perpetually on guard by the stairs, I'm not sure what we can do. And our resources are stretched fairly thin as it is. Excuse me, I see my husband, and there's something I need to talk to him about." And Claire, feeling moderately guilty, quickly crossed the room to where Brett was chatting with the rector. "Sorry to barge in," she murmured.

"Are you fleeing Mrs. Winnicott?" Brett said understandingly.

"I'm afraid so. She's angry about the graffiti."

"What graffiti?" Brett said.

"The drawings on the walls of the stairs," the rector explained.

"They must be fairly new," Brett said. "I used the stairs about a month ago, when the elevator was having an attack of temperament, and I didn't see any."

"They are fairly new," Mark said. "And Mrs. Winnicott isn't the only person to be in a state about it. Two of the vestrymen and three women from the congregation have been on to me about it."

"I had no idea people used the stairs that much," Brett said.

Claire heard the tension in his tone and realized it was not the happiest of subjects. It was at that moment that Claire was struck with the fact that Brett, who was usually surrounded by people during the coffee hour, had been standing for sometime only with the rector.

What an idiot I am! she thought. Their avoidance of him, something she had been too busy to notice before, was now obvious. Without even thinking, she put out her hand and touched his arm.

He hesitated, then put his own hand over hers. Mark, looking at them, smiled. "Brett, I've said this to you in private. I am now going to say it in front of Claire. I think the police have gone out of their minds to suspect you. And I shall state that loudly and clearly at all times to anyone who looks as if he or she were suffering the faintest doubt about it. Now excuse me, because I see Mrs. W. bearing down on us, and I owe you a favor, Claire. Last week you rescued me from the head of the Sunday school. Now I'm going to rescue you from Mrs. W."

"I must say," Claire said warmly as he walked off, "that was nice. Nicer and warmer than I've been used to giving him credit for."

"Yes," Brett said, and put his coffee cup down on table nearby. "I'm going to go on home," he said abruptly. "Probably you want to stay longer."

"No," Claire said. "I'll go with you. Maybe I should collect Martha."

"The last I saw of her she was having a heart-to-heart with a hippie type."

"That expression has gone out, darling. Do you mean the gloomy-looking young man with long hair and a long nose?"

"The same. I can't think what a girl would see in him. He looks like your ideal victim."

Claire was mildly puzzled. "Victim of what?"

"Does it matter? The essential thing is to be a victim. Any reason will do."

Claire rubbed his arm. "You're angry."

"Yes," Brett said. "I am."

Claire did not ask what he was angry about. Being wrongfully accused could do it. Appearing in every edition of every paper as a suspect could also do it, as could people staying on the other side of the room in droves. When he was treasurer of the church and then was temporary business manager Brett had gone out of his way to help the church in its various financial undertakings, and he had put himself out to be helpful to church members who for one reason or another fell on hard times. But not one of the latter had come to his side during the coffee hour—at least not while Claire was watching.

The ride home was silent. Martha had been left behind with her new boyfriend. When they reached the apartment, Claire said something about fixing lunch and went toward the kitchen, but when Brett had gone to his study, she turned towards Jamie's room. Her soft knock brought no reply, so she turned the knob and went in. Motley, who was asleep on the floor, looked up. Jamie wasn't there, but in the middle of his bed was a white envelope with "Mom" inscribed on the front.

As Claire went towards it, her heart started its tattoo. It means nothing, she told herself. He's probably doing homework with a friend. But somehow she didn't believe it. She ripped open the envelope and extracted a single sheet of paper.

I have to go away for a bit. There's a good reason. Will be back as soon as possible. Don't worry. I'm all right. Please take care of Motley and remember he has to be walked THREE times a day.

Jamie

6

laire did not know how long she sat there on the bed, the letter in her hand, immobilized by shock. Then her mind started coming to grips with the meaning of the words. Jamie, her son, was going away for a while, where he didn't say, or for how long, or with whom, or why—something he'd never done before in his fourteen years.

But he's only a child, she thought. He can't do that. He's too young!

But he'd done it. He'd gone, without consulting her or Brett or asking their permission.

Suddenly in her mind he stopped being the adolescent, taller than she. He was the little boy he once had been: square and rugged, but also sweet, kind and friendly.

Every horror story she had ever read, every headline in a

tabloid involving boys who had been victimized, taken advantage of, kidnapped, raped, went through her mind.

She was so wrapped up in her thoughts that she didn't hear the rap on the door or was even aware someone had knocked until the letter was taken out of her hand.

After a minute Brett said, "Stop thinking of the possible horrors, which, from your face, you obviously were thinking. Am I right?"

"Brett, he's only a little boy!"

"He's fourteen. That's not a little boy, and he's almost as tall as I am. He's also strong and could give a good account of himself if he had to."

"That sounds just like a man—all you think of is physical strength! He's not a man—he doesn't have a man's judgment!"

"I didn't say he did. And I understand how you feel. Supposing a mother came to you with this story about a son who'd gone off leaving a note like that. What would you say to her?"

Claire was silent. Brett put his hand on her shoulder and shook her gently. "It's not like you to be hysterical."

"You're not a mother!"

"That's certainly true. Now let's talk about this rationally. Do you have any idea of why he's done this? Has anything happened lately, at school, or here, or with his friends?"

Claire said slowly, "The only thing I've noticed lately is that—well, that there seemed to be tension between the two of you." She looked at her husband. "Did you notice it?"

"Yes. It would have been hard to miss."

"Do you know why? Did you have any words or a quarrel?"

Brett shook his head. "No. I can't say we have. As a matter of fact, what I noticed before I felt the recent tension was that he all but stopped talking to me."

Claire stared at him. "Yes, you're right. But since it came at the same time as his being more difficult than usual about everything—homework, grades, you name it, I didn't isolate it. And I put the whole thing down to his having exams. But that was last week."

"Christmas break hasn't started, has it?"

"No, it's due to start Thursday. Did you ever challenge him on the strain between you?"

Brett shook his head. "I thought at first it'd be best to ignore it. Certainly I wasn't going to do it during exam week. But I was thinking about getting him off somewhere for a talk when this whole business with the dean came up."

They started walking from the room. Motley, who had been standing, looking at them, started following them.

Claire looked back. "I suppose one of us ought to walk him."

"I'll take him out," Brett offered. "Sit down and try to relax."

When he was gone Claire, who found she couldn't either sit down or relax, went into the kitchen to make a stab at lunch. She was boiling some rice when there was the sound of a key in the front door.

"Jamie!" Claire called. Then, leaving the boiling rice to froth up over the pan, she ran into the hall.

"It's only me," Martha said, taking off her coat.

"Do you have any idea where Jamie went?" Claire asked.

Martha, in the act of putting her coat on a hanger, stopped. "Isn't he here?"

"No, he's gone, but wouldn't say where. He left this." And Claire took the letter out of her pocket and gave it to Martha.

"Holy cow!" Martha said. "So that's what he's been plotting."

"Do you have any idea of where he went?" Claire could hear the anxiety in her own voice.

"No. None. I haven't been his confidante for some time now. But I was fairly sure something was up his sleeve."

"Was he unhappy?"

"Yes, I think so. But I don't know what about."

"You don't have any idea?"

Martha looked at her for a moment. "No. I'm sorry. I don't."

Claire went back to the stove, turned off the flame, removed the pot of rice, wet some paper toweling and went to clean up the mess. "Ouch!" she yelled, and snatched her hand back.

"I'll do it," Martha said, taking the toweling from her and adding several layers.

"I wonder which of his friends I can call."

"He'd know you'd be doing that, so I'd be pretty surprised if he talked to any of them. Or, if he did, he'd have sworn them to secrecy."

"Then what can I do?" Claire's voice broke.

"Wait it out, I guess," Martha said.

Brett and Motley came through the front door and into the kitchen, followed by Patsy, tail in the air.

"Brett, what do you think we should do—about Jamie, I mean?" Claire said.

"For the moment, and hard as it is, nothing. Jamie had some reason for going. Knowing him, it was almost certainly a good one. I'm sure you'll be hearing from him soon."

All this time, Claire realized, she had been thinking in some corner of her mind that she could call Lieutenant O'Neill and ask him for his help. But would O'Neill and the police use this in some way against Brett?

● ■ ●

Lunch was a silent meal. No one ate much, and they were all glad when it was over.

"Motley didn't have what he obviously considered his usual walk just now," Brett said. "Getting him out of the park was not easy. How about our taking him for a real walk in the park?"

"No," Claire said. "Jamie might decide to call."

"I don't think he'd be calling this soon," Martha said.

"You don't know. And, if he did, I might miss him."

"All right," Brett said. "Martha, I'm still going to take Motley. Want to come?"

"That guy I met at church, of all unlikely places," Martha said. "He had to go somewhere for lunch but he thought we might go to a movie this afternoon."

"Who is he?" Claire asked. "And I don't think church is such an unlikely place to meet somebody, but he looked like an unlikely person to be there."

Martha grinned. "Just because he looks like one of the Beatles?"

Claire smiled wearily back. "All right. I'm prejudiced."

"I don't know why you are," Martha said. "After all, the sixties was your generation. Philippe de Mornay."

"Who?" Brett and Claire asked together.

"You asked his name. That's what it is."

"French?" Claire said.

"Yes. Just been here a week."

"There are French Protestants, of course," Brett said, "but somehow I expect them to be in Presbyterian churches."

"He was at St. Anselm's to listen to the boys' choir. He's a composer."

"Good heavens," Claire was momentarily distracted.

"Dissonant, atonal and cerebral—" Brett made a face, "speaking of prejudice."

"No, movie music. He's been hired to do the music for a British-French movie about a boys' choir to be made here."

"Why does a movie described that way fill me with vague forbodings?" Brett pondered.

"More prejudice," Martha said. "By the way, he knows Eric What's-his-name. In fact that's who suggested he do this research at St. Anselm's. He also knows somebody named Christopher Porritt, but I didn't learn what his connection was."

"Director of the Norwich choir, the one we're expecting this week," Claire said after a minute. She was having a hard time keeping her mind on the conversation.

The phone rang. Claire jumped to her feet and rushed

into the hall. "Hello?" she said, her voice full of anxiety. "Oh. All right." She turned to Martha. "It's your friend." Before Martha could get there Claire picked up the phone again. "I'm sorry if I sounded abrupt."

Martha talked for a moment, then hung up. "You'll get a chance to meet him properly. He's coming to pick me up in half an hour."

In about five minutes the phone rang again. Claire ran out to it. "Hello, Mark," she said. Then, after a brief pause. "Yes, all right. I'll take the eight-thirty tomorrow." She put down the phone.

"The early service?" Brett asked.

"Yes.

"I'm glad you decided to take it,"

"Jamie knows the church number as well as this one," she told Brett. Then, "I'm going into the study to do some work. Since it's Advent, Mark suggested I give a short homily."

In about half an hour the doorbell rang and a few seconds later Martha knocked on her door. "I'd like you to meet Philippe," she said.

He wasn't, Claire decided as she shook hands, as plain-looking as she had originally thought. Perhaps it was because he seemed to have combed his hair back so his forehead appeared higher and his nose therefore less prominent. Also, he had nice hazel eyes and an attractive smile. She knew that Brett and Martha were watching her anxiously. I have to get hold of myself, she thought.

"How do you do?" she said, and made herself smile back.

Evidently she was functioning on automatic, because without being aware of having thought of it she heard herself say to Martha, "Can I speak to you for a moment."

With a slightly alarmed look on her face, Martha allowed herself to be taken into the study.

"Don't tell him about Jamie," Claire said to her.

"All right, I won't. I wasn't planning to. But why not?"

Claire thought a moment. "I'm not entirely sure why not.

I can't give you a rational sounding reason. It's just something I feel."

"You and your friend Letty Dalrymple," Martha said, referring to the psychic from the Village, with whom Claire had worked in several of her cases.

"Letty," Claire said slowly.

"Oh-oh! I think I've put ideas in your head," Martha said.

Claire ignored that. "I suppose it's no use asking you when you'll be back."

Martha hesitated. "Normally, I'd say probably not, but in view of everything, I'll make it a point to be early tonight."

"Thanks." Claire smiled and went back to the study.

It was a while later when she found herself dialing a number. She heard the phone ring and ring and was about to hang up, when a breathless voice said, "Hello?"

"Letty" Claire said.

"What's the matter?" Letty asked.

"How did you know something was the matter?" Claire knew that was a silly question, but she added, "But I guess that comes with being a psychic."

"You don't have to be a psychic to know you're upset about something, Claire. Something serious. What is it? Brett? Jamie? Martha?"

"Jamie. And, of course, Brett. I was upset about him—still am—before Jamie walked out." She gulped. "I'm not making a lot of sense.

"Let's begin with Jamie. What do you mean, walked out?"

"I mean when Brett and I got home from church we found a note in Jamie's room saying he was going away for a while."

"Is that all?"

"Isn't that enough, Letty? He's only fourteen!"

"Yes. Broderick went away for a while, once. Of course he didn't write a note."

Claire assumed Broderick was a cat. Letty had a number of cats and a close relationship with each. "Did he come back?"

"Oh yes. And to this day I don't know why he went or where he was."

"Letty, a son, a child, is a little different."

"You're right. A cat is much more worrying. He couldn't telephone or write a note or tell me what was wrong. Jamie can."

Claire wished suddenly that she hadn't called Letty.

"And it's no use your wishing that you hadn't called me. I'll concentrate on Jamie and see what comes up. But you know, I somehow feel more worried about Brett."

"You don't read the papers, do you?"

"Never. Don't watch television either. They just muddle things and spread bad vibrations!"

"Brett has been virtually accused of the murder of an elderly English dean who stayed with us one night and was killed the following day in the parish house."

"Well he certainly didn't do it," Letty said. "The police can sometimes be as blind as a bat!"

Claire felt a surge of comfort come over her. "I know he didn't do it, too. But—"

"But there's something else, isn't there?"

To no one else in the world would Claire have said what she did. "The police say that somebody, they don't say who, saw Brett in the parish house the afternoon the dean was killed and say they saw him kissing a woman. When accused of that, he said he was more kissed than kissing, but I think that's a cop out."

"In other words, you're afraid for him and you're also angry."

As she heard the words Claire knew that for all her assurance to Brett of faith in him, Letty was right. She was frightened and she was angry, angry for again seeming to be involved with another woman as he had once before, only there was less excuse then because they weren't married.

"I suppose I am. And he doesn't seem to be as worried as he should be about Jamie." Those words popped out of her mouth, too. "At least, I guess what I mean is that he keeps trying to calm me down."

"And you don't want to be calmed down. What would you do with one of your patients or clients who came to you with the same story? Wouldn't you try to calm them down, too? Nobody thinks or acts for the best when they're all agitated."

"All right, Letty. You're right, of course!"

"And now you're upset at me. Well, it takes some of it away from Brett. I'll call you back presently." And Letty hung up.

Claire sat there staring at the phone. Then, using all her discipline, she forced her mind onto the short sermon for the next morning.

■ ■ ■

On Monday Claire left for the church at seven-thirty. Before she did, she called St. Stephen's, Jamie's school, and asked for the headmaster.

"Mr. McDermott isn't in yet," the receptionist said.

"Would you ask him to call the Reverend Claire Aldington at St. Anselm's Church when he comes in? He has the number. Please tell him it's very important."

When she emerged from the service and hurried to the parish house there was a message in her box saying the headmaster had called.

As soon as she was in her office Claire telephoned him.

"Yes, Ms. Aldington," Mr. McDermott said. "What was it you wanted to talk to me about?"

"Is Jamie there?" she said.

"I haven't seen him this morning. Which doesn't, of course, mean he's not here. Has something happened?"

Claire took a breath and told him about Jamie's note.

There was a short silence. "Let me talk to his faculty advisor," Mr. McDermott said. "As I'm sure you know, exams ended last week, and of course Christmas break begins on Thursday. So our normal schedule is off and most of the boys have been at loose ends, not where they usually are. I'll talk to his faculty advisor, Ms. Aldington. And I'll call you back as soon as I can."

Claire looked at her schedule. Hope Meredith was coming at nine and a new client at eleven. She glanced out to see if Joanna was at her desk. She wasn't, but came in carrying some water in a watering can and started to water the two philodendrons and three pothos plants sitting on the window sills.

"They get so dry over the weekend," she said.

"Maybe you should give them an extra dunking on Friday," Claire said. Joanna seemed to have some affinity for the plants and Claire was happy to encourage it. "By the way, I'm expecting an important call from St. Stephen's School. If it should come while I'm in a session, please interrupt me."

Joanna looked up. "It must be an important call. You've never said that before."

"It is important."

She was talking to Hope when the phone rang outside and her buzzer went. Claire had already warned Hope that the call might come in.

"Excuse me," she said, and reached for the phone.

"I'm sorry," the headmaster said, "but I don't have any news for you, good or bad. Jamie's exams ended last Thursday, he was here Friday. But he hasn't been here today. There are no regular classes, as I said, though he should, of course, check in with his home room. Because of the break, it's easy for him not to. But I'll call you immediately if he shows up. Ms. Aldington, try not to worry. Boys do strange things and seem never to understand why their parents get upset. Jamie's a very sensible young man. He'll be all right."

When she hung up, Hope said in her customary dreary voice, "I hope Jamie doesn't take up with some pervert."

It was seldom that Claire had to hang on to her self-control with a client, but she could feel her hands tense and counted to five.

"What makes you think he might?"

"Everything is so much freer these days. The kids know a

lot more about sex than we did at their age and you know teenagers want to experiment." Hope flicked a piece of fluff off her Irish tweed skirt. "And Jamie is a good-looking kid."

Claire, who had been on the verge of saying something totally different, said, "You speak as though you've seen him."

"Well, not recently. Adam Deane is my cousin. And when Jamie went to the choir school I used to see him at graduation and other events."

"I see. Let's get back to what we were talking about before the call, which was the possibility of your getting a job."

"I really think it wouldn't be right to take a job away from someone who needed it, when I have more money than I need."

"A job would do you a world of good," Claire said, hearing the sharpness in her voice and regretting it. "There are other reasons for taking work than material need."

"I don't really have any skills. Mother saw to that."

"Your mother has been dead five years."

"What she wanted me to do was marry."

"Why do you think you haven't. You are certainly attractive."

"Mummy didn't think so. Neither did Daddy. He always said I was too fat. He liked thin little girls, the kind I brought home to dinner sometimes, who sat at the dining table with me when I brought them home and said, 'Yes, Mr. Meredith' and 'No, Mr. Meredith' and what he got was me."

The sudden savagery in her voice startled Claire, who had never heard anything there but a flat, uninflected tone.

"I've never heard you speak of your father quite that way," she said.

Hope shrugged.

"Did he abuse you verbally?"

She shrugged again. "He told me no man would ever look at me."

"But you know that's not true. From what you've told me there have been several men who wanted to marry you."

"Daddy always said, and Mummy agreed, that the only

ones who'd want to marry me would be after my money." She
smoothed her tweed skirt. "It's not as good as being desirable,
but it's better than nothing. And anyway, attractiveness goes,
money doesn't. You should know that!"

"What do you mean by that, Hope?"

The amber eyes looked at her in surprise. "You're a therapist, aren't you? You have to know that kind of thing."

Claire's eyes caught the clock that was placed at the end of
her desk turned so that only she could see it. But Hope could
also be quick. She looked at her watch and rose. "I'll see you
next week."

. . .

Claire plodded through the rest of the day, trying not to listen
for the phone, trying to give her clients her full attention.
And feeling guilty that she had probably not succeeded. At
the end of the day she was exhausted. By the time she got
home she was numb with fatigue.

As soon as Brett came home she said, "I'm going to call
Jamie's friends. I suppose you disapprove."

"I doubt very much that they would know where Jamie is,
or, if they do know, if they haven't been sworn to secrecy."
He paused. "But you must do as you feel best." He left with
Motley for the latter's afternoon walk.

Claire called Andrew Fairborn first. He was Jamie's closest
friend.

"Gosh, Mrs. Cunningham, I wonder why he'd split like
that. No, I didn't know about it."

"And you don't know and can't guess where he might
be?"

"No, I can't."

"He hasn't said anything to you lately that . . . about
anything he might be upset over?"

"No. Honest."

She had the same reaction with the next boy, Bill Fraser,
and the next, and the next. In all she called five boys. All of
them denied knowing anything.

Brett and Motley arrived home just as she finished talking to the fifth boy.

"You were right," she said dully. "None of them knows where Jamie is, or says he doesn't."

Brett put his arm around her, and for a few moments of safety she clung to him.

Martha was not home for dinner, and Claire for the life of her couldn't remember whether Martha had told her she'd be out or in. But at ten, there was the sound of voices and a key in the lock. "Hi, everybody," Martha said. And she and Philippe came into the living room.

"Have a good evening?" Claire asked.

Brett put down the book he was reading. "What did you do?"

"Went to listen to a choir across town. I thought it was good, but Philippe says it's nowhere near as good as St. Anselm's."

"That's gratifying," Brett said. "Eric should be pleased." He looked at Philippe. "How's the movie music progressing."

"Slowly," Philippe said. His English, Claire noticed, was excellent.

"Have you spent a lot of time over here?" she asked. "You have almost no accent at all."

"My mother was an American. She grew up a few blocks from here." He hesitated. "Mrs. Cunningham, Martha told me about Jamie. When I was about his age I ran away from home."

Claire drew in her breath. "Did you now! And you were all right?"

"Yes. I didn't tell any of my friends where I was going because I knew that they'd be the first my parents would ask. I stayed quite safely with somebody they wouldn't have thought of, and when my—er—crisis had passed, I went back. Of course, they were enrage"—suddenly, Claire noticed, he sounded more French—"and punished me. But I was all right."

"Thank you," Claire said. "I realize you were telling us that to keep us from worry."

"But it doesn't help?"

"No, you're not Jamie. You strike me as far calmer, more given to . . . well, planning."

"But I wasn't at fourteen. My mother felt exactly as you did—I discovered afterwards."

Claire stunned herself by turning on him. "You must have known she'd feel that way before you went, and still you took off!"

"Philippe was trying to be helpful, Claire," Brett said.

"I know he was. But he doesn't understand. I'm sorry!" And she went off down the hall to her room. She was sitting on the bed when Martha came in.

"Truly, he was just—"

"Trying to be helpful. If anybody else says that I'll scream! Martha, if you ever have children you'll know what I'm feeling, but before that there's no way of my telling you."

"I don't know why you're angry at Brett, though. He hasn't done anything."

"I didn't realize it showed that much—at least to anyone but Letty."

Martha sat down, reached out and took Claire's hand. "You're a wonderful mother!"

"If I'm such a wonderful mother, why has Jamie run away?" Claire said, and burst into tears.

. . .

After a few hours' sleep that night, she found herself awake, staring at the dark, aware of Brett sleeping beside her. As though he knew she was awake, he woke up himself and simply put his arm around her, drawing her to him. And she found ease and comfort in his strength and warmth so she could go back to sleep.

The next day she bumped into Larry in the hallway and became vaguely aware that she hadn't seen him since Sunday. "Have you been away?" she asked accusingly.

"I have. Do you mean you're only just noticing?"

She gave a strained smile. "Business or pleasure?"

"Both really. We went to that conference in Philadelphia and stayed with Wendy's parents. What's the matter?"

"Well, you know about Brett."

"Something new there? There wasn't anything in the paper."

She paused. Why she felt so strongly against talking about Jamie she didn't know. But Larry was different.

"Jamie . . . Jamie's gone. I don't know where he is."

"You mean he just walked out?"

"Yes. When Brett and I got back from church Sunday he was gone. There was a note on his bed saying he was leaving for a while."

"Didn't say why, I take it."

"No."

Larry looked at her thoughtfully. "What about his school? Do they know anything?"

"No. And I called his friends last night. They don't know anything either." She paused. "I have to tell you that I loathed broadcasting to the world that my son had taken off. Sure I'd be blamed. How's that for ego?"

"Entirely natural, I'd say. I'd feel the same."

"You would?"

"I would. Do you have any ideas about why Jamie took off?"

"Not really." She hesitated. "There's been some kind of tension between him and Brett lately. Brett noticed it, too. Jamie just stopped talking to him. Brett said he was on the point of trying to talk to him to see what was going on, when the whole thing about the dean broke."

"Do you think it could have anything to do with Brett's being questioned?"

"I don't know. I can't believe it's that."

"Hmmm. Of course I can't take Brett in the role of murderer seriously." He paused. "You aren't having a very easy time of it, are you?" As Claire's eyes suddenly filled, he said gently, "Have you tried anything really revolutionary?"

"Like what?"

"Well, prayer, for instance."

"Yes." Somehow she managed not to mention what was on the tip of her tongue. I want suggestions for action, not pious exhortations!

Larry grinned. "Yes, I know how you feel but you have to give it time." He patted her arm with a plump hand and went down the hall.

Claire went back into her office, closed the door, and pulled her phone towards her. She dialed a number and said, "Lieutenant O'Neill, please. It's Claire Aldington."

When the lieutenant came on the phone she told him, as succinctly as possible, about Jamie's leaving and her efforts to locate him.

"Why didn't you call me sooner?" he asked.

"Because of Brett. I thought . . . well I thought it might make it more difficult for him."

"Do you think the two are connected?"

"No," she said. "I have no reason to think that they are. I'm calling you to see if you have any suggestions regarding Jamie."

There was silence at the other end of the phone. Then, "Since he's a child, technically, I can get the police into action right away. Tell me. He's your son—how well do you know him?"

"I thought I knew him very well. It seems I don't."

"It sounds to me as though he had thought out what he was going to do with a lot of care. That doesn't mean his judgment is adult or that he can't get into a scrape through misjudgment. But he always looked like a wise sort of kid to me."

"What are you saying, Lieutenant? Don't worry? You're a parent yourself."

"Have a little trust! He's doing what seems to him to be the right thing. He'll be back soon, I'm sure. By the way, I take it you don't want this spread across the tabloids if you can avoid it."

"No, I don't. Do you think you can keep it from being?"

"I don't know. I can try. It will be better if no one puts Jamie's disappearance and Brett's being questioned together."

"Why?" Claire said sharply.

"I have to go now and get this thing started. I'll be in touch."

7

he twenty-five boys of the Norwich choir arrived with their choir master, Christopher Porritt, on Thursday. Eric Fullerton and Larry went to Kennedy to greet them and to help them through the gang of reporters.

An editorial in one of the papers that morning expressed surprise that the choir's annual visit to St. Anselm's was proceeding, in view of Dr. Maitland's tragic death at the parish house.

When asked by the editor of the paper's editorial page whether he would like to reply, Mark Hastings drafted a statement that the editor assured him would be published on the paper's Op Ed page.

"Horrible and disastrous as Dr. Maitland's death was," Mark Hastings wrote, "the dean in his courage and profound faith would be the first to say that God's work goes on, not in spite of, but all the more in the face of disaster."

To make sure that it would not sound a false note, Mark sent for Claire, Larry, Eric and Joe the morning before Eric and Larry left for Kennedy and read what he had written to them.

"Please be candid," he said, putting down his sheet of paper. "Do you think that's all right?"

"It's excellent," Eric said. "Right on the button."

Larry nodded. "It puts the church's case very well."

"Claire?" Mark said. "Do you think the piece says what it ought to say?"

"Yes, I do." Claire said. "It's a good piece."

"Joe?"

There was an almost imperceptible pause, then Joe said, "It's fine!"

Mark looked satisfied. "The editor of the Op Ed page says it will appear in the editorial section on Sunday."

As the three went into the hall, Eric turned to Joe. "Did you like it?"

"If I hadn't, I would have said so." The sculptured nostrils flared. "Come on, Eric, did you think I was lying?"

Eric grinned at his friend. "No need to get in an uproar! I just thought there were a couple of unspoken comments hovering in the air."

"What were hovering were dollar signs. We don't sell tickets to the regular services they sing at, but the walls bulge with charitable and generous people who come to listen to the visiting choir, and there is a charge at the door at their official concert—all of which swells the church's coffers."

To Claire, the usual easy aimiability between the two unlikely friends seemed suddenly strained.

"Is that bad?" Eric asked defensively.

"No, of course not! As long as the money goes to good causes. We can certainly use it for our outreach programs and our homeless. I guess I wished the rector would say something about them, and how their need goes on, no matter what happens. As far as I'm concerned, they're a lot more important than proper deference to high British officials."

"But maybe some of us who revere old music and wish to keep strong the tie between the two branches of the Anglican Church feel differently. They're still a few of us around." There was color in Eric's cheeks and his eyes shone.

"And maybe that's the reason you don't have more minority boys in our own bloody choir—for all your fine talk about sitting behind a curtain when they audition! Let me tell you—"

"NO!" Larry's usually soft voice was so loud that everybody stopped talking out of sheer shock.

"I suppose—" Joe started.

"I said 'No,' " Larry turned to look at him. "If you want to win people over, as you say you do, for God's sake, don't bludgeon them! You may think you're acting out of love for the poor and the homeless, but you're not! You're using them as a respectable vehicle for your own anger over something that has little or nothing to do with them!"

Joe's cheeks got red. "When I think what my people—"

"Your people my—er—foot. As I know but maybe the others don't, your name may be Hispanic but you don't come from a downtrodden minority. Your father was an upper-middle-class Spaniard from Madrid—a lawyer, wasn't he? And your mother came from the Anglo-Irish ascendancy. Her grandfather on her mother's side may have marched with the Sinn Fein, but your mother's father was a considerable landowner. Right?"

There was a silence. "That doesn't make what I say wrong!"

"It doesn't make your advocacy of the poor wrong but with hostility like that, you're not going to win anybody to their side, if that's what you want."

There was a short silence. Then Joe turned on his heel and walked away.

"I shouldn't have let him rile me," Eric said. He sighed. "I really like him, but when he goes on about the choir he gets my goat, especially when we're into Christmas and the Norwich people are about to arrive." He stopped for a minute, then burst out, "And I'm still worried about young Malcolm being able to take Timothy's place if he has to."

"Don't tell me Timothy's voice has cracked!" Claire said.

"I'm just not sure. I haven't actually heard it crack, but something tells me either it has, and he hasn't told me and is trying to bluff or it will crack at any moment."

"Can he bluff it?" Claire asked.

"Not to me."

"What about Malcolm? Couldn't he step in?"

"Malcolm is very young. I'm just not sure whether he can take it on throughout all of Advent and Christmas. There's a lot of singing."

"But don't you have soloists beside Malcolm who could also?" Larry asked.

"I certainly have other good singers, but not one with that particular high clear sound. Oh well. We're leaving for the airport in an hour. Larry, I'll meet you downstairs."

"Timothy doesn't sound too up front about the state of his voice," Claire said to Larry, as they turned to walk down the hall, "especially considering how much depends on him. But I suppose he can't be faulted. What person, child or adult, doesn't want his moment in the limelight!"

"Yes," Larry said thoughtfully. "Didn't you say you thought Malcolm looked unhappy?"

"Yes. I did. Why?"

"Because I thought so, too. And I don't think an unhappy child works well."

"Wouldn't Eric know if something was seriously wrong?"

"He knows something is wrong, all right. That's why he's fussing about whether Malcolm can pick up if Timothy is overtaken by puberty. He just puts it another way, and, I guess, thinks of it another way." He paused. "Didn't Jamie go to the choir school for a while?"

Hearing Jamie's name brought a sudden clutch at her middle, but Claire answered evenly. "A brief while, about three years ago. He had a good enough voice, or Max, the then choir master wouldn't have let him in. But he hated it, and I think sang deliberately badly."

"Why did he go then in the first place?"

"I think he was trying to help me. Because of my being here, he was offered a full scholarship, which certainly eased the money burden. But when I saw how unhappy he was, I told him we could manage, and he was able to get a partial scholarship from the school he's at—thanks, I think, largely to Brett." There was another pang at his name, too.

Larry took her arm. "Listen, they're both going to be all right. I'm sure of it."

"I certainly hope you're right!" She took a breath. "How come you know so much about Joe's family background?"

"Wendy's mother was friendly with his mother. To hear him talk sometimes, you'd think he rose from the bottom of the bottom. Actually, his mother was socially quite prominent, and a member of one of the top women's clubs."

Claire started to laugh. "You're right, of course. Revolutionaries nearly all come from the middle class—vide Rousseau, Voltaire, and the others."

"Disaffected intellectuals—even Marx and Lenin. Do you think they're all angry at their mothers or fathers?"

"History according to Freud? It's an interesting thought!"

The elevator seemed to be stuck or held on the ground floor, so when Claire, whose office was the floor below, left Larry, she decided to use the stairs. That was when she noticed again the graffiti on the walls. There wasn't much light, but the scrawlings were clearly visible, because whoever had done it had used chalk. Claire stared at the white figures against the uninspired green. Somehow feeling as though she were subjecting herself to a Rorschak test, she tried to see if there were anything other than random swirls and lines. There was one word, BANG! But as far as she could see at first it bore no relation to any of the other scribblings. Some of the lines were joined at their ends, in a sort of concertina effect, and there was near it a round circular scribble with lines coming out. Signifying nothing, she thought to herself, and went on down. She was wondering why the whole thing made her feel so depressed when she remembered that when he was younger Jamie had developed a habit of furtively drawing on walls and fences unless he thought she was watching. It was a phase he went through, and she thoroughly deplored it, reprimanding him whenever she caught him at it. Fortunately, he also grew out of it. . . .

It was so fatally easy for her mind to slide back to Jamie, bringing its accompaniment of fear and anger. But O'Neill was now involved and Larry, who didn't deal in false or easy comfort, also knew what had happened, and they both seemed to be sure that Jamie was remarkably levelheaded for a fourteen-year-old boy.

Thank God, she thought, I have clients this afternoon.

Joanna had gone to lunch by the time Claire was back in her office. Claire glanced at her watch and decided to go down and get the mail which usually arrived in the middle of the morning. This time she used the elevator both ways and on her way back up ran through the letters and circulars that had jammed her box when she opened it. Correction, she thought: A letter.

She glanced though the circulars, mostly about seminars and lectures, and threw them in Joanna's waste basket when she returned to her office. She glanced at her watch. Her next client wasn't due for three minutes, so she slid her finger under the flap of the letter's envelope.

Like the envelope, the letter had been typed. There was a single line:

Bad things are going to happen to you and to those you love.

Claire dropped the letter onto the desk. My God, she thought. She was about to pick it up again when Lieutenant O'Neill's voice sounded in her head almost as clear as though he were there: don't touch it. Fingerprints.

Who on earth could have sent it and why? Obviously someone who wished her harm. Again, why?

Nothing occurred to her. She had no idea.

. . .

The English boys streamed through the parish house and into the choir rehearsal room. After a while their voices, almost unbearably clear and pure, could be heard throughout the building. Claire, pausing between clients, wondered if she could detect any difference between the English and the St. Anselm's singing and decided that while the English had the purer sound, the Americans had more body. She had just gone down the hall to the water cooler when she learned from Eric, approaching with a tall, dark man of about his own age, that she had it backwards.

"Christopher Porritt," Eric said, introducing his companion. Claire shook hands, taking in the wide, high-cheekboned, rather Celtic face and the narrow dark eyes. "That was your lot we were hearing just now," she said, "wasn't it?"

"No," Eric replied. "The last voices you heard were ours. The others only rehearsed briefly, just to make sure they still had their voices after all the trauma of the flight."

Claire made a wry face. "That'll teach me to make judgments."

Eric looked happy. Christopher smiled briefly.

"We're very sorry about the dean's death," Claire said. "It was good of you to come, anyway."

"Yes," Porritt said. He glanced at his watch. Eric said, "We're in a bit of a rush. We have to get together with Mark about schedules. See you later."

Am I being supersensitive, Claire wondered, as she went back to her office, or did the attractive Mr. Porritt want to get rid of me fast?"

. . .

The same feeling of being regarded with a certain suspicion came again that afternoon when she went to Mark's office to meet the dean's nephew and the Archbishop's chaplain who had come over on a later flight.

Larry and Joe were there when Claire walked in. Introductions were made, Claire shook hands with the two men. The chaplain was a stockily built man of about fifty, with blue eyes and thinning brown hair. The dean's nephew was younger, about forty, bearing no resemblance whatsoever to the dean.

"We're all so very sorry," Claire said, knowing that was the least tribute she could pay, yet feeling as though the phrase had become rote.

"Quite so," the chaplain said. The dean's nephew, George Maitland, said nothing.

"We've been asked to go down to the police precinct this afternoon and Mark has very kindly offered to accompany us," the chaplain added.

George Maitland turned suddenly to Claire. "I was extremely fond of my uncle," he said in a somewhat pedantic voice. "I gather Uncle Alec spent his last night in your home. Was there anything he said that could possibly throw any light on . . . on what happened to him? I realize," the nephew hurried on, "that I probably should be addressing this question to your husband, since it was because they knew each other that Uncle Alec stayed with you, but in the circumstances . . . perhaps it wouldn't be desirable."

There was a short silence. Then, "Why not?" Claire asked.

"Well, there's been a lot in the papers in London about your husband and all the evidence that points to his—"

Larry interrupted him. "I've known Brett longer than Claire has, and such an act would be impossible for him. There's no question about that."

"Well if it's that certain," Maitland said, "then why do the police seem to think he did it?"

Mark put in, "They haven't arrested him. He's just under questioning."

"I know that he and my uncle had some sharp disagreements when he was in London fifteen years ago."

"How do you know that?" Claire said.

"Because I was acting as my uncle's aide-de-camp." The old-fashioned words sounded odd but appropriate in Maitland's voice. There was something old-fashioned about him, Claire thought, though he couldn't be much over forty. "Uncle Alec would come home very upset."

"What was the disagreement about?" Larry asked.

"Something to do with putting together the funds from the New York diocese and the London mission, as far as I can make out," Mark said. He turned to Claire. "Isn't that about right?"

"As far as I know—" Claire started when there was a knock on the door and Joe Martinez stalked in. "Sorry to be late," he said.

"Late for what?" Mark asked.

Joe's brows shot up. "Didn't you summon the staff—to meet the English delegation?" Joe asked. "Or wasn't it supposed to include me?"

Mark put in hastily, "And this is Joe Martinez who has joined us, we're happy to say, but who used to be vicar of St. Matthew's before it was closed."

"Ah, the Hispanic church," the chaplain said, and stepped forward to shake hands with Joe with enthusiasm, in contrast, Claire thought, to his manner when greeting her. George Maitland then moved forward to meet Joe with the same warm greeting on his face.

They really do think Brett killed the dean, she thought, and an odd chill went through her.

She had planned to show the anonymous letter she'd received to Mark. But she excused herself as soon as she reasonably could and went back to her office.

Joanna was opening and closing the drawers of her desk, pushing things aside, obviously looking for something.

"Lost something?" Claire said as she walked through to her office.

"Yes, a ten dollar bill," Joanna said. "And please don't ask me if I'm sure I didn't leave it somewhere else. I came with two tens this morning, spent one on lunch and some errands, and was counting on the other to go to the supermarket before dinner. It's not in my wallet, and I haven't been leaving my bag around."

Claire stopped. "Where do you normally keep it—your wallet, I mean?"

"In my handbag, which I keep in the file drawer, which I keep locked."

"And you took it out to go to lunch, and then put it back when you returned?"

"Yes. Yes, I did."

"When you went to get it now, was the file drawer locked?"

She stared at Claire for a minute, surprised. Then, "No," she said. "I was in such a hurry I didn't think. I know I locked it when I came back from lunch. But when I went to open it now, the file drawer wasn't locked."

"Who else would have a key?"

"I don't know. But—they're so many file drawers, don't you think maybe some keys match more than one drawer?"

"Perhaps," Claire said. "Who's responsible for requisitioning files and things like that?"

"Maude Butler, the rector's secretary," Joanna said.

"I'll go and see her now."

"Deborah Quin called. Wants you to call her back."

Claire hesitated, torn between priorities. Then she glanced at her watch. "I'd better go and see if I can waylay Maude before she leaves for the day," she said. "I'll call Deborah when I get back." She hesitated, "Anybody else call?" Always there was the hope that Jamie would get in touch!

"No. There was a hang-up. The phone rang, but when I answered it, whoever it was hung up."

"How did you answer it?"

"The way I always do. 'Pastoral Counseling.'"

"All right." Claire went swiftly back down the stairs again and along the hall to Mark's office, her mind running around a now familiar track. Could it have been Jamie? Would he have hung up if someone other than herself had answered.

Maude Butler was putting the cover on her typewriter. Mark's office was open and there was no one in it.

"Maude, when the files are requisitioned and sent, I assume keys are sent with them."

"Of course. And are given to whoever is getting the file. Why?"

Claire explained. "If the keys are fairly standard, then I thought one key might fit another file. Is that possible?"

"It's possible, I suppose. But I don't think it's likely. The people who supply these files are pretty good. Undoubtedly they must have a master key that would open all the files. But I've never found one that would fit several. Why are you asking?"

"Because it looks like someone opened Joanna's drawer where she keeps her handbag and took a ten dollar bill out of it."

"Oh. Could the lock have been jimmied open?"

"I don't know," Claire admitted. "I didn't look."

"Well look when you go back. It shouldn't be too hard to figure out. There are usually scratches on the file and the metal of the lock inside the drawer might be a little distorted. And let me know tomorrow morning. I'm afraid I can't wait now, because I'm rushing off to meet somebody for dinner and a concert."

"All right," Claire said to Joanna on her return. "Maude said there shouldn't be any duplication of keys. Let's see if the lock is jimmied."

Joanna was standing beside her desk, holding her handbag, which was open. But she closed it and slung it over her shoulder as she came over to the file. "Not that being careful now is going to get me back my ten dollars."

It wasn't hard to see that the file drawer had, indeed, been jimmied. The files were a dark green and the scratches were fairly apparent. Also, the square lock mechanism inside had been pulled a little from the wall of the drawer itself.

Claire and Joanna stared at one another. Finally Claire said, "This was obviously done after you came back from lunch and locked up your bag. You must have stepped out at least once, do you remember when?"

"I went to the bathroom around three-thirty, and then about four fifteen, I went to the cafeteria to get some coffee."

"And I was in my office with a client and the door closed, I suppose."

"Yes."

Claire went into her office and took her own bag out of the bottom drawer of her desk. Extracting ten dollars from the wallet, she went back and held it out to Joanna. "There's no use your being short when you go to the market tonight. Take this to make up, and I'll speak to Maude Butler tomorrow. This makes about half a dozen items now that are missing. My pencil, your pen, your ten dollars—"

"My aunt's keychain with the charm on it, and the keys, too, so she's had to have her locks changed, Mr. Swade's secretary's china cat and somebody else's lion paperweight. Oh, and five dollars from Pedro's coat pocket." Pedro was one of the custodians.

"You mean he just hung his coat up with money in it?"

"He forgot about it, and then, half an hour after he hung it up, he remembered and went back."

"Where was it?"

"In that little cloak room just outside the transept of the church."

"What time of day was it when it happened?"

"Morning."

Joanna was still holding the ten dollar bill. "You know, you don't have to give me the ten dollars. I mean, it could have been yours. It burns me up, but you're not responsible."

This was such a mature attitude on Joanna's part that Claire promptly forgave her a variety of small inefficiencies. "Take it, anyway. You need it going home."

"Okay. Thanks."

Claire went back into her office, put her bag away again,

and locked the drawer. "Although," she muttered half aloud to herself, "that doesn't seem to do much good."

Then she dialed Deborah's number. The phone rang and rang. Then it was picked up and, before she could say anything, put down again. For a moment she stared at the phone, then rang the same number again, only to have it once more picked up at the other end and replaced.

Now what do I do, she wondered?

Turning her Rolodex, she checked the number. It was correct. Also listed was Deborah's office number. Claire tried that and glanced at her watch. Five-twenty. As she half expected, there was no answer at all.

Deborah calling could mean that her husband had started abusing her again. The odd business about the phone could also mean that she was unable to answer it.

Claire sat at her desk, her face in her hands for a while. Where was Jamie? Why in God's name had he decided to go away without giving her any idea where he might be or what might be the matter. Was he all right . . . ?

She picked up the phone and dialled O'Neill's number. "I know I'm bugging you, but have you had any chance to learn anything about Jamie?" she said.

"I'm afraid not." There was a short silence. "Are you okay?"

"That's an interesting question, Lieutenant. My husband has been practically accused of committing a murder, my son is missing, there is a really queer series of thefts around the church here and I have received a threatening anonymous letter. Apart from that I'm fine."

"You didn't tell me about the anonymous letter."

"It just got here this afternoon."

"Is it there handy?"

"Yes."

"Okay. Pick it up in a handkerchief. Put it and the envelope it came in in a manila envelope. I'll pick it up."

"All right." There was something tense about his silence.

Summoning her courage she said to him, "Has anything else happened that I should know about?"

"Somebody else has been killed. A woman."

"Who?"

"Her name is Lavinia Barton."

The name rang a faint bell in Claire's mind, but she couldn't track it down. "Who is she?"

"A wealthy lady from the South—South Carolina, I think —who is, we learned, a recent member of your congregation."

"But that doesn't necessarily have anything to do with us!"

"I'm afraid it does. She is the woman Brett was said to be —er—embracing, when he was seen in the parish house shortly before he was heard quarreling with the dean."

"Oh." Now she remembered! This must be the woman whom she herself had described as a stunner at the coffee hour.

"I see." she said. "Where—where was she found?" she asked.

"In the choir school, where she had been visiting her son."

8

he reporters this time were not only in front of the parish house, they were also thronging around the front door to the choir school across the street.

The questions came hurtling at Claire, even though she felt that for the moment she was not the main focus of attention.

"Do you think your husband is involved with the murder at the choir school?"

"Were you and your husband close friends of Lavinia Barton?"

"How do you feel now that your husband may be the suspect in not one but two—?"

Claire set her teeth and pushed her way through the mikes and hands stretched out holding them, determined not to give way to temptation and land a punch. Fortunately, she was rescued by Lieutenant O'Neill to whom she had talked only minutes before.

"You got up here fast," she said to him.

"I left the moment I talked to you. Okay, now," he said to the crowd at large. "Stand back!" To Claire he said, "I'd like to talk to you for a minute. Come over here to the car."

Claire felt a little sick as she got into the front seat of O'Neill's car. "Just for the record," she said as O'Neill went around and got in beside her, "Brett didn't do this."

"What makes you so sure?"

"I know Brett. He doesn't go around killing people."

"Well, we know your husband couldn't have killed Mrs. Barton. She's been dead only about an hour and a half at the most, and he's been ensconced in a meeting for the past three hours, in full view of about twenty people. And before that he was at his downtown club for lunch with two other bankers."

Despite her conviction that Brett was incapable of murder, she felt relief wash over her. "So how does this affect his involvement with the other murder?"

"Officially, it doesn't. I've felt for several days, in fact from the beginning, that he wasn't responsible for the death of Maitland."

"Then why in God's name did you act like you thought he was and get him spread all over the papers?"

"I can't take responsibility for what the papers do, but I guess the answer is that we were under a lot of pressure because of the importance of the dean."

"So are you going to say maybe that you no longer suspect Brett?"

"No. But about twenty reporters have already asked if the police thought Brett Cunningham was the suspect here and we were able to give them his solid alibi." He paused. "I do have to ask you, though, whether or not you were aware that Brett was involved with Lavinia Barton?"

"Did you ask Brett that question?"

"Yes, the captain himself went down to see Brett in his banker's tower."

Claire could feel her whole body stiffening. "And what did he say?"

"He did not deny knowing her. He denied absolutely being involved with her sexually or romantically."

Claire heard her own voice, filled with certainty. "Then if that's what he said, that is the truth."

There was a few minutes' silence. "Is there anything you can tell me about this murder?" she asked.

"It seems she came to the choir school more or less on impulse, since she hadn't had an appointment. Apparently, she wanted to see her son about something. But she didn't get to see him. She had obviously been shown into the reception room, because that was where her body was found."

"How did she die?"

"A ferocious blow to the head."

"How horrible! Who on earth. . . . Does anyone have the faintest idea why?"

"No one. We've talked to her son a little, but, understandably, he's upset."

"Who was the boy?" Claire asked.

"Malcolm—Malcolm Richardson. He was the child of a previous marriage."

"Malcolm," Claire repeated slowly.

O'Neill looked at her sharply. "I take it you knew him. I mean, I know you're attached to the church, but I didn't think you had anything to do with the choir."

"I don't—other than seeing them tear around sometimes and hearing them rehearse. I was only aware of Malcolm because Eric Fullerton, the choir master, seemed a little worried about him. He was supposed to be able to take over the main soprano role in a pinch, but Eric wasn't sure he was up to it."

"Yeah, that's what Fullerton told us. And this whole thing isn't made easier by all the English kids who are there."

"And their choir master, Christopher Porritt, of course," Claire said. "Who's with Malcolm now?"

"The choir master, the headmaster of the school and the

school nurse—any of the three or all of them. They were all circulating anxiously. Why?"

"I wondered if there were anything I could do, but I hardly know the boy and he'd probably need to be with friends or relatives, if he has any. By the way, where is his father?"

"He's married again and lives in France."

"And Lavinia's husband?"

"He died a year or two ago."

"Poor little boy." She thought for a minute. "Did you say the school nurse was there?"

"Yes. A good, practical-looking soul, the kind who'd be marvelous if you have a royal stomach ache. I'm not sure how good she'd be in this."

This was Claire's impression of Miss Reynolds, who had always struck her as somewhat dry and precise, a bit of a cold fish. Then suspicion crossed her mind. "Are you trying to get me to go over there?" she asked suddenly. "Painting this heartrending picture?"

"Well, it would be a help to have somebody whose power of observation I trust around the boy right now."

"You know me well enough to know which way I'd jump if I came across something that you might want to know but I thought it'd be better for Malcolm if you didn't."

"Yes, but I'd be willing to take the risk."

"All right. I'll stick my head in if you clear the way with the police." She stopped. "One more question: do you think this murder and the dean's are in any way connected?"

"I haven't the faintest idea. I wish I did. The only real link between the two murders is that they both occurred on St. Anselm's property. If you can find another link it would be a help."

"Aren't you being a little unorthodox asking me this?"

"Very. And if the commissioner heard about it, he'd have my badge. But we're being pushed even harder than before. There's some kind of international element here that nobody's made very clear. Political, I think. When I ask politely or impolitely what it is, I get stonewalled. But I'm sure of it. Did you bring the anonymous letter?"

"Yes." She dug in her sizable bag for the manila envelope. "Here."

"Thanks." He put the folded envelope in his pocket. "All set?"

"Yes. Let's get on with it."

While Claire had come to know by sight some of the other choir boys, she had only glimpsed Malcolm at occasional choir rehearsals and on Sundays, standing in his white ruff and red robe next to Timothy Bentham. So she didn't feel she knew him at all well, but her heart certainly went out to him in a moment like this.

"Was he the one to find his mother?"

"Yes, unfortunately. The receptionist showed Mrs. Barton into the reception room, rang for Malcolm and then, as far as the hysterical woman's been able to tell us, went toward the back of the school where there's a ladies' room. Whatever happened to Lavinia Barton happened in those few minutes. Malcolm came down the stairs, went into the reception room, and when the receptionist came back to her post, she saw him simply standing there, his face as white as paper, stuttering, 'Mom, Mom, Mom . . .'"

As O'Neill described the scene it was horrifyingly vivid. Claire's sense of pity and compassion for the child increased.

Being with O'Neill certainly made it easier to get through the crowd of reporters, police and idle watchers. For all her years in the parish Claire had rarely been in the school before, and was surprised at how modern and compact it looked, although a moment's reflection made her realize it had been built within the past few years.

There was no question as to where the reception room was. A clutch of people stood in a doorway to the left, looking down.

"Let us through please," O'Neill said, and they stepped aside.

Claire caught her breath. Mrs. Barton, still wearing her

fur coat, was on the floor, blood congealing in her hair and on the carpet around her head. One hand was thrust out, a tissue still clutched in it. Her handbag was a few feet from her hand. One shoe was off. Beneath the dark mink where the coat had fallen open was an equally stylish turquoise wool dress. Bending over her was a man Claire was fairly sure was the police doctor. Other men were there, one of them snapping photographs. The whole scene made Claire feel a little sick.

"Where's Malcolm?" she asked O'Neill.

"I'll ask. Stay here."

Two hours ago, she thought, looking again at the woman she had described only the previous Sunday as a stunner, two hours ago Lavinia Barton had been alive and full of life. It was a banal thought, but nonetheless true for being banal. Who would want to kill her in such a savage manner? And how little room she took up on the rug! She seemed tiny, not much bigger than a medium-sized child.

"Malcolm is up in the headmaster's study," O'Neill said coming back. "I've been instructed to take you there. The nurse hasn't turned out to be too efficient, and the poor kid is in a state of shock."

What Claire saw, when she and O'Neill entered the headmaster's study upstairs, was a sight that would stay with her for a long time. In his desk chair, turned around toward the room for the occasion, was Adam Deane, headmaster of the St. Anselm's Choir School for the past fifteen years. Across from him was a woman in a fussy dress adorned with ribbons and bows. But the plain face above registered what Claire found to be an odd mixture of sentimentality and impatience.

Between them was Malcolm, looking, in his gray flannel suit, even smaller than she had remembered him. She knew from Eric Fullerton that he was at least eleven, but he could have easily passed for a boy of eight. His straight brown hair fell over his forehead, which was high and wide. His face was down, his arms braced against the arms of the chair in which he sat. He seemed to be examining his feet, but Claire realized he could simply be keeping his head lowered, trying not to cry.

When she and O'Neill entered, he looked up. His eyes were brown, the lids puffy. His most devoted friend would not have called him good-looking, because the face below the strong, prominent forehead seemed to shrink to almost nothing. Or perhaps it was just the frozen look on his face, an expression of extreme grief, Claire told herself, and pushed away a curious feeling that that was not the right diagnosis. Whatever it was, she knew that the small face would haunt her for a long time, and the important thing now was to give whatever help she could.

"Malcolm?" she said gently, and walked over to him. "I'm so sorry about your mother and about your being the one to find her. That must have been dreadful for you!" Tentatively she put a hand on his narrow shoulder.

Malcolm gave a convulsive shudder and then a sob. As Claire slid her hands around his prominent shoulder blades he suddenly wrapped his arms around her and rested his head against her. She could feel his small body shake with sobs as she held him to her. "It's all right, Malcolm. Cry as much as you want!"

After a minute the nurse almost flounced to her feet. "Well you seem to be doing better than I did," she said, "and I do have other things needing my attention."

As she walked out of the room the headmaster rose. He was a stocky man of medium height. "I'm glad you're here," he said to Claire. "Until now the boy didn't seem to be able to express anything."

Claire, unwilling to talk over Malcolm's head, nodded.

"I think perhaps I should go and see how the police—" he paused as Malcolm at the word seemed to shrink even closer to Claire—"how they are getting along."

As she held Malcolm, murmuring words of encouragement and support, she found her mind inclined to stray, trying to remember what she had ever heard about Deane. No one she'd known had ever had any doubts about his ability as a headmaster and as a teacher, though some occasionally gave him higher marks for scholarship and discipline than for intuition. But as one of them said, "You can't run a school like that without a good working knowledge of what could go on in the heads of some seventy-five boys ranging from nine to fourteen." By fourteen, of course, the boys had passed the age at which their purpose for being at such a school existed, and they all went on to prep schools. At that moment, she remembered, as in a frame of film, Malcolm's face as he stood in the choir stall, his soprano voice soaring out, neither as high nor yet as strong as Timothy's beside him, but still remarkable.

Malcolm lifted his head from Claire's skirt, leaving a wet spot where his tears had soaked in. He astonished her then. "Can I come home with you tonight?"

"Home with me?" she repeated, feeling stupid. Such a recourse hadn't occurred to her. "I don't know, Malcolm, what do you think Mr. Deane would say?"

"He'd say no," Malcolm burst out. "He doesn't like kids to spend the night away from school."

Claire groped in her mind. "Well, you have very early choir practice, don't you?"

"Yes."

There was the guest room, of course, Claire thought, the room where the dean had stayed. And, her mind went relentlessly on, Jamie's room. She had been blessedly free from consciously thinking about Jamie's absence for the past half-hour, so that for a few seconds the reality struck her anew. Thrusting that aside, Claire forced her mind back to Malcolm and decided he could stay there and be comforted by Motley and comfort the big dog in return.

"Do you like dogs?" she said now.

"Yes. Real dogs. Not poodles."

"What's wrong with poodles? They're dogs, too."

"They don't look like dogs."

"Well . . . let's see what Mr. Deane says." Until that moment she had been playing for time, not sure what she herself thought about taking Malcolm home. Would it help him? Or would it be merely an escape?

At this point, her mind argued, what's wrong with escape? Everyone needs it from time to time, and that would certainly apply to an eleven-year-old boy who had just discovered his mother's murdered body in the school reception room. Claire pushed aside an entirely irrational fear that to let Malcolm stay in Jamie's room would be tantamount to forgetting Jamie himself and his rightful ownership should Jamie choose tonight to come back.

"Can I?" Malcolm's urgent, searching expression was painfully intense.

"I don't see why not."

Now she'd have to square it with Adam Deane. "Just let me speak to the headmaster, then if he says yes, you can go up and pack a few things."

"I don't need to pack anything."

"What about a—a change of clothes?"

"I put on clean clothes this morning."

For some reason that reminded Claire of the old joke her father used to tell her about the boy who said indignantly, "What do you mean wash my neck? I washed it last week." She smiled a little. Jamie never said those actual words, but his expression and general attitude of mulish obstinacy when she was trying to drive him to a bath often reminded her of them. Did boys of a certain age congenitally dislike being told to take a bath?

I'm woolgathering again, Claire thought. She looked down at Malcolm. "Why don't you stay here while I go and talk to Mr. Deane?"

"I'll go with you. Please!"

Obviously he didn't want to be alone with his grief, Claire thought. At that moment O'Neill appeared in the doorway. "Everything okay?"

"Fine," she said. "Malcolm wants to come home with me. I guess he doesn't want to be around the school here, especially after—" she glanced down—"especially now." She looked up at O'Neill. "Is that all right with you?"

"Sure. Do you have the principal's permission?"

There were principals and there were headmasters, Claire thought. And to some degree the difference in terms reflected the difference between the public and the private systems of education. She herself and, obviously, Lieutenant O'Neill had gone to public schools which had principals; her first husband, her son and Brett had all gone to private schools with headmasters. "I don't know, yet. I—Malcolm and I—are going to ask him."

O'Neill stepped aside. "Okay. Let me know."

"Oh, I don't think that'd be at all necessary," Mr. Deane said when approached. He glanced down at Malcolm clinging to Claire's arm. "If Malcolm is feeling at all—strange—he could sleep in the sick room."

"I don't want to sleep there," Malcolm said passionately. "I want to go home with Mrs. Cunningham."

The headmaster didn't exactly frown. His face suddenly became rigid. "I'm afraid—"

Help came from unexpected quarters. "I'd be grateful if you allowed Malcolm to go home with Mrs. Cunningham," Lieutenant O'Neill said. "She is a trained therapist, and good as your nurse is, I don't think she has that training, does she?"

Claire was astonished, but she was also grateful. She glanced again at the headmaster.

The latter's face got, if anything, more rigid, but he said, "If, of course, you think that best. Very well, run upstairs to your bedroom, Malcolm, and put a few night things in your bag."

"No!" Again the passionate refusal, and he started to cry again.

"He'll be all right," Claire said hastily. "My son, Jamie, you may remember, came to the school here briefly. I'll . . . I'll borrow some of his things."

"As you wish!"

Going back towards the front door was not easy, because they had to pass the reception room. The body, visible between various policemen, was now covered with a cloth. Malcolm clutched Claire's hand, the fingers so tight Claire was sure they'd leave indentations.

"I'll take you in my car," O'Neill said.

As they left the school, they hurried out between ranks of reporters, mikes and television cameras. Once again Claire was grateful for the lieutenant's escort.

Malcolm sat between them as they drove up Park Avenue. The Christmas trees, lining the mall in the middle of the avenue, were ablaze with their Christmas lights. Wreaths were on doors. Back of the car as they drove uptown was the Helmsley Building. Later, when all the lights from the business offices had been turned off, lights in the shape of a huge cross—so many windows going straight up, so many across on one of the floors—would pay a public tribute to the season.

No one said anything until they arrived at the apartment house.

"Here you are," O'Neill said, and got out of the car. He accompanied them up to the front door. "You'll be all right from here," he said.

Brett flung open the door before Claire had inserted her key in the lock. "I was worried about you—" he started, and then caught sight of Malcolm. "Hello," he paused. "Is your name Malcolm?"

"Yes," Malcolm said.

Brett stepped back. "Come in both of you." He then disappeared. As Claire took off her coat and urged Malcolm to remove his she heard the television set turned off. Unlike so many men, Claire thought, Brett could be trusted to be imaginative and thoughtful. And then, despite herself, came the traitorous question again, had he really been involved with Lavinia Barton?

"No," she said aloud. She had settled that question to her own satisfaction a while back. Hadn't she?

Oh God! she thought. There were times when the layers

of the conscious and the unconscious were too complicated for her.

"Let me have your coat," she said again to Malcolm, and helped him as he started, slowly, to pull himself from his coat.

Boys didn't wear coats anymore, she thought. They wear zip jackets, quilt jackets, leather jackets. Unless they wore uniforms, which, of course, Malcolm did. She took the dark blue, lined raincoat and hung it up in the hall closet.

Brett emerged again from the living room. Suddenly his and Claire's eyes met. Claire heard herself ask, "Have you and Malcolm met before?"

"No. We haven't."

"No," Malcolm said. He looked frightened, and she reproached herself for having asked this question of Brett for emotional reasons of her own when Malcolm was present. But then, Claire forced herself to realize, since she had known him, Malcolm had looked frightened most of the time.

"This is my husband Mr. Cunningham, Malcolm."

Brett held out his hand. "Hello, Malcolm."

For a moment Malcolm, who had taken Claire's hand again, didn't move. Then he let go her hand and walked towards Brett and shook his hand. "Hello. Sir," he added, as an afterthought.

"I'm very sorry about your mother," Brett said.

Claire, watching Malcolm's face, saw once again the expression she had seen there before, but it passed too quickly for her to identify it.

"Yes," Malcolm said, and looked down at his feet.

All three stood there for a moment, then Claire said, "Malcolm, I'm going to let you borrow my son, Jamie's, room for tonight." She paused, forcing herself to continue. "Come along and I'll show you where it is. Then I'll go and fix dinner."

Malcolm trotted with her down the hall. Claire forced herself to switch on the light and walk into Jamie's room. She had done it, of course, every day since Jamie had gone away—

how long was it now? she asked herself. Two days? It felt like a year.

The room to Claire looked achingly the same, as though any minute Jamie would walk in. There were pictures of Motley all over the wall. One of Claire was above his desk. On either side of that were one of his father, and one of himself and Brett. The rest of the wall space was taken up with pictures of animals of all kinds cut from magazines and papers.

"He liked animals, didn't he?" Malcolm said.

"Yes, he does." Claire replied, emphasizing the present tense. "The bathroom's through that door there. I'll go and get a pair of pajamas from the cupboard. I think I have an old pair left of Jamie's that would fit you."

"How old's Jamie now?"

"He's fourteen."

"Where is he? Won't he mind me being in his room?"

"He's . . . visiting a friend. No, he wouldn't mind. I'll go and get the pajamas. Why don't you wash your hands."

She half expected an argument. But Malcolm went obediently off to the bathroom.

She went down the hall to the living room. "I hope you don't mind," she said to Brett, who was sipping his drink. "He—I don't know quite what happened, but he—he was the one who found his mother's body. O'Neill felt the nurse at the school was not good for this kind of thing and asked me to go over there and see him. He—he seemed frantic about not wanting to spend the night in the school. He asked if he could come home with me. Brett—I couldn't—"

"Of course you couldn't. Did you think I'd object?"

She went over and put her hands on his shoulders. If only there were not that wall of suspicion between them, everything Brett said would have seemed right and exactly what a generous, imaginative man would say. She bent down and kissed him. When she straightened, she saw Malcolm in the doorway. He looked extremely small.

She turned to him and smiled. "What would you like to eat? Malcolm?"

"I'm not very hungry."

"What do you usually like when you're not very hungry?"

"Pizza."

"That's a good idea," Brett said.

"But I'm not very hungry."

"That's all right," Brett said. "I am."

Motley, who had paid little attention to Malcolm, now got up and wandered over. Claire, who was watching idly, saw Malcolm stiffen, his face white.

"It's all right, Malcolm," she said, going swiftly to his side. "Motley's very gentle, and he likes little boys. Motley, come here." She held one hand out to Motley's nose, while with the other she held Malcolm's hand. "Now let him smell the back of your hand. He won't hurt you, Malcolm. I promise you."

Malcolm held out his hand, palm down. Claire, who was lightly holding his arm, felt how rigid it was. Motley sniffed and sniffed. Then gently he licked the small hand, his tongue almost as big as Malcolm's hand and wrist.

"You see," Claire said. "He likes you."

Dinner was a somewhat stilted meal. Malcolm didn't talk much. However, he ate more than Claire expected him to. The pizza, a frozen concoction, was fairly good, and Claire added a salad. Malcolm's attention was divided between his plate and Motley, who stayed under the table but kept his muzzle on Malcolm's knee to encourage handouts.

"Can I give him some pizza?" Malcolm said at one point.

"If you want to, but put it on some paper. Here!" Claire jumped up and got one of the sections of the morning paper and put it down on the carpet. "Motley's not proud. He'll eat it off of that, that is if decides that he likes pizza."

Apparently Motley decided that he did. He gobbled up every bite Malcolm tore off his piece and gave to him.

Right after dinner Claire said to the little boy, "Would you like to go and watch some television in the living room, or would you rather go to bed?"

"There's television in my room, isn't there?"

Claire sighed, acknowledging that she could hardly expect

a child, however upset, not to notice the modest television set that Jamie had bought for his room with some Christmas money. "Yes, Malcolm, would you rather watch it in there?"

Malcolm surprised her then. "No. It's just that I saw it in the room. I'd rather watch it in the living room with you and Mr. Cunningham."

"You're very welcome to," Brett said. "Let's put the dishes in the dishwasher and then go the living room."

"Isn't there a maid?" Malcolm asked innocently.

"Just me," Claire said.

Malcolm looked bewildered. "You're not a maid."

"No," Claire said. "I was just joking." He looked so forlorn that she went over and hugged him. Unlike the previous time when he had clung to her, this time he remained stiff.

"All right, Malcolm," Brett said. "Let's go find a television show."

Claire busied herself in the kitchen, trying to interpret the sounds that came from the living room. She admitted to herself that, while she felt desperately sorry for her young guest, she also found him bewildering. There was no question but that he was in a state of shock, which was entirely natural. But the word "grief" that she kept trying to apply did not fit as easily. As she knew from personal as well as professional experience, grief could wear many different faces, not all of them attractive or sympathetic. Yet Malcolm's odd, antiphonal reactions of extreme need and rigid independence were not that unusual. Why did she keep coming back to the feeling that it was not grief he was feeling.

Around eight that evening Claire said to Malcolm, "What time do you go to bed at school?"

There was a short pause. "About eight-thirty."

Claire was then visited with what she thought was a brainwave. "Would you like me to ask Mr. Deane if one of your friends from school could come and spend the night with you?" Why she suddenly thought of that she didn't know, except perhaps he seemed so small to be spending the night all by himself in a good-sized room. There was another bed hidden under the regular one, and bringing another boy in would prove no problem. She had been congratulating herself and was therefore unprepared for the vehemence with which he said—almost shouted—"No!"

"All right, Malcolm, you certainly don't have to. It was just an idea. Forget it!"

His white look was back again, Claire noted with concern. "Are you all right?" she asked.

"Yes. Yes thanks." Malcolm got up. Because the chair was rather tall for a small person, he was as tall sitting down as he was when on his legs. "I think I'd like to go to bed," he said.

"All right. Would you like me or Mr. Cunningham to go with you?"

"No. It's all right. Good night." He walked out of the living room. Then, just beyond the door. "Do you mind if I ask Motley?"

"Not at all," Claire said.

"Motley," Malcolm called.

Motley raised his big head.

"Come on, Motley."

Motley pulled himself up and wandered out to Malcolm, his tail slowly wagging.

Malcolm put a hand on his head. "Let's go to bed," he said. Then once again he turned. "Do you think he'd bite someone if I asked him to?"

Claire was too astonished to reply.

Brett pushed his reading glasses down his nose. "If he or she or it would be attacking you, possibly. But short of that, I doubt it. He's basically an affectionate slob."

"Oh," Malcolm said.

"Anyone particular in mind?" Brett asked.

"No," Malcolm said, unconvincingly.

Brett and Claire watched as Malcolm and Motley walked down the hall and turned.

"What do you make of that?" Brett asked.

"I haven't the slightest idea. What do you make of it?"

"I can't give you any good reason, but I have a strong

feeling that (a) he isn't that grief stricken about his mother, and (b) he's scared of somebody."

"I think you're probably right on both counts," Claire said slowly.

· · ·

The phone calls started coming in later that night. The first two were from newspapers and then two from local television news stations.

"This is the *Morning Journal*," one smooth-voiced woman said. "Is Malcolm Richardson there with you?"

"Why do you want to know?" Claire said, playing for time while she thought out an appropriate response.

"Considering his mother has been killed, his stepfather is dead and his own father is half way across the world, then his fate should be of interest to any right-thinking person," the voice replied smugly.

"I'm sorry," Claire said with all the authority she could muster, "As you know I'm a psychotherapist, and I don't think for me to discuss Malcolm's state of mind under the present circumstances would benefit him or the city or the state. Good night."

Her hands were shaking as she put down the receiver.

"What did they want?" Brett asked.

Claire told him.

Brett hesitated a moment, then asked, "Why are you so upset? Reporters can be a bloody damn nuisance. You've had enough dealings with them to know that. But it's their job."

"Yes. I know that. And I can't answer your question. It was something to do with that woman's sanctimoniousness. No nonsense about 'sorry to be asking this but—' "

Brett sighed. "If you don't have a skin made of leather before becoming a reporter, you sure as hell will have it after a year or two."

Claire went back to catching up on some professional articles that had been piling up in the past weeks.

When the phone rang again Brett answered. Claire listened to his end of the conversation. "In answer to those questions," Brett said in his most aimiable voice, "No, no and no." He hung up.

"The same?" Claire asked.

"More or less."

They endured two more calls from various members of the media. "You'd think," Claire said furiously, "given what Malcolm has been through and the fact that he's only an eleven-year-old, they'd be a little less aggressive in their hounding."

"Not if you'd had any experience with them, you wouldn't."

"Why are you calmer than I am?" Claire asked. "After all, you haven't had an easy time of it in the past few days."

"True. But I think the answer is Jamie." He looked at her. "Isn't it?"

"Aren't you worried at all about him?" Claire said.

"Of course I am. But I also think my confidence is greater than yours, which is natural. I'm not his mother. I'll grant that if he walked in now I'd have a hard time not wanting to shake him till his teeth fell out—mostly because of what he's put you through. But I still depend on his good sense not to get in trouble—even if he failed the imagination test by a mile."

"What do you mean?"

"I mean, by thinking that anything warranted his taking off just like that and putting such a burden on you!"

Claire felt her eyes fill.

A few minutes later she was saying, "I wonder if I ought to go in and see if Malcolm is all right," when the phone rang again. "My turn," she said, and reached for the receiver.

A high voice said, "Tell Malcolm he can hide there as much as he likes. It's not going to do him any good!" In the background somewhere there was giggling.

"Who is this?" Claire said angrily. "Do you realize you're talking about a child who's just had his mother killed!"

"Serve him right!"

Another treble voice said. "Lousy sneak!" and the receiver was banged down.

Claire, knowing it was useless, rattled the buttons on the telephone.

"What was that all about?" Brett asked.

Claire told him, and added, "I can't believe it!"

"Sounds like it might be some of the boys at the choir school."

"But why would they do such a thing? Do you suppose poor little Malcolm is that unpopular?"

"Who can tell? Kids can be ferociously hard on one another, and their methods of allotting praise or disapproval can be as ruthless and savage as those of a primitive tribe."

"I suppose you're right. Still it's a shock!"

"I'm not a sentimentalist about children. The great myth, out of the Enlightenment, out of Rousseau and Wordsworth and still revered in our society, that children come trailing clouds of glory, only to be mauled and distorted by carnivorous adults until they are clones of themselves, has never appealed much to me."

"But, Brett—you know what parents can do to a child, I see it all the time!"

"Yes, my lady therapist, I do. But have you ever studied what children can do to children? Visit a schoolyard or locker room or dormitory, I don't care whether it's P.S. whatever or St. Swithin's of large fees and even larger repute. Some of them sometimes can make the jungle look benevolent."

Claire stared at her husband. "I've known you for several years and lived with you for one, but you still surprise me. Do you know what you sound like?"

"I'm afraid to ask."

"You sound like an old-fashioned hell-fire puritan talking about the Fall!"

"As opposed to a new-fashioned psychology major talking about what Mummy did during toilet training?"

"Ouch!" Claire said.

Brett got up and kissed her. "Present company excepted."

"Still," Claire said, after a pleasant moment, "I think I'll go and see how Malcolm is."

Malcolm, his arm around Motley, was asleep. Claire did not want to risk waking him up with a direct light, so she couldn't be sure whether or not the faint stains on his cheeks were fresh tears.

Claire was on her way to bed when the phone rang again. She was walking past the hall extension, but something made her deliberately hold off answering. Instead, she stopped and waited to hear Brett's side of the conversation when he picked up the receiver.

"Claire," he said in a minute. "It's for you. Lieutenant O'Neill," and he handed over the phone.

She put the receiver to her ear. "Yes, Lieutenant?"

"That letter you gave me, the anonymous one."

She'd forgotten about that. "Yes?"

"Whoever sent it knew what he was doing. There are no prints on it. He/she must have used gloves. There are prints on the envelope, of course, but so many they're blurred and probably belong to people at the post office. It was typed, but unless I could identify the machine in some way—that is, had other letters typed on the same machine—it's worse than the proverbial needle in a haystack. I'll hang onto the letter to see if anybody comes up with anything, but I'm afraid that's all I can do."

"That's all right, Lieutenant. Thanks for trying."

"How's young Malcolm."

"Asleep, thank heaven. Which I hope will do him some good. He's certainly been through a wringer. . . ." Her voice trailed off.

"What is it you're not saying?"

"After he'd gone to bed we had a strange phone call." And she told him about it. "It must be some of the boys at the choir school—actually I think it was two boys—who got to a phone, but it's not attractive."

"No. It isn't. I don't suppose you've the remotest idea as to who the boy, or boys, might be."

"None at all. I was horrified, but my beloved husband Brett expressed his opinion that children, so far from being little bits of heaven sent down to delight us, can really be monsters."

"I think I'm on his side in this. That much applauded sentiment from the founder of Boys' Town, 'There's no such thing as a bad boy,' etcetera, is for the birds. I know you're a therapist and therefore think it's all the parents' fault—"

"I'd like both you and Brett to realize that Freud, so far from sentimentalizing children, was the one who talked about 'His Majesty the Baby.' "

"All right, all right, don't take offense."

. . .

Claire was planning to talk to Adam Deane about Malcolm and the phone call, but he was unavailable when she called him right after she got to the office the next morning, and after that she had a string of clients, one following the other. She kept the anxieties gnawing at her inner self—Jamie, Brett and the accusations leveled at him, the anonymous letter, and now little Malcolm—behind a wall she had learned to put up when working professionally, but keeping the wall in place took its toll in fatigue and a readier irritability than was usual with her.

"Come on, Hope," she heard herself say, "lighten up. It's not that bad."

There was a pause, and then with more anger than she'd heard before from the depressed young woman. "You sound just like my mother, and like all the dear people at the various boarding schools I went to."

"I'm sorry," Claire said after a moment. "I shouldn't have said that."

"I realize that I'm hardly in the category of the oppressed of the earth. But just because I have a private income, I don't think what I feel is . . . is less important."

"No, it isn't." Claire was shocked at herself for her lapse, if it was a lapse. She was so busy trying to work this out that

she missed the next few words Hope said, and came to as
Hope continued, "and when I talked to Adam he agreed with
me."

"Adam?" Claire said. "Who is that? I don't think you've
mentioned him before. Do you mean Adam Deane?"

"Yes, I told you that," Hope said, her voice losing its angry
edge and relapsing into its customary depressed monotone.
"Only you weren't listening."

"Then tell me all over again. I am now listening. Is Adam
Deane a friend?"

"I told you, or at least I think I did, he's my cousin. That's
why I'm here at St. Anselm's. When I left Dr. Rhinelander
and didn't know where to go, he suggested you."

"Yes, Hope, you did tell me. I'll admit I am having a little
trouble this morning with my attention for reasons that even
you will allow are fairly overpowering and for which, again, I
apologize. What is it he agreed with you about?"

"That Lavinia Barton was probably a lousy mother."

"How did you arrive at that?" Claire asked.

Hope gave an elaborate sigh. "You weren't listening," she
spoke with happy long suffering. "I arrived at that because she
never cared about anything but herself." As Claire continued
to stare she said, "As I just finished telling you, Lavinia and I
went to school together."

9

"You went to school together?" Claire repeated. "Then you must be—to say the least—shocked at what happened to her."

Hope shrugged. "It was pretty awful. But . . . well, terrible as it sounds, there must be a lot of people who'd like to hit her over the head. I guess somebody just went too far." She added defiantly, "I suppose that sounds horrifying."

"Here, the only thing that is important is that you say what you honestly feel. There is no 'awful' or 'terrible' or, for that matter, 'good.' " Claire hesitated. "I don't know whether you know it or not, but I took Malcolm home with me last night. He didn't—he didn't seem to want to stay at the school."

"No, that's what Adam said. I think he was a bit put out. Singing and rehearsals are what the school is about. They have rehearsals every morning at seven-thirty, and of course Malcolm missed this morning. I suppose losing his mother like that, would knock him out, anyway. But—"

"But what?" Claire asked after a moment.

"But he wasn't that crazy about her, you know. In fact, he spent a lot of the time hating her."

Suddenly Claire remembered the look she had seen on his face once or twice that had puzzled her. She had told herself it was grief, because that was what she was expecting to see. What had it been? "Why did he hate her?" she asked slowly.

Hope shrugged. "I haven't seen her more than once or twice since she married and divorced Malcolm's father, plus one or two others, and of course the person she really set her sights on—" she glanced quickly at Claire—"but that's not important. Anyway, she turned him over to baby sitters and nannies, the usual story. I suppose," she said with a certain irony, "you'll accuse me again of self-pity if I say, 'the way my own mother did me.' "

"No, I don't think I will accuse you of that again."

Hope then surprised her. She stared down at her clasped hands and said, "Not that you aren't right. I've spent a lot of time feeling sorry for myself. Sometimes I think it's the one thing I do successfully."

"That's a little harsh. You've been successful in other things."

"Like what?"

"You've helped out in the soup kitchen. I know you're active with the local bread pantry."

"Well, you can't go wrong doing things like that, can you?" Hope looked up at her. The hazel eyes had an expression of honesty and self-knowledge that Claire had never credited her with.

Have I been unfair to her, Claire wondered? On an impulse she said, "If you could do what you wanted to—and don't think about whether or not you'd be any good at it— what would you do?"

"I'd teach," Hope said. "I've always liked children. I think a lot of them have a rotten time, and it has nothing to do with whether or not they have money."

"Then why don't you get a teaching certificate, if you want to go into the public school system. You don't even have to do that if you're content with private education."

"Mummy said I'd be taking a job from somebody who needed it."

"You would also be acquiring a degree of independence that might not have suited your mother."

"It wouldn't." She paused. "Maybe I will."

⋅ ⋅ ⋅

As soon as Hope had gone Claire telephoned home. She had left Malcolm in Martha's care, figuring that he might not want to go straight back to school. She also couldn't rid herself of her sense of anxiety over that phone call from, she was convinced, some of Malcolm's less kindly schoolmates.

Martha answered the phone. "He's fine," she said in answer to Claire's question. "We took Motley for a long walk in the park. Right now he's watching television."

"I haven't heard from the headmaster yet. I'll call him as soon as I finish this call. He wasn't happy for Malcolm to miss choir practice, but it didn't seem to me he ought to be plunged straight back in school so soon. Tomorrow is soon enough, I should think. Have you talked to him at all?"

"Well, he chattered away quite happily in the park, but nothing crucial or revealing."

"Do you have any idea as to whether he's eager to get back to school or not?"

"I'd say not, except that I can't tell you exactly why I think so. It's just a feeling."

Claire sighed. "All right. Thanks for your help."

"He's a nice kid." Claire was about to hang up when Martha added, "I think he's afraid of something."

"What?" Claire asked, more sharply than she intended. "Sorry," she said. "I didn't mean to bark that out. It's just— well, it's just that I've had the same impression—but more before his mother . . . before his mother was killed. Do you have any idea what of?"

"No. It's nothing he's said. And, somehow, I don't like to ask him. I have a feeling it might scare him off."

"I think you're right," Claire said. "You'd make a good therapist."

"Well—"

"That's not a push, it was just an off-the-cuff comment. Thanks again. As I said this morning, don't hesitate to call if there's anything that bothers you. By the way, do you mind taking care of him the rest of the day? It's an imposition, I know, and what about your boyfriend, Phillipe? Weren't you supposed to be seeing him?"

"I was going to ask you anyway. Malcolm says he likes zoos, so Phillipe and I thought we'd take him to the Bronx Zoo. Would that be okay?"

"That'd be fine. But are you sure you don't mind?"

"No, truly. If I did, I'd let you know."

. . .

Just before lunch Claire put in a call to the school and asked for Adam Deane.

"I was just going to call you," he said. "I'm afraid we must get Malcolm back here. Next Sunday is the third Sunday in Advent, and of course Christmas is the week after. I realize he's been through a wretched time and I fully realize he had to get away for a bit. You were very kind to take him, and we're most grateful. I certainly don't want to put too much of a burden on him. But I have been talking to Eric, and if Malcolm isn't here for the next services and rehearsals, then we'll have to cancel him out for this season. I know that sounds harsh," he went on hastily, "but it's a small choir, each part is vital, and a boy who isn't properly rehearsed can stand out a mile and ruin the whole thing."

Claire, however sympathetic to Malcolm, saw the headmaster's point. And though he didn't say so, the fact that the Norwich choir was here complicated everything. "All right.

I'll bring him back. But I think he ought to have one more night away from the school." As she said that she remembered the phone call of the night before. "That reminds me, we got a strange call last night from, I think, some boys in the choir school." And she told the headmaster about the call.

"I see," he said. And then, "Of course it could have been boys from anywhere. You realize that, don't you?"

"No, I don't realize that. I'm not sure Malcolm even knows any other boys in the city. And what about that reference to 'lousy sneak'? That sounded like some personal grudge!"

"Perhaps it is. You can be sure I'll look into it. But what time did the phone call come in?"

"Around nine to nine-thirty."

A second before he replied she knew the point he was about to make. "By that time the whole wretched affair about his mother and his finding her body had been on the news on every television and radio station. And almost everyone knew that you had taken Malcolm home. Certainly, without my telling anyone, everyone at school knew. Any boys anywhere, fond of playing cruel tricks, could have made that call."

"But—" She hesitated. "All right. You have a point. But don't you think it's equally likely, if not more so, that boys from the school would do it?"

"I would if I didn't know that the only pay telephones in the school are on the first floor and are in offices that are locked at night. The only other phones are in the masters' rooms, and they keep them locked also. And at nine or nine-thirty, I can assure you, two or more boys would not be out on the street in some public phone booth. There is such a thing as room check every night, and if they were missing, it would be known—and something would be done about it—within minutes."

"The boys on the phone sounded like boys from a prep school."

"All sorts of boys play tricks." He hurried on. "However, I will certainly make the most stringent inquiries."

It was pointless to push the point further. "What time do you want Malcolm there in the morning?"

"Seven-fifteen. I'm sorry to put it at such an early hour, but that's when Eric comes here and rehearses them."

"All right. I'll see if I can change with one of the other clergy and I'll take the early Communion. I'll have him there at seven-fifteen."

"Thank you." After a moment he added, "You've been most kind."

■ ■ ■

Just before noon Claire went to the vesting room and put on her surplice and stoll. She didn't have a part to play at the noon service, but she knew Mark liked as many of the clergy as possible to be present in the choir stalls.

When she lined up with the other clergy behind the boys in the outer hall, she saw that Mark had persuaded the English canon to join the procession. She wondered if the dean's nephew would be out front.

There was a pause, then the Processional hymn, "Oh, Come All Ye Faithful," sounded. It was one of Claire's favorites, and despite everything, her heart rose a little. This was, indeed, the Christmas season. Nothing, however grim and frightening, could take away from the basic message, the tidings of great joy. Standing, waiting with a huddle of other clergy for her end of the procession to start moving, Claire listened with intense pleasure knowing that the part of the carol she loved most—the stanza sung in descant by one or two of the boys—would be next.

But before that rang out there was an odd and mildly upsetting interlude.

"All right," Mark said quietly from his position at the back of the procession, "let's get ourselves in some kind of order. Canon, why don't you go with Claire, and Larry and Joe Martinez can process behind you."

Claire turned and smiled at the British canon who was standing a few feet from her talking to Larry. He looked right through her, then went and stood just in front of the rector. "I think I'll stand here if you don't mind."

Into the brief silence that followed, Claire heard a voice she was sure was Timothy's soar up. "Sing, choir of angels, sing in exaltation . . ."

Then Larry stepped up beside Claire and lightly put his arm around her surpliced form. "My gain, etcetera," he said cheerfully. "Timothy sounds in good form, doesn't he?"

"Excellent," Claire said. In her own ears her voice was a croak. At that moment the procession started moving.

"Sing all ye citizens of Heaven above . . ." Claire, still in shock, mouthed the words. Suddenly she felt on her wrist Larry's hand, holding it firmly. And, to her horror, felt her eyes fill with tears.

"Hang in there," Larry whispered.

The service passed in a haze. Every now and then Claire would check with the leaflet, forcing herself to pay attention. I should concentrate, she scolded herself. Gripping the leaflet she examined the list of anthems and psalms that were to be sung. At least two of them, a baroque Benedictus and the Cantique de Noel, were among her favorites. But the moment she stopped forcing herself to listen, everything around disappeared in a kind of fog.

Do I care about the stuffy old canon that much, she wondered? No, it was just that his snobbish unkindness had thrust back in her face the realization that he, along, no doubt, with others, considered Brett guilty.

Then, as though it had been lying in wait for the moment when she was most vulnerable, her worry about Jamie appeared and ballooned up. She realized now that she had consciously accepted Brett's and O'Neill's reassurances about Jamie's maturity, good sense and reliability—probably because she had wanted to so much. Now, sitting in the choir stalls, staring at the boys in their red Advent robes and white ruffs, all energetically singing, she suddenly saw her son as he was during his brief tenure at the choir school, the square little boy with his passion for his dog and a belief in a fundamentally kind universe. Anybody who wanted to get his attention could plead an emergency, talk about a hurt animal. Pictures, as though from some macabre cinema verité opened in and out of one another in her mind. Horrifying stories of child abuse that she thought she had long forgotten played in technicolor—

"Are you all right?" Larry whispered.

"I'm frantic with worry about Jamie."

"Do you want to leave? If you do, I'll slip out with you."

At that moment the congregation sat down and it was too late. The boys stood, faces turned towards the mirror over the organ in which Eric conducted.

"It's all right," she said, and then found herself wondering, which of those boys had made the phone call the night before?

The spasm passed, the horrifying pictures receded. She closed her eyes. "Please let him be all right," she prayed. "Please!" And she tried not to think about or argue about those who had prayed the same prayer to no avail. Following along those lines she recalled a professor of theology at her seminary who had replied in indignant tones to a questioner, "What do you mean God didn't answer? He did. He said no."

The pictures started to come back. She opened her eyes and fixed them on the choir. The boys had their music open, and she could see, here and there, the Order of Service leaflet stuck into the music book almost as a bookmark. As she felt her control and her balance coming back she glanced into the congregation. Most of the people there looked to be what they were, shoppers, people from nearby offices, families in the city on Christmas visits. Brett, of course, she thought, would be downtown in his Wall Street office. If he were at a service, it would be at Trinity.

Inevitably, her mind went to Lavinia Barton, and at that moment words that Hope had said and she had passed over came at her like a screaming bomb. ". . . of course she'd set her sights on—" and then she had stopped and looked at Claire and broken off the sentence.

It was painfully easy for Claire to finish the sentence now. The seductive Lavinia had set her sights on Brett. Brett's words, "I was more—er—kissed against than kissing" fit and made ugly sense of the situation. She had set her sights on Brett many years before but never got him. Now, twice divorced, the ending could be different—or so she had thought.

Why am I thinking these horrible things? Claire wondered. It was as though the ugly pictures had taken on a life of their own in her mind. I must stop this, she thought, and forced her attention back to the boys who were now finishing their anthem. As the rector climbed into the pulpit she noticed that an Order of Service leaflet must have dropped out of one of the music books onto the stone floor of the chancel. It was lying face down. Obviously whoever had had it originally had doodled on it. There was a drawing on the back, an oddly familiar drawing. . . . There were the same disjointed, concertinalike lines, linked end to end, looking like . . . she turned her head to the side . . . looking like, well, stairs. And there was the same rough circle with squiggles at one side, as though it were a . . . a head. And the word "BANG!"

Where had she seen that before?

"And now to God the Father, God the Son—" Mark announced in his clear, ringing voice, and turned towards the altar. The sermon was over. Along with the others in the choir stall, Claire stood up. One of the seminarians going up to the altar stooped and picked up the leaflet. Claire could imagine Eric demanding who had had the stupidity and carelessness to drop such an inappropriate doodle on the chancel floor during the Eucharist? Thinking about it, she smiled.

The Recessional hymn was "Hark, the Herald Angels Sing," and once again, Claire looked forward to the descant. It started in the third verse. The superb boy's soprano began the flight up to the high note. But something happened, quite what Claire couldn't be sure. Nor could she see Eric's face from where she was slowly walking out beside Larry. But an electric shock seemed to go through the choir for a second before another boy's voice immediately picked up the climb to the high note.

"What happened?" She whispered to Larry out of the side of her mouth.

"Sounds like his voice broke. If that's it, it's the end of his singing. Eric can't risk that again."

"Timothy?"

"Yes."

It was impossible to see ahead how the boys were reacting to this. The procession, like a colored snake, worked itself along the corridor leading from the church to the parish house. Finally they were entering the huge room where the procession came to a halt and most of the participants looked around for coffee. The boys seemed to be in a huddle at one end of the room, Timothy's golden head rising above the others.

"Excuse me," Eric said and went past towards his choir.

"You mean Timothy can't sing again?" she asked Larry.

"No. His voice might do that now any time."

"I suppose that's why Adam Deane was so determined this morning that I produce Malcolm early tomorrow."

"Probably." Larry looked at her. "The scuttlebutt is that you whisked him home with you. If so, I think it's marvelous. Poor lad! What a horrible thing to happen. How bright of you to think of it!"

"I didn't, if you want to know. O'Neill took me over to the school and up to the room where Malcolm was with Adam and the school nurse. Malcolm flung his arms around me and begged me to take him home with me."

"Umm. Not surprising."

"The trouble is, Larry, according to Hope Meredith who, I discovered this morning during her session, went to school with Lavinia Barton and is Adam Deane's cousin, Malcolm didn't like his mother much. In her words, he sometimes hated her."

Larry's round light blue eyes fixed on Claire. "Interesting."

"Also, Martha, who's been looking after him today, said on the phone she thought Malcolm was afraid of something."

Larry thought for a moment. "That sort of fits in, doesn't it, with the unhappy look he's been wearing off and on lately."

"But who could he be afraid of? I mean, it could have been his mother. But then he wouldn't still be afraid, would he?"

"I shouldn't think so. Have you asked Adam or Eric?"

"No."

"Well maybe you should."

Claire glanced over to where both Adam and Eric were standing surrounded by various members of the choir, Marguerite and Joe Martinez. Near them, talking to the rector, was the English canon.

"I think I'll wait until our Brit moves on," Claire said.

"It gives me great sorrow that he's too old for me to punch," Larry said. "That was one of the less Christian pieces of behavior I've witnessed in the sacred confines of St. Anselm's."

"I must say, I didn't much like being cut dead."

At that moment Adam Deane came up. "I suppose you heard what happened," he said to Claire. "You can see now why we need to have Malcolm back as soon as possible."

"I'll bring him tomorrow morning at seven-fifteen," Claire assured him.

Eric had come up behind Adam. "Is there any chance you could bring him back this afternoon in time for the rehearsal right after Evensong? Now that Timothy is out we need all the trained soloists we have. And Malcolm, when he tries, and is working hard, is good."

Claire hesitated. Her feeling that Malcolm needed a little time before returning was strong. On the other hand, she owed loyalty to the church and its activities, and there was no mistaking what had happened to Timothy. "Adam," she said suddenly, "May I speak to you for a moment?"

"Of course." Adam spoke rather stiffly. "Although I don't

see how anyone can dispute the need for getting Malcolm and his voice back here as soon as possible."

"A moment of your time," Claire said firmly and led the way down the hall to an empty room.

"Perhaps I didn't say it to you, I can't remember, but it struck me before Malcolm's mother was killed, that he looked unhappy. Larry Swade noticed the same thing. And today, when I called home, my stepdaughter, in whose care I left him, said she thought he was afraid of something." Seeing the rigid expression on Adam's face, she said, "I didn't ask her a leading question. She came out with it on her own."

There was a silence. Claire had the odd impression that an internal battle was going on within the headmaster, not unlike the one that went on within him when she told him about the phone call of the night before. He was plainly not a man who found it easy to acknowledge imperfections.

Then he said, "I think she must have been reading things into a small boy who, after all, had not only just lost his mother, but had been the one to find her body."

"I don't think that was it." Claire pondered the idea of telling Adam that according to his cousin, Malcolm's feeling for his mother went from indifference to dislike. But she decided against it. Hope had made this statement during her therapy session, and Claire didn't want to put her in the position of being scolded by Adam for what she said in confidence.

"Have you anything, anything at all, to substantiate this idea of yours that Malcolm is afraid of something or someone?"

"No."

"You know," Adam pointed out, "therapists, as well as others, can frequently imagine somewhat exaggerated sets of feelings."

"As other people can. No, I have nothing to back my feeling up with, but I wish you wouldn't just dismiss it."

"Of course I'm not going to dismiss it. I shall investigate it thoroughly. Just as I intend to investigate the phone call you reported. But in the meantime Eric and the choir can use the training young Malcolm has had these past years." He paused. "So he'll be brought back this afternoon before evening rehearsal?"

Claire held her breath, then let it go. "Yes, all right. I'll bring him back as soon as he gets back from the Bronx Zoo."

"The Bronx Zoo, is it? Well, probably a good idea. Take his mind off of various things."

. . .

Claire talked to one or two of the parishioners and after that removed her vestments in the vesting room. Then she returned to her office to telephone home to find out when Martha and Phillipe were planning to bring Malcolm back from the Bronx Zoo. But, as she feared, they had obviously already left. She debated calling Adam Deane and telling she could not guarantee Malcolm's return in time for the afternoon rehearsal, but decided to wait on that.

She thought about lunch. She was not hungry, but she knew she ought to eat something before her afternoon sessions. She glanced out the window. The sky was blue, the air was clear. She told herself she should go out and drop into a nearby coffee shop. But she didn't move. The street beneath her was almost invisible under packed crowds and gridlocked cars. Further down and out of sight was Bloomingdale's and Claire did not doubt that a fair portion of the people moving slowly in that direction were on their way there. Remembering her visit with the dean, she smiled to herself, a smile that vanished when she recalled what had happened to him. . . .

I'll order in, she thought, and went hastily through her desk drawers to see if she had a menu from a nearby delicatessen that delivered. It wasn't there.

"Joanna—" Claire called out, and then remembered that Joanna had left for lunch.

For a moment she toyed with the thought of not worrying about lunch, but she knew she owed it to her clients not to become faint in the middle of the afternoon. There was also the cafeteria, but Claire did not think she could cope with the many questions about herself and her family, however kindly intended, that would probably come her way.

"Damn!" she said aloud, and crossed the office to Joanna's room. As she did so, she heard a faint sound on the other side of the door between the two offices. She noticed then the door was closed. Had she closed it? She couldn't remember. Even when Joanna wasn't there she often shut it as a matter of habit and privacy.

As she turned the doorknob, she thought she heard the faint sound of the outer door closing. Pushing her own door open, she stood there, listening. There was no sound. She crossed Joanna's office and flung open the door to the hall. Had those been running steps she had heard? If so there was silence now, and no one was visible.

The whole thing seemed eerie, and she shivered a little. The menu she had been looking for was stuck in the back of a letter rack on Joanna's desk. Pulling it out, Claire returned to her office, this time leaving the door between the two rooms deliberately open.

Reading the list of sandwiches, bagels and salad plates on the menu did nothing for her appetite. Suddenly changing her mind, Claire took her coat off the hanger in the closet and left, carefully locking the outer door behind her. Joanna, she knew, had the key.

Pushing her way among the people, she finally went into a small coffee shop, sat down at the counter and without thinking ordered a tuna salad sandwich and some coffee. It seemed the most basic, neutral and least bothersome dish she could accomodate. Then, sitting there, waiting for it, she wished she'd brought something to read—anything, because when not actively occupied, her mind had a tendency to run around some well-worn and unpleasant tracks.

"I suppose you'll think I'm following you," a familiar voice said beside her.

Claire turned and gave a rueful grin. "Why aren't you in the cafeteria?" she asked.

"Somehow, the prospect of all those assorted clergy filled with Advent goodwill was more than I could bear," Larry replied. "I decided the materialistic servants of Mammon out here would be more restful. And you, why aren't you in the cafeteria?"

"Much the same reason." She looked with lack of enthusiasm at the somewhat limp sandwich dumped down in front of her. The waitress pushed a coffee cup over, spilling some of the light colored contents into the saucer. She then scribbled on her pad and shoved a check under the sandwich plate. "Happy holiday," she muttered, her eyes on the door where standees were watching those at the counter with angry anxiety.

"I wish I really wanted to eat this," Claire said picking up one half of the sandwich.

"Close your eyes and think of England," Larry quoted.

Claire started to giggle. After that it seemed easier to swallow the slightly greasy sandwich.

"I must report that when I finally accepted that I couldn't punch the dear canon," Larry said, "I decided to take the lower road and go and tell him what I thought of his loving attitude."

"Did he freeze you out?"

"No, surprisingly, he said he was entirely aware of how atrocious his behavior had been and had, in fact, tried to go to your office and apologize. But you weren't there."

"Thank heaven! I know that's probably not very generous of me, but I'm not sure receiving his apology wouldn't have been worse."

"Yes, I rather thought that, too. His excuse, in case you're the least interested, is that his sorrow over the dean's dreadful and untimely death—I am now quoting—blotted out every other thought."

"In that case he should have cut the rector and the entire clutch of clergy."

"Yes, but I decided not to look a—er—gift apology in the

mouth, if you can stand the mixed metaphor." Larry took a large bite of his own cheese sandwich. "Every time I order a cheese sandwich I think of Wendy's strictures on the subject of cholesterol, overweight and bad eating habits."

"I notice it doesn't stop you."

"No. If anything, it spices it up."

"You're scandalous! When I think of all the worry you probably put Wendy through—"

"Wendy is one of the least worrying people I know, thank God! She worries far more over Dudley than she does over me."

"I don't believe that for one minute, but I sometimes wonder who is the more clucked-over canine, Motley or Dudley."

Motley made her think of Jamie, and brought back the dark shadows that Larry's presence had pushed away. "You know, I haven't said this because I didn't want you to go into paroxysms of embarrassment, but you're a great comfort."

"Fortunately," Larry said, swallowing the second half of his sandwich in what looked like one huge bite, "there's no such thing as too much praise. When I think of the opportunities Wendy has missed—"

"Liar!" Claire said, and punched him in his arm.

"One other thing," Larry went on, putting down his coffee cup. "The good canon said he knocked on the door of the pastoral counseling office because he was certain someone was inside. But there was no answer, so after trying again, he left."

"That's odd. When did he try?"

"I couldn't pin him down, although I tried, but I thought it was strange, too. He talked to me about half an hour ago, so it was obviously between then and the end of the noon service."

"The service usually runs an hour, and half an hour ago would have been—" she checked her watch—"about one-forty." She paused. "I was up there phoning home, but not immediately. There were a couple of people who were obviously hovering to talk, and I had to go to the vesting room. I'd say I was there after one-fifteen or one-twenty."

"So the canon, technically, could have gone up immediately following the service to make his amends. But wouldn't he have seen you milling around the coffee room?"

"No," Claire said slowly. "I'd been talking to Adam Deane in the adjoining study, and that's where Mrs. Walker and Liz Hammond cornered me. They wanted to talk about the Tuesday study group. I went from there to the vesting room without going through the coffee room, so the canon could easily not have seen me."

"Since he seemed concerned about this, I told him it could have been Joanna on a long distance call or something, which would explain why she might not have heard him knock, or might have ignored the knock."

"Or she might have been chatting with Jimmy, her boyfriend. She's inclined to space out when they have contact. Still—I've never known her to ignore somebody trying to see me."

Larry collected his check. "Don't worry about it, for heaven's sake. I almost didn't tell you, but decided that fairness to the canon—however little inclined I am to be fair to him—demanded it."

"The funny thing is," Claire said, "when I'm there alone, I don't usually close the door between the inner and outer offices, but when I got up to rummage for the deli menu in Joanna's office, I found the door closed. And I could have sworn there was somebody in the other room. There was nobody there when I pushed the door open, but there may or may not have been steps going down the hall. Of course they were gone, too, when I opened that door."

"As Alice would say, 'Curiouser and curiouser.' "

• • •

Claire got back to her office barely in time for her first afternoon client. Her mail was waiting on her desk, having been picked up by Joanna, but she didn't get to look at it till the end of the afternoon. There were the usual circulars and second class mail. At the bottom was an envelope with a typed address. Claire stared at it, her heart beating quickly. Then she tore it open. There was a single typed line:

"Now it's your turn."

10

Claire called O'Neill, but he was out.

"Can I help you?" Sergeant Glass asked.

"Just tell the lieutenant that I got another threatening note."

"Wanna bring it down here, Ms. Aldington?"

"I'd rather talk to the lieutenant first." She hesitated. "Have you got any further on the case—that is, that you can talk about?"

"I'm afraid I can't discuss that," the sergeant said, almost audibly withdrawing.

"All right."

Claire then called Brett, but he was in the middle of a conference. Claire debated telling the superior young woman to get him out of the conference, but decided she could wait.

Feeling bereft, she hung up.

At that moment, Joanna stuck her head in the door. "If it's okay with you, I'd like to leave a little early."

"All right," Claire said automatically. Then, "Wait a second. What time did you go out to lunch? No, no," she said in answer to the look of alarm on Joanna's face, "I'm not asking that because you want to leave early. But it seems the English canon knocked on the door some time between one and one-forty this afternoon. He said he heard somebody in here, but nobody answered and he went away. I got here about one-thirty. It must have been before that."

"You didn't say positively when you wanted me to take lunch, so I went out at around twelve-thirty."

"And you locked the door?"

"Of course I did, particularly after the last time when somebody robbed my handbag."

Claire thought for a moment. "If you were out, you obviously had your handbag with you. Have you missed anything else?"

Another look of alarm came over Joanna's face. Quickly she went back into her office and Claire heard the sound of drawers being opened and shut. One, two, three, four, Claire counted, aware that Joanna's desk had four drawers. So far, so good. Then there was the squeakier sound of file drawers being opened.

"Oh no! Oh my God!"

Claire got up and hurried into the outer office. "What is it?"

"The petty cash. I always keep it at the back of the top file drawer. It's empty."

Claire walked over and stared at the metal box, now open. Inside were a few papers. There was no money, coin or bills. "How much did you have in there?" she asked.

"Twenty-four dollars and thirty cents," Joanna replied.

"I take it that was the exact amount."

"Yes. I'm very careful, Claire, about keeping the account straight. The book is here," and Joanna pulled a ledger out of the same area of the top drawer. "Everything I spend petty cash for I put down. You can look at it if you want!"

Claire touched her arm. "I don't doubt you about that for a moment, Joanna." She was about to push the drawer in with her hand, when she turned and shoved it in with her arm. "No use handling the handle or the outside of the drawer more than's necessary," she said. She paused then said, "Just for the record, when did you last look at the petty cash?"

"Day before yesterday. You told me to get you some more telephone answering pads. The storeroom had run out, so I went to Bachman's and got half a dozen. It's there in the ledger."

"All right." Claire thought for a moment. "Have you had the file drawer open since?"

Joanna thought for a moment. "Yes. I had to put your afternoon clients' files away yesterday afternoon. That's the Baker and the Carr files."

"There were also the Saunders, Meredith and Katz files."

"Yes, but the petty cash box goes in the top file, and those were in lower ones."

"So yesterday, you didn't actually look in the cash box?"

"No."

"But you're sure you saw it—I mean, it was there in its usual place?

"Yes, positive."

"Was it open, like it is now?"

"No. And I know I closed it when I got the money for the pads."

"Did you lock it?"

"No. I always figure it's not necessary because the file drawer is locked."

"And you locked the file when you were finished with it yesterday?"

This time there was a hesitation. Finally Joanna sighed and said, "I always do. I've become neurotic about it. But— now don't yell at me—but Jimmy called just about that time and we'd had a fight. Maybe I didn't remember to lock the files."

"And you had no reason to open that particular file today?"

Joanna shook her head. "No." She glanced at Claire. "That means, I guess, that whoever took the money could have taken it yesterday as well as today."

"I'm afraid so. I'm going to have to talk to the rector about this."

"I suppose he's going to say it's all my fault."

"Joanna, it's no more all your fault, than it's all mine. If blame is to be allotted, then how about whoever took the money?"

Claire turned around to go back to her office. "I know you're in a hurry. So, go on if you want to."

Joanna looked slightly put upon, but said, "I suppose I ought to stay, since I'm at least partly responsible."

"No, you've told me all you can. I'm going to have to handle this myself. The rector is not going to be happy to have this dumped on him—least of all now."

"You're sure?" Joanna said from the door.

"Yes, sure. Run along!"

When Joanna had left Claire sat there a moment or two. Then she picked up the phone and dialed the precinct's number. "Has Lieutenant O'Neill come back yet?" She thought it highly unlikely, but asked anyway, and was not surprised when the officer at the other end said, "No, 'Fraid not. Who's calling?" Then, before she'd had time to give him her name, "Just a minute, this looks like it might be the lieutenant. No, my mistake. Who shall I say called?"

"Please tell him Claire Aldington would like to talk to him as soon as possible."

As she hung up, she glanced outside. In the time she'd gone into the outer office and returned it had become dark outside. It happened fast at this time of year, a day or two from the shortest day of the year. It was also raining, she noted, and the murk hid any sign of stars. Straight down

Lexington Avenue in the shop windows the motif of Christmas still blared and shone, but the almost cozy quality that stores, streets and offices carefully developed and cultivated at this time of year seemed, this evening, missing. Claire shivered and wondered if the ever-watchful budget committee had given instructions to turn the heat down (or off?) earlier.

Surely not, she thought. There might be a few hardhearted types who felt the church was doing more than it ought to feed and shelter the homeless, but no one would ever think of trying to freeze out the unfortunates by cutting down on the heat.

All this time Claire had been making massive efforts not to think about the second anonymous letter, or, when she did, to remind herself that somebody was most likely playing a cruel prank. She shivered again, this time from fear.

She picked up the telephone preparatory to pushing the buttons of Mark's extension. But she hesitated. Possibly by this time he would have gone home, too. Claire hoped so. It would postpone her having to do anything about the missing petty cash. It seemed such a small, niggling matter to bring to the rector's attention at a time when the church had not one but two violent deaths on its hands. Unless, of course, the events—the deaths and the thefts—were connected in some way.

How could they be? Claire thought. And then, who was she to pass on what seemed possible or impossible? A month ago she would have stated with conviction that the violent deaths would have been unthinkable.

She was about to press Mark's extension when she heard faintly the swelling voices of the choir from the basement far below. It took a moment for her to take in what that meant.

"Oh—" Quickly she punched the phone number of her apartment and then waited impatiently while it rang. But eventually there was the familiar click and Brett's voice asking whoever was going to leave a message to wait for the beep.

What did that mean? That Martha and Phillippe had not

brought Malcolm back yet from the Bronx Zoo? That they had, but had taken him out again, perhaps for dinner.

"Blast, damn and hell," she said quietly to herself. The anonymous letter and the disappearance of the petty cash had driven out of her head Adam Deane's insistence that Malcolm be returned for the rehearsal that even now was going on. Was there the faintest possibility that Malcolm had come back anyway? There was only one sure way to find out. To go down to the rehearsal room and see.

Once more Claire dialed her home number. Once again Brett came on the tape, asking the caller to wait for the beep. Claire hung up.

Claire glanced at her watch. It was now nearly six. She felt suddenly overwhelmingly tired. Even her body seemed to ache. Move it, Claire! she said to herself. The room seemed suddenly dark, and she realized she had put on only her desk lamp. Walking over to the door she switched on the overhead light. About to leave the office, she hesitated, then went back to her desk and dialed Brett's direct line. It was unlikely, though not impossible, that his meeting was still going on, but she decided that she would hang on till he came out and spoke to her. She had never had this feeling of need before in this intensity, and tried to laugh at herself. But it didn't work. She wanted—no, she needed—to talk to Brett, to hear his strong, reassuring voice, and then jibed at herself for acting like the tearful heroine of a paperback romance. The trouble is, she thought gloomily, I feel like one.

But there was no answer on Brett's phone. After four rings an electronic voice came on suggesting that the caller call back after nine o'clock the next morning.

"Thanks a lot," Claire muttered. She then went to the door, then, after further thought, returned to her desk, picked up her handbag and returned to the door. She was just about to open it when the phone rang.

Brett, she thought, and flew back.

But it wasn't Brett. "Claire?" said Letty Dalrymple's rather quavering voice.

"Yes. Letty?"

"Claire dear, I know this is a dreadful time to call you, but I've been overcome with the strongest feeling—really an urgent feeling—that you should not be hanging about that building. Now I know you'll probably laugh, but I've been right before, and I want you to listen to me . . ." What she said after that was lost for Claire who, in between Letty's words, heard the sound of the doorknob to the outer door being slowly turned.

Whether it was Letty's warning, or the anonymous letter or her own sense of isolation in the darkened building, Claire could never afterwards be sure. But saying quietly "Just a minute" into the receiver, she put down the phone, flew over to the door and pushed the button inside the knob on her side, locking the door. The doorknob stopped turning. There was a pause. Then whoever it was tried again.

Claire waited, her heart beating. Curiously, though, in her head, she felt calm. Stepping over to Joanna's desk, she picked up the receiver there. "Letty?"

"Yes, my dear. Please be careful."

"I'm going to hang up now. I want you to call Lieutenant O'Neill at 555-1246 immediately and tell him to come over here to my office right away. I don't know what's happening, but strange things have occurred, and somebody is on the other side of the office door trying to get in. It may be perfectly innocent, but if it were, I'm sure whoever it is would call out and ask if anybody were inside. I've managed to lock the door, but he or she hasn't gone away and now certainly knows that somebody is here." With no one else except Letty, she thought, could she make that statement and know that Letty wouldn't waste time asking what she meant.

Then she hung up, paused, took off her pumps and flew into her room to replace the receiver on her desk. Quickly she returned to the outer room and retrieved her shoes. She was thinking of turning off the light when it occurred to her that since whoever was out there knew she—or someone—was inside there wouldn't be much point to it. Also, the hall was lighted, so what difference did it make?

The door of the outer office was the only possible exit from her room. Claire looked around and finally saw a heavy tape dispenser on Joanna's desk. Picking that up, she stationed herself where, if and when whoever was out there broke in, she could hit his/her head.

"Who's there?" she called out, not expecting an answer.

What followed surprised her. The would-be intruder ran away. She could hear the steps running down the hall towards the elevator. She was about to open the door when it occurred to her that she couldn't be positive the person had been alone. Someone else could be there now.

.   .   .

She sat down again at Joanna's desk, telling herself to wait it out until somebody—preferably Lieutenant O'Neill—came along. But as she sat there, the sounds of the choir rehearsing were a reproach about her forgetting to have Malcolm there.

Finally she got up. She respected Letty and her psychic abilities, but she was a little ashamed of her panic reaction and announced to herself that she was a rational woman who did not have to be ordered about by them. Pushing the button inside the doorknob, she opened the door and looked out. There was no one there. She pushed the button again, locking the door, made sure she had her keys, and went towards the elevator. After punching the DOWN button, she waited. After a while it occurred to her that she had not heard the sounds of the elevator on another floor starting up. She punched the button again. Still no sound. This time she punched the UP button, but the shaft remained silent. Twice more she pushed the DOWN button, more out of frustration than any hope that it would be working.

It became obvious that, for whatever reason, the elevator was not functioning. It was not an unheard-of occurance. The elevator was fairly old and had been installed when all elevators were manually controlled, then converted later on.

Claire walked slowly back to her office, unlocked the door and went in. Going over to the phone she tried to get the switchboard operator, but knew almost immediately that the latter would have connected the automatic answering machine and gone home.

At this moment it came over her again how isolated she was. It gave her an eerie feeling which she didn't much like. She pressed the buttons again to Mark's office, and got the answering tape. She then tried Larry's, and heard it again. Then she called home, and once again heard Brett's voice asking her to wait for the beep before leaving a message.

Almost slamming the receiver down, she sat there for a few seconds, then put her handbag strap over her shoulder and turned out the desk lamp and the overhead light. Crossing over to Joanna's desk, she turned that lamp out and reached for the wall switch to turn off the overhead light. The room went dark. She was reaching for the doorknob when she was overcome with the conviction that there was someone outside the door, waiting for her to come out.

The feeling was so strong, she paused. Then, fed up with herself, with Letty and everyone else, she flung open the door. There was no one there, and she was about to remind herself to think about this when she was next overcome with ESP and other like phenomena, when she heard footsteps running along the hall at right angles to the one she was standing in. Then there came another sound: the creaking and wheezing and the noise of the elderly elevator door sliding open.

Furious at having—in her mind—been made a fool of, she flew down the hall herself, determined to catch the elevator door before it finally shut and force whoever was there to explain what he or she thought she was doing. But as she rounded the corner and faced the elevator door, it slid shut and the contraption, now working perfectly, proceeded to descend.

Going over to the wall beside the elevator, she saw the light indicating that the car was descending, and she angrily pushed the UP button with the idea of sending it back up as soon as it hit a lower floor.

But when the elevator got to whatever floor it was heading for it stopped, and the indicator light went out. Claire pushed the DOWN button, not once but several times. When that had no effect, she pushed the UP button. That, too, proved useless. Obviously, the elevator call system worked on some floors but not on Claire's. Unfortunately, because to install a floor indicator on each floor at the time the building was renovated was considered too costly for a church anxious to spend the bulk of its income on those who most needed it, there was no way for Claire to know on which floor the elevator now rested. It could be the floor below, or on any of three floors below that.

It would have to be the stairs.

Claire started towards the staircase, opened the door and hesitated. True, it was not down the stairs leading to this floor that the dean had fallen. That was two levels below. The words of the anonymous letter hovered, as though in a brilliantly written sign in her head:

Now it's your turn.

Being scared is exactly what this crazy wants, she told herself, and started down the stairs, determined to enter the floor at each level to see where the elevator was.

But when she got to the fourth floor and tried to open the big door below the EXIT sign, the door didn't yield. She pushed again, turning the knob as strongly and as far as she could. But to no avail. It was locked.

She stood there for a moment, forcing herself to be calm. The door from the stairs on the floor above was not locked, she could always go back there, and it was not as though it were a highrise. Her own floor, the fifth, was at the top.

Determined not to let herself give in, she started down the stairs to the third floor, remembering suddenly that that was where the graffiti had been. It was still there, and she saw again the linked lines, now completely identifiable as stairs, and the circular whirls that appeared to represent—what? A head, of course. If there was any doubt, the word "BANG!" would have made that clear. Whoever had done it was obviously making a crude comment on what had happened to the dean.

As the full import of that broke on her, Claire stopped her descent. At that moment the stair light went out. She was in total blackness.

She stood there, her heart pounding, panic clawing at her. For the first time it really occurred to her that someone was out to harm—or kill—her. Before now it had seemed, at the least, ludicrous. Now it appeared obvious.

As she stood there she remembered again the words of the letter, Letty's warning, her own intuition. Claire was not much on psychic phenomena, but she had developed in her work an extraordinary respect for the intuitions—frequently ignored, ridiculed and overlooked—of ordinary people. Someone—who was it?—in her seminary had once said to her there is a Mind within our mind that knows far more than we realize or want to acknowledge. It is wise to pay attention to it!

Drawing in her breath, she decided to stop fighting her inner conviction that she was, indeed, in danger. When she let that go, she felt, first, an appalling vulnerability. Then the faces of Jamie, Brett, Martha—even the images of Motley and Patsy, all those whom she loved and who loved and depended on her—slid through her mind. And she prayed with all her strength, not so much to be rescued, as to have whatever courage she needed to cope with whatever was before her.

Then the door immediately below her opened, sending in a shaft of light. A voice she recognized as Lieutenant O'Neill's called her name. "Ms. Aldington, are you there?"

"Yes," she said. "I'm here." Her knees, she found, were trembling. "I'm very glad to hear you," she said, and at that moment the light went on.

"What the hell," O'Neill said, slowly mounting the stairs, "were you doing using the stairs in the dark with the light off when the building is all but empty. I understand you've had another anonymous letter?"

"You've no idea how glad I am to see you!" Claire said.

The lieutenant was regarding her closely. "Scared?" he said.

She nodded.

"Serves you right. Come on, come on down the steps."

She started down the remaining steps, then saw that her rescuer hadn't moved. He was staring at the drawing on the wall.

"Graffiti!" he said. "You think you get rid of it one place and it crops up another. But I sure as hell wouldn't have expected to see it here at St. Anselm's." He glanced at Claire and said, half kiddingly, "Come on, now! Move lively. I want to see that letter."

When they got to the third floor and turned down the hall, Claire saw the elevator standing there, its door obediently open. "I sent for that aging mechanism when I was on the fifth floor," she said resentfully. "Much good it did me!"

"You mean it wouldn't come up when you summoned it?"

"That's right."

"It was working perfectly well when I made the custodian let me in."

"I have no explanation for that, Lieutenant," Claire said tiredly, "anymore than I have for the off-the-wall things that happened for the half-hour preceding that."

By this time they were in the elevator going slowly but steadily up to the fifth floor.

"Tell me about it—in detail."

So while they creaked to the top floor and then walked to Claire's office she told him about the turning of the doorknob, her punching the button so that the door would lock, about her calling out and the running footsteps. "And before that, before Joanna left," she said, "we discovered that the petty cash had been burgled." She tried to unlock her door, but found that the key wouldn't turn for the simple reason that the door was unlocked. "I know I locked it before I left," she said. "Or else I am really going mad! I swear to you, Lieutenant!"

She put her hand out to feel the button when O'Neill said sharply, "Don't touch it. If what you're saying is true, then somebody knows how to work this lock or has a key or something. Leave it. Now, where is this letter?"

But the letter, which had been on her desk, open, was gone. Just to convince herself and O'Neill that she wasn't as crazy as she looked, she searched the drawers of her desk, her own personal file in the bottom drawer and all the file drawers in the inner and outer office. "I can't go through every file at this moment, Lieutenant," she said despairingly, "it could easily be hidden in any of the I-don't-know-how-many files we have in the office going back over years."

"You can get your secretary to do it tomorrow. But I don't think it's there. I think, like I said before, somebody who knows how to work the locks here came in and got the letter."

"At least you're not claiming I made the whole thing up!"

"If I didn't know you, personally, over several years and other cases, I might be inclined to. But I'll admit, I don't see you making up this crazy-quilt story, unless of course—" she suddenly found his hard, probing blue eyes on her—"unless you think you're protecting either Cunningham or your son —or daughter, for all I know!"

"You've left out the dog and the cat!"

"Don't give me any smart alec answer. You know what I mean! You'd do a lot more than fuzz up the evidence if you thought it would distract me from Brett or Jamie or Martha."

"Then why don't you arrest me?"

"I don't have what you could call solid evidence of your participation in some grand plot right now. That's why."

"But you still think I could be engaged in some elaborate cover up on behalf of Brett or Jamie."

"I just said could. I didn't say you were. Come on, Claire, don't give me a hard time."

Claire blinked her eyes a couple of times. "I'm tired, I'm going to go home."

"That's good news," Brett said from the doorway.

"Brett darling!" Claire went across to him and put her arms around him, police presence or not. "I'm so glad to see you!"

Brett, the reserved, returned her hug. "And I you."

"What are you doing here? Or is it ESP?"

"Nothing so romantic, or at least I don't think so. I was at home, wondering why you weren't, when several things happened. Martha and whatever-his-name-is came home, bringing Malcolm, Eric Fullerton called and said Malcolm had to come back right away as—I'm not sure I've got this right, but I could swear he said Timothy's something was broken. My hearing was a little faulty largely because Motley started barking to go out, and I'd no sooner hung up than your crazy friend Letty called and said I should get over here right away because you were in great danger. So I threw young Malcolm into a taxi, brought him back here, took him down to the rehearsal room and then came up here. Now it's my turn. Why do you look as though you'd been steam-rollered?"

"Because I have." And Claire told him everything that had happened since she last tried to call him.

Brett looked at her, then at O'Neill, then back at her. "And you say this letter is now missing?"

"Yes."

"What did it say?"

"It said, 'Now it's your turn.' "

"And somebody was obviously able to get in and collect it while you were being lured down the stairs."

"Yes."

Brett looked at O'Neill. "I wish you and the other police would find who the hell is doing this, or are you so determined that I'm a double murderer you can't get your mind on it?"

"I don't blame you for being put out, Mr. Cunningham. I

am here trying to figure it out. And incidentally, I never said or accused you of being a double murderer."

"I guess I should be grateful for small mercies. Come on, Claire, I'm taking you home."

At that moment Joe Martinez's form appeared in the doorway. He was dressed in black clericals and sported a black rabat, not unlike the Roman Catholics. He then surprised Claire by saying, "Are you okay?"

O'Neill put out a hand just as Claire was about to answer. "What made you think she might not be?"

The sensitive nostrils flared. "Is this a police inquiry? Where is your stick?"

"For Chris sake!" Brett said.

"Come off it, Joe," Claire said. "I sent for the lieutenant, if you must know."

"Who do you suspect now?" Joe said.

"How about you?" O'Neill said. "You're the one who talks about the glories of the Sinn Fein."

"Don't, Lieutenant," Claire said. "He has no sense of humor."

"You mean I don't get a charge out of harrying the poor and the helpless the way you cops do—"

"I never thought of you as helpless, Mrs. Cunningham," O'Neill said smoothly.

"I'm going home," Claire said flatly.

Brett pulled her coat from the closet. "Joe, I have a suggestion: Why don't you consider a New's Year's resolution to stop being a horse's ass?"

"I'll have you know—" Joe shouted, when Claire surprised everyone, including herself, by bursting into tears.

"Come along, darling." Brett said. "With any luck the lieutenant will shove him in a dungeon."

"It would be a pleasure," O'Neill said.

Joe looked slightly aghast. "Claire, I'm really sorry. You know how I run off at the mouth! As Ja—" He caught himself, but no one, least of all Claire, was in any condition to listen to him further. "Is there anything I can do?" He finished meekly.

"Yes," Brett said. "Shut up!"

. . .

She must, Claire decided later, look worse than she realized, because everyone—that is Brett, Martha and her boyfriend, Phillippe, who happened to be in the apartment when she and Brett arrived home—were so overwhelmingly nice to her.

"Let me get you a drink, darling," Brett said, pushing her gently down in her chair. He was going off to hang up her coat when Martha appeared, took one look at her, and said, "I'll do that."

"I'm not dying," Claire said, feeling curiously irritated and rather ungrateful. "Just because I shed a few tears—"

"And almost got yourself killed," Brett said, handing her a mild Scotch and water. "I wouldn't even have put water in, except that I know you wouldn't drink it straight."

"I just don't like the way straight whiskey makes me feel," Claire said.

"Well, should you ever have any doubt about the matter, that should prove to you beyond doubt that you do not have any tendencies towards alcoholism."

"Why's that?" Martha, who was hovering, asked.

"Because," Claire said, sipping her drink, "alcoholics aren't interested in the taste—what they want is how it makes them feel."

"I'm cooking dinner," Martha announced. "And Phillippe is helping. He says he's a gourmet cook."

"What I really said," Phillippe amended, "was that I like cooking."

"Well, Frenchmen have led the world in matters of cuisine," Brett said. "Just don't get too free with the garlic. I know it's chic, but I remain a hick when it comes to that."

"No garlic"—Phillippe glanced at Brett—"or so little you won't notice it."

"I'll notice it all right," Brett said, as Phillippe and Martha walked off toward the kitchen, "but I don't suppose I should discourage them. Is there anything more I can—"

"No," Claire said. "I'm sorry, I don't mean to sound unappreciative, but right now I'd just rather be let alone. Could we watch some news?"

"If you want to—I thought you might not like it." He went over and turned on the television set.

Claire watched it mindlessly, aware only of something hooked into the back of her mind that she couldn't extract and look at. It was something set off by what Brett had said in the past few minutes, but she couldn't even recall that coherently. Then her attention was jerked up.

"Cyrus Richardson, former husband of Lavinia Barton, whose body was discovered at Manhattan's St. Anselm's Church earlier this week, was reached today at his Paris office. Richardson, who has since remarried, said that pressing business matters prevented him from coming to New York at this time. His son, eleven-year-old Malcolm Richardson, a student at St. Anselm's Choir School, discovered the body of his mother in the choir school. Now, from Washington . . ."

"That's a nice loving father," Brett said, switching off the set.

"He ought to have come," Claire emphatically agreed. She remembered Malcolm's face and his passionate desire not to spend the night at the school. "You say you put Malcolm into a cab and took him back to school. Did you have any trouble persuading him?"

"Yes and no. Yes, because it was plain he didn't want to go back. No, because I didn't give him much chance to make his case. At that moment my mind was on you and getting you out of the parish house. Malcolm's lack of desire to go back to the choir school came way down on my list of priorities."

There was a silence for a minute or two. Claire thought about asking Brett again about Lavinia Barton, but didn't think she could cope with it right now.

A while later, she forced herself to eat some of the dinner Martha and Phillippe had concocted, but she had no idea what it was, and was unable to finish what had been put on her plate.

"Phillippe, don't be offended, it has nothing to do with your cooking. It's just—"

"No, I understand." He smiled. *"Je tous comprend."*

I wish I did, Claire thought. And then pushed it aside. At eight she rose from the table. "Please, no one get up or be upset. I am going to have a hot bath and go to bed. Good night, Martha and Phillippe, and thanks again. Brett, I'll see you a little later."

Brett glanced at her and smiled. He didn't say anything, and she was grateful.

She was already tired. The bath soaked out the remaining tension and she went to sleep a few minutes after pulling the covers up.

Sometime later she awoke and lay without moving for a minute or two. She could feel Brett beside her, although his body was not actually touching hers. It was a big bed, and he was, deliberately, probably, giving her plenty of room.

After about ten minutes she realized she was not going to go back to sleep immediately as she had hoped. Lying on her back, she stared up at the ceiling, at the lights from the occasional traffic that played across it, revealing the moulding and the small curlicues at the corners. This, she reflected, was one of the more beautiful buildings on the block and had the high ceilings and thick walls that had gone out shortly after World War II.

Whatever was sticking at the back of her mind was still there, but she had learned from experience that if she tried to dig it out, she would most likely drive it deeper and make it irretrievable. So she let her mind drift where it would, and was beginning to feel a slight drowsiness wash over her when suddenly she remembered that she had been unable to reach Deborah when she had tried to return her call. The phone had been picked up but then put down again. She would have to try again and suggest to Deborah that since she did not plan continuing therapy she should consider making a call to Alanon.

. . .

The next morning, in order to avoid what was sure to be a gang of reporters crowded around the front of the church, Claire deliberately took a roundabout way to work that would lead her to a little-used back door of the parish house. It was when she was walking across town that she suddenly remembered her typewriter. The repair shop was in this block between Lexington and Third.

Approaching the store cautiously, she peered in, wondering if she would encounter Carl Quinn and what she would say if she did. But he did not appear to be there, so she went in.

"Where's Carl Quinn?" she asked as casually as she could, as she paid for the repair.

"You tell us!" the older man who ran the store said. "He just didn't turn up a couple of days ago and hasn't been back."

"Did you call him?"

"We called the number he gave us. There was no answer."

"I think I might know his wife's office number. I'll call her."

"Well, don't tell him to hurry back. I'm not interested in employees who don't show up. And I've already arranged for somebody else to come in tomorrow."

Claire slid her portable in its case off the counter. "All right." She hesitated. "I have a reason for asking this. Did you have trouble with him?"

"When he was sober, no. But that was less and less of the time. Do you know that guy graduated from Princeton? For Pete's sake, he'd be lucky now to get a job cleaning up basements."

. . .

She was in a session with one of her clients when her buzzer went.

"It's Lieutenant O'Neill," Joanna said. "He insisted that I break in."

"All right." She turned to her client. "Excuse me. I'll only be a moment." She watched her client's mouth assume a sulky expression, but knew she had to find out what O'Neill wanted. "Yes, Lieutenant?" she said.

"I can't believe that you're so stupid as to go back to that place where somebody showed every sign of wanting to do you in," he said.

"Maybe not so much that as wanted to get into the office. Which, we know, he or she did, finally."

"Yeah? And who turned off the elevator so you couldn't use it?"

"Look, lieutenant, I don't like getting threatening letters. But I refuse to hide. I have obligations, and one of them is sitting here right now. We are talking on her time."

"Excuse me. Please let me talk to your slavey!"

Claire pushed her buzzer. "Joanna," she said, "the Lieutenant wants to speak to you." Then she turned back to make her peace with her client.

■ ■ ■

That night she took the portable typewriter home, and after dinner set it up in her bedroom to type up some notes. She'd been typing a while when something about the letters and words in front of her made her pause. The typewriter ribbon paraphernalia, which had been broken, had been fixed, but certain letters out of alignment had remained out of alignment. They looked unpleasantly familiar. For a moment she sat there, staring, wondering where she had seen that particular set of uneven letters. Then she remembered.

Getting up, she ripped the paper from her typewriter and went into the living room where Brett was reading a book and listening to television.

"How can you do that?" she asked. "Doesn't one blot out the other?"

"Yes, but I was too lazy to turn it off." He got up and turned the switch. Then he looked at her and asked sharply, "What is it?"

"I have a feeling that whoever . . ." She felt short of breath and started again, "Whoever wrote those anonymous letters, was using my own typewriter."

11

She was put through to O'Neill as soon as she gave her
name.

"Don't touch the machine anymore," he ordered. "I'm
coming up there right now."

"You have the first anonymous letter, don't you?" Claire
asked. "I gave it to you."

"Yes, we have the first, and I'll bring it along to make
comparisons. What are the letters that are out of alignment?"

"The tail of the y is cut off and the i and the v ride above
the line."

"Okay, stay put. And, like I said, don't touch the machine
anymore."

"Yes, maestro." Claire hung up.

O'Neill, accompanied by two other men, was there in
twenty minutes.

"You must have broken all speed records," Claire said as she let them in.

"That's what sirens are for. Now, where's the typewriter?"

Claire took them into the bedroom and waved in the direction of her desk and the portable.

O'Neill and the two men went over and stared at the little machine. "Okay, Ed, you'd better print it before I try anything." While Ed was puffing powder over the machine and another man was photographing it O'Neill turned to Claire. "Now, tell me from the beginning about this guy Carl Quinn and how you met him."

"I met him at the repair shop where they fix typewriters from the church. I brought this one"—she waved at the portable—"in about a month ago. A young man was making out the ticket. When he learned I was from St. Anselm's, he said something about his wife wanting to go there. 'She's into this church business,' I think were his words. And then he added, 'I'm not.' "

"So what did you say?"

"I could see from his scowl that he meant what he said, so I deliberately didn't come on too strong. I said something like why don't you and your wife wander over some time? We have nice music and so on."

"You didn't push it."

"No. I made it casual, figuring that any kind of pressure would just drive him in the opposite direction."

"And then?"

"Then, the next Sunday I was reading the First Lesson from the lectern and saw him sitting in a pew about halfway down the church, and with him was a young woman. I introduced myself at the coffee hour afterwards and then the young woman, Deborah, called me a week or so later to make an appointment to come and see me."

"Okay, what was your impression of this guy?"

"Tall, good-looking, very uptight, angry, which, of course, goes without saying if he's a drunk—a therapist I studied with once called alcoholism bottled anger—and I'd say of a somewhat more affluent background than his wife, Deborah. She's more your working-class, middle-American girl-next-door." Claire went on to relate what the boss of the repair shop had said about Carl's being a graduate of Princeton.

"And he beats up his wife."

"Yes. When she called and said she didn't want to come for therapy anymore, one of the reasons she gave was that her husband seemed to resent my—er—influence with her. So when I said, 'But he told me you were interested in going to church,' she said, 'Well, I've thought it over and I really am not. I agree with Carl about this. And I don't want to discuss it any more.' And then she hung up."

"How long was the typewriter in that shop?"

"They said—or rather Carl said—it would be ready in about a week. But what with one thing and another I forgot about it. Then suddenly yesterday I remembered it because to avoid the press I detoured down the side street where the shop is. I went in, got the machine and was told that Carl wasn't there anymore. Had failed to show up. And obviously the boss there knew that alcohol was his problem."

"Okay. Have you talked to Deborah—Mrs. Quinn—since she said she was stopping therapy?"

"No. She called, but I haven't been able to reach her."

"What's her number?"

Out of habit, Claire hesitated. Information about clients, even former clients, was confidential.

"Come on, come on, we don't know what this guy could have done."

"What do you mean?"

"I mean, if he sent those anonymous letters, and it looks like he might have, then he's up to no good."

Brett, who had been listening to this exchange, said, "Has he been in touch with anybody at the church—or has Deborah, for that matter?"

"I don't know. I'll ask Joanna." Then the thing that had been in the back of her mind, but which she had not been able to retrieve, suddenly surfaced. "Wait," she said. "Jenny, the receptionist downstairs, said something the other day about a drunk coming in there. She said it was long after she'd gone home and it was the custodian, Jeff, who'd left her a message about it."

"Is he on duty now? Can you get him on the phone?"

Claire called St. Anselm's and asked for Jeff. Apparently he was not on duty, but would be back tomorrow morning at nine. Claire passed the message on to O'Neill.

"Okay, what's the Quinn's home phone?"

Claire gave it to him. He dialed the number. After a minute he hung up.

"No answer?" Claire asked.

O'Neill shook his head. "Do you have any other number for him or her?"

"There's her work number. She is some kind of editorial assistant at a publishing house."

"Number?"

Claire gave it to him. He wrote it down. "Okay, I'll try this tomorrow." He looked up at Claire. "Don't call her yourself, and if she calls you, don't tell her anything about the typewriter or my trying to be in touch with her. You can ask her about her husband, how things are, if she's still with him, that kind of thing. But don't give her any idea of police involvement. She'd almost certainly tell him and he might take off."

Again Claire hesitated.

"You're surely not nuts enough not to know what I say is right?" O'Neill said.

"No. All right. I'll do as you say. But I'll be surprised if she calls me. Unless—you know I'm really worried that he might have done something to her."

"Unless he's had a total change—which is unlikely this fast—he almost certainly has."

"If he has any idea that she's talking to me, or that you're involved, Lieutenant, he might kill her!"

"Since we don't know whether or not that's the case, then don't assume it's true."

"Do you think he has anything to do with the murders?" Brett asked.

"He's the most promising suspect we have right now."

"But the dean was killed the same night that Deborah called me for the first time about his beating her up."

"She'd been having therapy with you, hadn't she, for several weeks before that."

"Yes, but—why would he kill the dean?"

"Who knows? If he's a chronic drunk he might also have other problems, such as paranoia. Sometimes—not always but sometimes—one masks the other. If he had decided that you were leading his wife to rebel against him, and hated the church and all the clergy anyway, and he's nuts as well as a drunk, which he might be, he could have come into the parish house, run across the dean and killed him in an alcoholic rage."

"That doesn't sound too logical," Brett said.

"Have you ever dealt with crazy people—I mean certifiably crazy people?"

"No, but we don't know he is. We only know he's a drunk."

"People who can be reasonably sane when sober, can become close to paranoid when they're drunk. That's one of the things alcohol does—bring out a lot of latent problems. He could have run into the dean, demanded to be told where you are, and received some kind of stiff, English response to the general effect that he had no business being there. What do you think a man, too drunk to have the slightest control and with a major grudge against the church and its workers, might do?"

"And Lavinia Barton?" Brett asked.

"Don't push me. I didn't say we had a solid case. And I'd think you'd be glad to get the eye of suspicion off of you!"

"Maybe it's because I have a fellow feeling for anybody who's center stage as suspect number one."

"Even though it looks very like he wants to hurt your wife

—regardless of what he did or may have done to the other victims?"

"You have a point, Lieutenant. I'm sorry, Claire."

Claire gave him a quick smile and took his arm. "Well, Lieutenant, let me know."

Just as he was leaving O'Neill said, "Heard anything from Jamie?"

"No." Claire said. As always her heart started beating more rapidly. Hope that she knew to be foolish surged up in her. "Have you?"

He shook his head.

   · · ·

After a restless night during which her thoughts churned among Jamie, the dean, Malcolm and Mrs. Barton and back to Jamie, Claire remembered that one of the better cures of tension was exercise and realized she hadn't had enough lately. So she decided to walk to St. Anselm's, deliberately going out of her way to go down Fifth Avenue. For one thing, she thought, if she walked on the park side, there was not the interruption of having to cross all the blocks and/or wait for the traffic light. For another, she could look into the park. The trees were bare, of course, but she'd always found a winter scene as attractive in its way as a summer one.

It was when she looked over the wall into a meadow near the southern end of the park and saw some boys playing ball that she stopped. The boys were young, ranging in age, Claire guessed, between about nine and about fourteen. As the two figures crossed her mind, she thought of the choir school. Of course these could be students at any private elementary boys school in the city, because she knew that many of them practiced ball in one or another of the meadows in Central Park. On the other hand several of the boys looked familiar.

That tall, fair-haired boy, wasn't that Timothy Bentham? She was so used to seeing him in his choir robes that it took a moment for her to be sure. She'd always thought that the robes made the boys look taller, but here he seemed to tower over the others and, in his white T-shirt and red practice shorts he also seemed stronger and more mature. No wonder his voice had broken, she thought.

Claire found her eyes then searching among the smaller boys for Malcolm, but even though it was difficult to keep up with the running, dodging figures, she became reasonably convinced that Malcolm was not there. A small sense of alarm snaked through her. Why wouldn't he be at football practice?

She was still standing there when the man in charge blew a whistle and the boys stopped playing, went over to a heap of what looked like jackets and sweaters.

They would, of course, be going back to St. Anselm's Choir School, and since Claire was headed in the same direction she decided to wait until they emerged from the park.

As they came through a gate in the park and passed her, she ran her eye over the smaller boys in front to make sure she hadn't missed Malcolm, but there was no sight of him. Then she looked to the back where Timothy was walking with another boy in front of a man Claire recognized as the athletics director. Timothy's face was turned away as he talked to his companion, but Claire saw, hooked into the pocket of his windbreaker, a pen that looked vaguely familiar. She stared at it and then realized it reminded her of the pen that Joanna's boyfriend, Jimmy, had given her.

A curious chill seized her. I have to be mistaken, she thought. The pen was a clear, bright blue with little marks and shapes on it. She knew because Joanna had made such a point of showing her and bragging about Jimmy's taste.

Upset and preoccupied, she watched the boys cross Fifth Avenue, and then hurried across herself. As she stepped up on the pavement a little behind the boys, Timothy turned and looked right at her. For a second or two she saw the brilliant blue eyes on her. He smiled and waved.

"That was a good practice you were having," she said, and thought how lame it sounded. "I'm Claire Aldington," she added by way of explanation to the athletics master as he stepped forward.

"I know you are. If we'd known you were going to be watching, we'd have been even more brisk and energetic, wouldn't we, boys?"

"Yeah," they all howled in a friendly fashion.

Now that she was up close to Timothy, she saw that the pen was indeed a replica of Joanna's. Since she didn't think that she could disguise her interest, and sometimes the bold approach was the most successful, she said, "That's a handsome pen you have there Timothy. Where did you get it?"

He put his hand up and touched it. "It's nice, isn't it. My godmother gave it to me for my birthday."

"Where's Malcolm?" Claire asked. "I didn't see him."

Nobody answered for a moment, then the coach said, "Lazing away, I'm afraid. But in view of everything I decided not to be too bullying about it. He didn't feel like coming out, and Matron thought it might be a good idea if he rested."

"I see. Well, see you in church, as they say!" she said, wanting to hurry on and for lack of anything else to say.

"Bye," several treble voices said.

"Bye," she said, waved and walked quickly on.

．　．　．

When she got in to the pastoral counseling offices she said to Joanna, "What color was that pen that Jimmy gave you?"

"I showed it to you!"

"You undoubtedly did, but please refresh my memory."

"It was a bright blue—almost a turquoise, with little black line drawings on it. Why, have you seen it?"

Claire didn't answer right away. Then she said, "I think I've seen one like it."

"Where. Where?"

"I'm not going to say right now—no, Joanna, the person I saw with it . . ." she paused, not wanting to even identify the sex of the person by saying in "his" pocket. "The person I saw who had it said it had been a present. I have no reason not to believe that."

"Jimmy told me that there was only a limited number in the store and they were all snapped up practically right away."

"I'm sure it's true, but the—er—giver of the pen to the person I saw could have been one of those who, as you say, snapped one up."

Joanna turned back and stared at her typewriter, her anger clearly visible.

"If somebody else had reported it as a theft and I saw you with the one that Jimmy gave you, wouldn't you want me to give you the benefit of the doubt?"

Silence. Then a long sigh. "Yes, I suppose you're right. But I really loved it." There was another silence. Then, "I don't suppose you'd even let me know where you saw the other pen, would you?"

"No. Not until I am sure whether it is yours or not."

∎ ∎ ∎

Somehow Claire got through the rest of the morning. She attended the noon Eucharist and was only mildly gratified when the canon carefully came and marched with her in the procession. Of the late dean's nephew she saw nothing. Larry, she knew, was not coming in until after lunch.

When the carols and the Christmas anthems rang out, Claire found she didn't and couldn't feel Christmassy. The basic message was still there and still profoundly valid, under all the sadness and anxiety, but she still couldn't feel it.

After a sandwich at her desk while she got through some paperwork, Claire picked up the phone and rang Larry. "Any chance of a chat and a cup of coffee?" she asked. "Or even a chat without the cup of coffee."

"A pleasure," he said, "as always. Give me a minute and then come along. I have to make one phone call."

When she got down to his office she found Larry staring out of his window into the inner court, looking, in profile, more like Pooh Bear than ever.

"Do you know how much you resemble Pooh Bear?" she

asked. Then added hastily, "That is an extreme compliment. I adore Pooh."

"If I didn't know now it's not for lack of being told. Wendy mentions it every now and then, not to mention my two daughters, who think telling me about Pooh the height of wit." He turned back. "And how are you?"

She sat down, and again found, to her embarrassment, that an honest question like that from her good friend nearly always produced a rush of tears. "Okay," she managed to say, "except when you ask me. Then I seem to become a water-fall."

"Heard from Jamie?"

"No."

"It's not pleasant for you, and the next time I set eyes on him he's going to find that Edward Bear has other facets to his personality than being bumbling and lovable. But I still remain convinced that he's perfectly all right, and has taken himself off for some addlepated but not life-threatening rea-son."

"I hope to God you're right. There are times when I'm convinced of it, too. Then somebody, like O'Neill last night, asks me if I've heard and all the horrible doubts and fears come rushing back. Poor Brett, I kicked and tossed around last night enough to give him back pain."

Larry looked at her and smiled a little. "Somehow I don't feel desperately sorry for him. What did you want to talk about?"

Claire told him about seeing the pen in young Timothy's windbreaker. "It seems outrageous to think he could have taken it, but so many strange and awful things are going on, if he did, then I wonder about all the rest."

"Have you asked Adam Deane about this?"

"No. I don't think he was too happy about my taking Malcolm home, and probably looks on me as a thoroughly interfering female."

"Umm. He was married once, but his wife left him, and I think he's been slightly untrusting of women ever since. If you like, I'll sound him out. In fact, why don't I do it now?" He reached for the phone.

"Won't he resent it?"

"If Timothy has had nothing to do with the thefts and disappearances, then Adam will be mad as a hornet if he's unjustly accused, and who could blame him? But there is always the remote possibility he might have."

Larry picked up the receiver of the telephone and punched in Adam Deane's number. "Larry here," he said in a moment. "I was wondering if Claire and I could come across and talk to you about something that has come up. All right. Five minutes."

"I thought you were going to soften him up first," Claire grumbled.

"Courage," Larry said. "Let's go."

When they got down to the first floor they heard the sound of the boys' voices soaring up from the basement. Larry stopped, and then said, "Timothy's not there."

"You're very good. I couldn't have told that—at least I don't think so." She stopped as she heard a soprano begin the climb in a descant, this time to "Hark, the Herald Angels Sing." The boy who was carrying the main soprano part was good, but Claire understood what Larry was talking about. His voice, though clear and carrying, did not have quite the strength or that peculiarly golden quality that Claire had come to associate with Timothy.

"I wonder if that's Malcolm," she said.

"Possibly," Larry replied. He glanced at Claire's face and said, "We can see them through the window from the staircase going down from the main hall to the practice room. Shall we spy on them and see?"

"Yes," Claire said. She found she was feeling anxious about Malcolm.

They went down the stairs from the main lobby, and sure enough, there in their choir stalls in the practice rooms were the boys, their faces turned to the piano in the middle where Eric was playing and conducting.

After they'd stood there for a few seconds Claire said, "There's Malcolm, on the opposite side."

"Umm," Larry said. "I don't think the voice we heard was his, though."

"What makes you say that?"

"Well, as an ex-choir boy, I do know when a chorister is giving his all. The boy we heard singing is the boy standing two from Malcolm, the one with red hair. Listen!"

Claire stopped and listened. Larry was right. The boy had a clear, strong voice, not quite as outstanding as Timothy's but good. And it certainly wasn't Malcolm, who was barely opening his mouth.

"I see what you mean about giving his all. Malcolm's hardly saying the words."

"I know. Of course, there is the matter of his mother's violent death . . ."

"I have been led to believe that he wasn't that crazy about his mother."

"Yes, I've heard that, too."

Claire glanced at him quickly.

"Let's go over and talk to Adam," Larry said. He took her elbow as they mounted the stairs.

■ ■ ■

Adam Deane listened to Claire, who made her comment about the pen in Timothy's pocket as uninflammatory as she could. "I just thought that might be one of the many mysteries that could be cleared up if . . . if we could be reassured about his godmother giving him the pen."

"I will, of course, make it my business to find out," Deane said. "But I'm bound to say that I am shocked that you would even think such a thing. I'm sure pens like that—"

"I don't think Claire is a suspicious person," Larry said peaceably, "but so many strange and queer things have occurred, she thought, and I'm bound to say I agree with her, anything that can be eliminated would be helpful."

Adam Deane's flushed look faded a little. His rather narrow mouth relaxed. "Well, I can assure you that this will be completely investigated and I will report to you both in the very near future."

"I'm afraid that whatever Adam's problems with women are, I don't think I improved them," Claire said, as they walked back across the street.

"Never mind," Larry replied. "We were right to do what we did. And however little you may credit it, Adam will get to the bottom of it. He's ferociously protective of the boys, as well he might be, but he's not blind."

 . . .

Late that afternoon as Claire was going out the front door of the parish house, Jenny, who was about to close the switchboard said, "Damn!" and answered yet another incoming call.

"She's on her way out," Jenny said, looking at Claire. "Can it wait till tomorrow morning?" She listened for a minute. Then she sighed. "Just a minute." She put the call on hold and said resignedly, "There's a Deborah Quinn on the line. She says she's your former client and she seems to be having hysterics. Something about her husband being picked up by the police."

Claire, overcoming a strong reluctance to dealing with this particular problem, came back from the door. "All right. I'll talk to her."

"I'll put it in the reception room," Jenny said grudgingly.

Claire walked into the small waiting room that opened off the lobby and picked up the phone. "Yes, Deborah," she said.

Hysterical just about described Deborah's frantic statements. "It's all because of something *you* said. They've taken him away and accused him of all kinds of horrible things including killing that wretched clergyman. Carl is right, the church is an oppressive instrument, going after all the people who don't agree with it. I want you to know that through somebody in my office we know Jason Rosenthal, the defense attorney, and when he gets through with you—"

"Deborah, listen to me. No, listen. I did not, repeat not,

accuse Carl of killing the dean, or suggest that he did. But I do think he may have had something to do with those anonymous letters I've been—Deborah, listen to me!"

But she'd already hung up.

Claire sat there with the receiver in her hand. She could, of course, call Deborah back. But that meant she had to go back upstairs and look up her number in her file up there. It all seemed too much. And Deborah would probably hang up on her again. But all the while Claire was reciting these probabilities to herself, she was walking over to the elevator and pushing the UP button. Back of all of these arguments was the painful memory of another time when she felt she should have made an extra effort—when she still felt she should have seen the old dean into the elevator instead of merely directing him. . . .

Claire got into the elevator, pushed the top button and rode to the top of the building. When she fitted her key into the lock she found it wouldn't turn for the simple reason that once again the door was already unlocked.

Had she locked it when she left, pushing in the button in the middle of the inside knob so that it would automatically lock when she pulled it closed?

She could swear on the proverbial stack of Bibles that she did. Yet, as she went back in her mind, she knew she could not accurately remember. Locking the door before closing it was such an automatic thing. She had done it when leaving for the day, or when she knew the office would be empty, for so many years, she did it without thinking, and therefore could not now—for sure—recall doing it.

She pushed the door open. Curiously, she did remember turning off the light, and it was indeed still off because the room was dark. Before entering, she reached around the door and flipped the switch. Joanna's office lit up. Walking in slowly she looked around. Was there any sign that someone had been here in the few minutes since she had left?

She walked over to Joanna's desk. Everything there seemed in order, and looked more or less the way it had when she'd left. But, of course, she couldn't be sure, because she hadn't stopped to examine it. Reaching around the open door to her own office Claire again flipped a switch. The big ceiling light went on. Did the things on her desk look different because she so seldom used that light, preferring instead the softer light from her desk lamp, or had someone been in there moving her things around?

After a moment or so of staring, Claire finally resigned herself to the fact that she could not be sure of the answer to that, since she was far from obsessively methodical and orderly. She knew she could recall the color of the eyes and hair of everyone with whom she had had any contact. She was good at noticing people. But she would be hard put to tell anyone the color of the walls of her office if the question was sprung on her.

Had the phone, the notebook, the Rolodex file been moved? She didn't know.

Walking over to the desk she fipped the file to Deborah's two numbers, copied them down on a small piece of paper, put it in her pocket and left the room, switching off the ceiling light as she went. She was starting to walk towards the outer door when she was suddenly struck with the conviction that she was not alone in the room.

She stood absolutely still and experienced the sensation that she had heard described as the hair on the back of the neck standing up. She had always thought it was an exaggeration and an over-repeated cliché. Now she knew it perfectly described what she was feeling. She started to say, "Who's there?" and found herself unable to speak.

Why? she thought. Why did she feel she mustn't say it? She then realized she was thinking of—of all people—Letty, and as clearly as though the sound were coming through her ears she heard Letty's high English voice saying, "Leave, Claire dear. Leave now. Go!"

She stood, her legs shaking a little. Shouldn't she resist this? After all this was a therapist's office with files full of confidential information. She took in a breath preparatory to forcing herself to speak. Then the light in the outer office went off. She was in the dark. The outer door opened and slammed shut.

Forcing herself to put one foot in front of the other, she walked towards the door, reached out with her left hand for the switch and flipped it. The light went on. Quickly she looked around the room. There was no one there. But there was across from Joanna's desk a closet used for coats and supplies. The closet door had been closed. It was now open. Claire turned toward the outer door and tried the handle. It opened.

She stood there for a while, listening. A door around another corridor slammed. What doors were there in that location? None, except the big door marked STAIRS leading to the inside staircase, the staircase she would have to take if, as had happened before, the elevator had been put out of commission.

Carefully she pushed the button to the lock position in the door then closed it behind her. The walk to the elevator was longer than she had ever known before. Finally she found herself facing the elevator doors and the two buttons. She pushed the button marked DOWN, and waited, half sick with anxiety for there to be no answering sound at all, no elevator creaking shut and then coming up to get her. That would mean, of course, that someone had turned it off. But it arrived and she got in.

Horrid questions haunted her mind as the ancient lift wheezed down. Could the cable have been tampered with? How often had she heard over the news that someone, usually in a housing project, had got into the elevator only to have it smash to the bottom of the building? Every ugly elevator mishap or accident she had ever heard of slid in front of her inner vision in glorious technicolor. When the cab door creaked finally open on the first floor she was almost too paralyzed with fright to get out.

But she was safe and left the elevator as the door started to wheeze shut again. Never had the lobby looked so reassuring, so safe.

Several of the homeless were sitting on chairs that were scattered here and there and were put out each night. "Evening, Ms. Aldington," a fairly familiar voice said. She turned. There was the man named Seldon.

"Hello, Jim," she said, surprised to hear that her own voice sounded normal. "How are you?"

"Not so bad. Maybe a shelter isn't the greatest place to be, but it sure beats jail and the cops!"

Claire looked quickly at him. Was there reproach or anger there? But the expression on Jim's face seemed unambiguously friendly.

"I'm sorry you were held, Jim," she said.

"That's all right. Least, it was all right after Mr. Martinez came down to see that nobody was pushing me around. He somehow talked them into seeing it wasn't me that pushed the old priest down the stairs. Him and the nice young guy who was with him."

Claire pulled the big book over to sign out. "Must have been some friend of Mr. Martinez's," she said. "Maybe one of his youth group from St. Matthew's."

"Yeah, I guess so. When Mr. Martinez was off talking to the cops, him and me talked about our dogs. He has one, too."

Something about what he said penetrated the maelstrom of thoughts and feelings in Claire's head.

"How can you have a dog, Jim? You can't keep him in a shelter."

"No. But a friend of mine has him and I go and see him every day. He's always real glad to see me."

Claire, closing the book, saw something come over Jim's face when he talked about his dog that reminded her of Jamie. She felt a familiar jab of pain. "Maybe some day, if you . . ." if he what? she wondered. Got a job? Found some way to pay the rent that was always somehow beyond the poorest New Yorkers to pay? She asked gently, "What kind of dog is he?"

"He's a mutt, but the boy said he was like his dog, part shepherd and part retriever. Mine's named Sam." He paused. "I can't remember exactly what he said his was named. Something funny."

Claire, who in her pastoral work for the church often came across women who did not have homes for their children, found herself strangely moved by this man who had no home for his dog. It seemed a hopeless proposition, but she said, "Maybe one day you'll be able to find a place for both of you so you and Sam can be together."

He sighed. "Yeah, I hope. But, like I said, being here sure beats being in jail."

Claire, still shaky from her experience upstairs, smiled. "Have a good night," she said.

12

*K*nowing that what she ought to do was walk home and calm down, Claire nevertheless took a taxi and sat back, trying not to think about her overwhelming sense of danger in her office and her conviction that someone who did not wish her well was hiding there in her office. And there was no question where he—or she—might have been: the closet in the outer office.

Had she known it then, when she was standing there, frozen? The truth was, she didn't know. But the answer could well be that she had deliberately not let the possibility drift up to her conscious mind because that meant she would have to —have to what? Call out? Walk over to the closet and fling open the door? Suddenly she found herself thinking about Letty's voice that seemed so clear at the time, telling her that she was in danger. There, in the taxi, bumping up the potholes of Madison Avenue, Claire shivered.

Talking to Brett about it would help—help enormously.

But Brett wasn't there when she got home. A note propped up on the hall table next to the phone said, in Martha's handwriting, that she and Phillippe would be out for the evening and that Brett had called, had said he had tried to get Claire again and again in her office but that her line was always busy, and that he had to attend a late meeting that was obviously going to be a dinner meeting. He was sorry and would see her when he got home. There was a p.s. Motley had been walked before she (Martha) had left, but he would need it again when Claire got home.

"Thanks a bunch," Claire said aloud.

About to shrug off her coat, she closed it again and buttoned it up.

If there was any doubt that Motley wanted his walk his presence, bounding around, making eager noises, and holding the leash in his mouth would have convinced her.

"All right," she said, and then, because she knew she had sounded cross and his tail had sunk down, she patted his head. "Good dog," she said, and was rewarded with a lick on her hand and his tail again going up and waving.

Twenty minutes later, having walked around the block, they were back. Claire hoped that, now that she was used to the idea of no one being there, she wouldn't feel as abandoned and let down as she did when she first read Martha's note. But the apartment was unquestionably empty, and she could not psych herself into feeling any less forlorn.

The thought of making dinner for herself was less than appealing, but she knew she ought to eat something, so she pulled a frozen dinner out of the freezer, put it in the oven and went in to watch the news. If she had just followed Brett's suggestion of several months before and bought herself a microwave, she thought grumpily, she wouldn't have to wait fifty minutes to eat. He should have bought it for me, she thought angrily, and then laughed at herself.

There was nothing in the news to cheer her up. The first item was the fact that the police had announced a new suspect in the case of the murder of the English dean. There was a shot of one of the reporters at the press conference that had been called by the precinct asking if the new suspect, one Carl Quinn, were also suspected of Mrs. Barton's murder.

"No comment on that," Lieutenant O'Neill said. "One thing at a time."

"But—" another reporter yelled.

"I'm afraid that's all we can give you at the moment," O'Neill said.

"What made you realize this—" the reporter glanced at his note—"this Carl Quinn was implicated?"

"Certain information received," O'Neill said briefly, and Claire felt a spasm of gratitude that he did not go into the matter of the anonymous letters.

But she had congratulated herself too soon. "You mean somebody actually saw him kill the dean?"

"No," O'Neill said. He hesitated, then added, "but there is no doubt at all that it was Quinn who wrote anonymous letters to one of the clergy at St. Anselm's threatening . . . various kinds of violence."

"To the rector?" several voices shouted.

"To Cunningham?" another voice yelled.

"We really can't say more at this time," the lieutenant answered, obviously trying to be patient.

"Yeah? But what made you suspect this Quinn?" an angry voice asked.

"I'm not at liberty to discuss that right now," O'Neill said.

Which means, Claire thought, that, press conference or no press conference, he isn't entirely sure about Carl and the dean's murder. As though in answer to her thought the telephone rang.

Claire went over to it. "Hello?" she answered.

Whoever it was hung up.

Claire stood with the receiver in her hand. It was at that moment that she remembered Deborah's hysterical phone call. With everything that had happened after she had gone to her office to get Deborah's number and then written it down, her decision to call Deborah back had entirely slipped her mind.

Damn! she thought. She hung up, went to her handbag to find the piece of paper on which she had written Deborah's number and could not locate it anywhere. Just to make sure, she checked the address book in which she carried the names and numbers of friends. It was not there. She looked in two zip pockets in her handbag. It wasn't in either. She emptied her handbag out onto the table beside the phone. Half of the contents rolled on the floor but there was no paper with telephone numbers written on it.

Putting the various contents of her handbag back, she considered other possibilities. Of course, her coat. She was wearing it when she went up to her office.

The paper proved to be in the left pocket. She was about to go back to the phone when the timer bell, set for the length of time her frozen dinner was to bake in the oven, went off.

Going into the kitchen, Claire opened the oven, all but burned her fingers before she remembered to use some pot holders, and got the slightly overdone dish out onto the kitchen table. Then she turned off the oven and went back to the living room.

She dialed Deborah's number and it was picked up on the second ring.

"I don't want to talk to any newspaper," Deborah's voice screamed. "If you want to know what happened call that bitch at St. Anselm's!"

"Deborah," Claire said quietly. "Listen to me—" The phone was slammed down.

It rang almost immediately.

"Mrs. Cunningham," a male voice said, "I am from the *Daily Herald*. We have been told that the reason Carl Quinn is in custody is because you have given information about his

implication in the crime to the police. Did you do this to take
the heat off your husband?"

"Of course not. I wouldn't do such a thing. I had been
getting anonymous letters—"

"Yes, we know about that," the voice went on, "but we
still want to know how much your desire to exonerate your
husband was part of your motive."

"It was no part of my motive," Claire said angrily.

"Naturally you would say that," the voice went on
smoothly, as though she hadn't spoken.

"I say it because it's the truth," Claire said, and hung up.
The phone rang almost immediately again. This time Claire
let it ring until the message tape came on. The caller turned
out to be from one of the local television news services. It had
no sooner finished than the phone rang again. This time it
was another newspaper.

Claire left the phone, unable to listen to the probing questions and unctuous voices. For a moment, to stop them, she
thought of simply taking the phone off the hook. But she
reflected then that if Brett called—or Jamie—she would not
know. So she decided to go into the kitchen and eat her
dinner there as far away from the phone as possible.

First she fed Motley, who was leaping around and Patsy,
who had emerged from Martha's room and was making hungry noises as she wound in and out of Claire's legs.

"Watch it, Patsy!" Claire said, as she almost stumbled.
"You'll get nothing to eat if you don't get out of the way,"
and she gently moved Patsy with her foot.

As Motley and Patsy were eating with every sound of en-
joyment, Claire pulled the cover off her dinner. It now looked
rather dry and brown.

Sitting down, Claire pushed a spoon inside the casserole
and took a bite. "Yuck!" she said aloud. After a moment or
two of staring at the unappetizing mess, she scooped it into
the garbage and made herself a tuna sandwich, of which she
managed to eat about two-thirds. At that point her stomach
rebelled.

Claire glanced at her watch. It was now seven thirty-five. But she felt tired enough for it to be eleven. Going into the bathroom she ran a full, hot tub, filled it with various kinds of bath salts and made herself soak for half an hour, while she listened to a Mozart symphony in her cassette player propped on the bathroom floor.

At a quarter to nine she went to bed and went to sleep almost immediately.

$$\bullet \quad \bullet \quad \bullet$$

She was looking frantically in room after room, running through doors and pulling open closets. Motley was with her and it was because of him that she realized finally she was looking for Jamie. "He's here somewhere, Motley, I know he is," she said in the dream. But Motley wasn't happy, he kept scrabbling on the doors, whimpering and crying, and it was because of that she knew that Jamie was in some kind of danger. Then suddenly she was in the prison with Jim Seldon and Joe Martinez, who was talking. "Ja—" he shouted.

Claire woke up, her heart pounding.

"Ja—" she said aloud.

A grunt beside her indicated that Brett was in bed and asleep.

"Ja—" she repeated. And then she remembered where she had heard that. It was from Joe Martinez the other day. "Ja—" he said and then stopped and went on to something else. And only a few hours ago at the parish house Jim Seldon had been talking about Jamie. She was sure of it. The young guy who was with Joe Martinez, he'd said, who had a dog with a funny name who was part shepherd and part retriever . . .

"Brett—" Claire said, and then she said it louder. "Brett. Listen—" she pushed him in his back. "I'm sure Jamie's at Joe Martinez's or at least Joe knows where he is."

Afterwards, when the damage had been done, she realized that Brett would never have answered the way he did if he hadn't been exhausted and sleeping soundly when she woke him. But at her third punch in the back he said, "What'd you say?"

"I said I'm sure Jamie's with Joe Martinez."

"Umm . . . I thought he might be."

All the strain of Jamie's absence, of the dean's death, of the lack of various explanations from Brett, of her overwhelming fear in her own office and the nerve-shattering effect of the phone calls came together.

"You bastard!" Claire yelled. "You knew all along where Jamie was and you never opened your mouth. Do you know what I was going through? Do you?"

By this time Brett was sitting up. "Take it easy!" he said disastrously.

"Take it easy? My son's missing and you tell *me* to take it easy?" Do you have any idea of how I must feel?"

"In case you've forgotten, I have a son myself."

"Yes, I do remember. And I also remember that I don't want my son to turn out to be a chronic druggie and thief like him!" Claire shouted.

Brett swung his legs to the side and pushed back the covers. Then he got up and went into the bathroom. When he came back he was putting on his robe. "Leave my son out of this." He collected the pillow from his side of the bed. "I'm going into the guestroom," he said. "I didn't say, by the way, that I *knew* Jamie was with Joe. I said I had begun to *suspect* it. I knew they'd been having talks from time to time and, in a sense, had become friends."

"Well, why the hell didn't you share this information or suspicion or whatever it was with me?"

"Because, as I just finished telling you, I wasn't sure. Why don't you get a grip on yourself." He tied the knot of his robe. "Good night!"

"Oh, no, you don't." As though from a great distance Claire heard her voice, harsh, angry, accusative. Some tiny voice deep within her was saying, "You'll be sorry about this, calm down." But it was drowned out by her anger, fear and anxiety. Angrier than she could ever remember being in her life, Claire picked up the book from her bedside table and threw it at Brett, just missing him as he closed their bedroom door behind him. She heard his slippered feet going down the hall and then the door of the guest room slam. This sound was followed by another: the key in the door being turned.

Somehow that added the last spurt of flame to her rage. "You didn't have to do that," she shouted. "I have no desire to share the room or the bed with you!"

Her hand shook as she opened the church directory to Martinez's home number, and then punched out the figures on her phone. She glanced at her watch. Three-fifteen. Tough!

"Hello?" Joe's voice, sleepy but unmistakable, answered.

"Joe, this is Claire Aldington." Aldington was her own name and she'd damn well see to it that people used it. At that moment it occurred to her that Aldington was the name of her first husband, but she pushed the unwelcome reminder aside. "Is my son Jamie there?"

There was a pause, then, "Ma?" Jamie's voice said.

Claire burst into tears. "Jamie, how could you do this? Do you have any idea what not knowing where you were could do to me?"

"I'm sorry, Ma. It just seemed the best thing for me to do."

"Why?"

"Let me tell you when I get home."

"No. Now!"

"Ma, it's the middle of the night."

"I am aware of that. I want you to answer my question."

There was another short silence, then Jamie said, his voice calm, even cold. "I was at the parish house the day that the dean was killed. I went there to see if I could get any idea from Joanna or maybe Mr. Swade or Maude What's-her-name what you might like for Christmas. You remember, I tried to ask you before but you wouldn't even think about it. I asked Brett about it, but he said he couldn't come up with any ideas. Anyway, I was there and I heard the dean, and . . . and

Brett having a knock-down-drag-out. I didn't know what to do. I didn't want to tell the police, but I also didn't feel too much like being around him, so I called up Joe and asked him if I could stay with him. I didn't think you'd mind, even though you do think he's some kind of nut! He's really a nice guy."

"I want you to come home, Jamie. I want you here."

"I can't come home in the middle of the night."

"All right. But I want you here tomorrow morning, before I leave for the office so I can know you're here."

"You know, you sound like you think I'm in some kind of danger. I'm not. And what about what I told you about hearing Brett and the dean? I know how you feel about him—how would you feel if he got convicted because of me."

"If Brett's guilty of anything, then he ought to be convicted."

"Are you okay, Ma? That doesn't sound like you. You love him!"

"Jamie, just come home. We'll work out the rest. Please!"

"Oh, all right." There was a pause. "Motley okay?"

"You deserve for me not to answer that, or to tell you he's run away!"

"Ma, don't joke. Is he there? Is he okay?"

"So, you'd feel bad if Motley ran away! Now you know how I've been feeling."

"Ma—"

"Yes, he's okay." She looked down at the dog who, possibly because he was able to hear Jamie's voice on the phone, was whimpering. "Listen," she said into the receiver, and then held it down towards Motley for a few seconds. Then she raised it to her ear again. "Did you hear that?" she asked.

"Yeah, that's cool. Thanks."

• • •

She couldn't go back to bed. She found she was too overwhelmingly aware of the closed and locked door down the hall. Going into the kitchen, she turned on the light and, after standing in the middle of the floor for a moment, opened the refrigerator and got out the milk. Pouring some in a pan, she put the pan over a flame, and began rummaging in the cupboard shelf for some crackers.

The unmistakable sound of boiling milk turned her around in time to see the white foam from the pan pour over the side and hiss down to the flame. She leaped across and turned the jet off.

"I hope you like boiled milk," Brett said from the door. He was fully dressed and was shrugging into his coat. A small suitcase was beside him on the floor. "I've decided that we'd do better in different establishments for the time being, so I called my club from the guest room and am going there."

"Brett—" Claire started.

"But before I go there's something I've decided to explain."

"Brett—" Claire went towards him with her hand out, some idea of what she had said and done beginning to penetrate the self-protective armor around her.

"No, I want to tell you something—" He put her hand away and stepped to the door. "If you don't want to hear me out, then I'll find a way to tell you later. What I want to say should not go in a letter. It's up to you whether you want to hear me out or not."

Claire stopped. "Please let me at least—"

"No. Will you listen to what I have to say?"

She stiffened. "Since you put it like that, all right."

"Why don't you sit down?"

"I'd rather stand."

"As you wish. Mark Hastings was at Cambridge a long time after Philby and Blount, of course. But there was still a fairly strong pro-Soviet feeling, and Mark got enamored of the dream of a rosier world as promised by the Marxist manifesto. For all that he was an American—or maybe because he was an American, I don't know—he became an avid opponent of what he described as the greed of a society based on the capitalistic principle.

"Whether he actually joined the Communist Party or not, I don't know. He says he didn't, and I believe him, and certainly one of the ways they used people was not to have them join openly but work for them wherever they happened to be —usually in government. Mark did a few errands for their network in England. Then something—I'm not sure what— disillusioned him, and he broke with them and went into the Church. The nearest thing I've ever heard him say about it was that he decided he preferred to work for peace and justice through apostleship rather than through secular action.

"When I went over to London fifteen years ago, Mark was already ordained and doing a stint with the London mission, and he was specifically involved in the distribution of the fund from the English Church. Washington thought it had reason to suspect that those same funds, intended for the needy and starving, were being laundered through some bogus organization to end up in the hands of antiAmerican rebels.

"Maitland was one of the people I questioned, because they had known each other in Cambridge. Maitland took a considerably more relaxed view of this than my colleagues at Intelligence did and was angry that I was poking around. That was the basis of our quarrel when I was there. He was a man who—despite Philby, Maclean et al.—still believed in the old joke about the dear vicar who was asked how his son at Oxford was doing and replied, 'Splendidly, splendidly, he's now a Communist.' In other words, Maitland felt that Marxism was a phase that young intellectuals went through. No, Claire," Brett said, as Claire looked as though she were going to speak. "Please don't interrupt. Let me finish. You had your say—at length and with considerable force! Now let me have mine."

It was not until that moment that Claire realized how angry Brett was. Some of the words, names and accusations that she had flung at him and then wiped from her mind were now back in her memory in full force. She felt she couldn't blame him. And made a gesture for him to go on.

"I disagreed with him—the dean—then. But nothing was turned up that would throw any doubt now on Hasting's loyalties, and so gradually I came around to his viewpoint. But when Maitland showed up in New York he made it clear to me that *he* had changed his mind and now decided that Hastings should, as he put it, make a clean breast of it to, at least, the bishop and the vestry. I told him that these many years later no good would be served by that, and there were those who might insist that Hastings leave his rectorship at St. Anselm's, although I was fairly sure if it became public knowledge the young people would understand. But, having switched sides, the dean was now as vigorous for Hastings to tell all as he had been against it. That's why he had come over early, to try and persuade Hastings to confess, so to speak, before the first of the year.

"We had disagreed about it over lunch at the club. He left in a huff and said he was coming to the church. I gave him a half hour to cool down, then I came up to the church myself and ran him down in the parish house where he had gone to look for Mark. I made my case again that, if he had to, he could tell the bishop, but all he'd do is raise trouble if he made it any more public than that.

"By this time we were shouting at each other. He said he would think it over. I was running for the elevator, knowing I was due in my office at four, when Lavinia burst out of one of the rooms—Eric Fullerton's, I think—and threw herself—and I mean just that—at me. She and I had had a fling many years ago, before I was married for the first time, but I soon became unenchanted. I unwound her arms and fled. That is the true and full account of my participation in this whole miserable, dreary affair. Now I'm going. Good night."

He was out the kitchen door and into the apartment hallway before Claire had had a chance to move. Then, "Brett, please, please let me say something now."

Brett had the front door open. "No, I don't think I will. And while I'm on the subject, I'm probably a candidate for the prize in old-fogyism, but I really don't like being called a bastard by my wife, nor having her throw things at me."

Claire, standing in the apartment door, cursed the speed of the building elevator, which arrived seconds after he had finished talking.

. . .

Jamie arrived the next morning shortly after eight. Claire, who had spent the remainder of the night sleepless, tried to hug him. He acquiesced without enthusiasm and then called to Motley who came down the hall yelping.

Watching the emotional reunion, Claire felt more rejected than she had ever felt in her life before. Numb and miserable, rather than walk as she usually did, she took the Lexington Avenue bus downtown and found she was longing for the day when the Christmas decorations would finally come down and she could stop feeling that, in addition to her many other failures, she was casting a blight over the season.

Salvation Army men and women in their uniforms stood outside stores, buckets hung from tripods for contributions, trumpets and other instruments playing carols. "Hark, the Herald Angels Sing." Next Saturday would be the Feast of Christmas. She was due to read the First Lesson at the celebration of the Vigil. Where would Brett be? In his club? Spending the day with his many friends, all of whom would be glad to have him around?

How could I have talked to him like that, Claire wondered? Such a temper tantrum had not exploded since she was a rebellious teenager.

. . .

As Claire got out and prepared to force her way through the press milling around the street outside the parish house, she finally conceded to herself that if Brett never returned home, never said another affectionate word to her, it would be her own fault. He had asked her to have faith in him, and she had failed. True, he had not told her about his suspicion that Jamie was with Joe Martinez, but he had what seemed to him a good reason.

Something within her tried to work up some of the resentment that had been simmering in her about his failure to explain his relationship with Lavinia Barton, about his not immediately telling her his reasons for his argument with the dean, for demanding blind faith and for not offering his suspicion as to where Jamie had gone to. In all fairness to herself, he had not been particularly forthcoming. Her overreaction had been understandable.

Did she feel better because of that?

No.

An overwhelming desire to be near him, to feel his arms around her, to have the relationship back where it was, washed over her. She found herself glancing at the pay phone just inside the deli across the street. But somehow the thought of calling up and begging forgiveness and restitution over a public phone was more than she could bear. The thought that he might not forgive her made her feel sick. Some words from a book read long ago, first in her own childhood, then in Martha's and Jamie's, skimmed through her mind: " 'I'll be judge, I'll be jury,' said cunning old Fury; 'I'll try the whole cause and condemn you to death.' "

How did it begin?

"Fury said to a mouse, that he met in the house, 'Let us both go to law: I will prosecute you . . .' "

"Guilty as charged." The words in Claire's mind seemed to come in the voice and accent of her father.

So what do I do now? she thought despairingly.

Put one foot in front of the other. How often had she said that to clients for whom the dailiness of life was unendurable.

Physician, heal thyself. Doctor, take your own medicine.

At this point, one of the reporters turning around, saw her, and the entire mob descended on her like sharks smelling blood.

She had an overwhelming desire to turn and run, but she decided instead to just push through them and not say anything. It wasn't easy. "No comment," she said. And then repeated it over and over again. There seemed an enormous number of microphones shoved in her face, and behind them and with them more faces.

"Come on, Mrs. Cunningham, it was you who put the police onto Quinn. What was he threatening you with—"

She was determined not to lose her cool, certainly not with the memory of how disastrously she had lost it only a few hours before. But not responding in kind, not yelling back, was getting more and more difficult.

Suddenly a hand slid under her elbow. "Now, now, ladies and gentlemen," Mark Hastings's voice said. "Let Ms. Aldington breathe. Please don't push. Step back . . ."

That calm, mid-Atlantic voice was having an effect. Claire saw the arms and mikes part. The demanding, intrusive voices faded a little. Gratefully, she saw the parish house steps immediately in front of her and walked up them, Mark's hand firmly on her arm. Then he was pushing one side of the big door open and they were in.

She let her breath out. "Thank you Mark. I'm extremely grateful—that's no exaggeration!"

He smiled down at her. But it did not, she noticed, take away strain in his face. "The quality of mercy is not very high with them." He looked grim for a moment. "It makes one's loyalty to a free press a little difficult sometimes."

"Yes, indeed." She hesitated, remembering what Brett had told her.

"Come to my study a minute," he said.

Mark's study faced the inner court and, when he shut the door, seemed remarkably full of peace. "I'll be glad when they finally discover who killed the dean and Mrs. Barton and we can get on with it. That sounds a little cold-blooded. Of course, we'll all be glad and hope that justice will be served. But I wish so much we could also be left alone to celebrate the birth of Christ. And I know the dean, anyway, would certainly wish that. He could be difficult and grumpy and rigid and dictatorial, but he was one of the most sincere and effec-

232   ISABELLE HOLLAND

tive Christians I have ever known." He smiled. "English style."

Claire was struggling with a temptation to tell him that she knew why the dean had come to the States. But would it be violating Brett's confidence. To play for time she said, "And I suppose that style is different from place to place—"

"And from time to time." He went over and stood in front of the window. "Having the advantage of being brought up according to two cultures has great advantages. People always tell me how lucky I was to have schooling both here and there." His voice trailed off.

"But I expect it has its problems," Claire said.

"Yes, it does. Did you ever think about that implication? Christianity is primarily based on four gospels, the Acts of the Apostles and a handful of epistles. Out of that relatively short canon we get the Christianity that exists in Italy, Spain and Greece. We also get the Christianity according to John Knox and Luther and Calvin. The one filled with images, the Virgin, the Holy Family, a pantheon of saints. In the other we get bare churches, a fierce patriarchal structure, little if any mention of any female, let alone the Virgin, and an overwhelming sense of sin. Since all of that is derived from the same canon, the differences have to be rooted in the people themselves, don't you think?"

"I don't think I'd thought about it," Claire said, trying to put her mind to the fence of his philosophical discussion.

"H. G. Wells thought about it. And it has occurred to me a lot recently when Alec came over not only with a schoolmasterly impulse to make me do what he considered my Christian duty, but also to fulfill a rather English Sense of Honour—all in capitals."

"Which was—?"

"To tell my current employers, the diocese, and the vestry and congregation of St. Anselm's that I was once of considerable interest to the Intelligence services of two continents." He turned around. "Did Brett mention it to you?"

"Yes. Last night. Or rather this morning."

"I'm impressed that he only just told you. Frequently such matters get exchanged in pillow talk far more quickly."

"Brett has a pretty acute sense of honor himself."

There was a silence. Then Mark sighed. "He—Alec—was probably right, of course. But I thought—well, I suppose the truth is that I was so turned off by the McCarthyism of the fifties that I didn't think a balanced viewpoint would prevail even all these years later."

"Yet I gather it was Brett who felt there was no reason for the dean to force your hand. Apparently Brett changed his mind from when he argued the matter fifteen years ago in England."

"Yes. I think Alec thought he—or the American Intelligence service—was exaggerating my relatively minor role in left-wing politics. But his almost mediaeval sense of honor evidently had changed his view."

There was a silence. Claire's mind kept reverting to the problem between her and Brett, and she felt she had nothing helpful to say.

Mark sighed. "Sorry about that horde outside. I know you were the one to put the police onto Quinn and I've heard various abbreviated versions from them. Could you tell me exactly what happened?"

So Claire told him about Deborah, and about Carl. "I told O'Neill about the threatening letters, but it wasn't till I went past the typewriter repair shop that I remembered I'd left my portable there and went in to get it. When I got it home I saw that some of the out of line letters were the same as those in the letters. So I called O'Neill."

There was a silence. Then Mark said, "You've met Quinn, do you think he was capable of murder?"

"In a drunken rage, yes. I think he might be capable of an act of violence like that. And he is prejudiced against the church and the clergy—even more than he had been, because he thought I'd been inciting his wife to rebellion." She stopped.

After a minute Mark said, "Is the answer then yes, you think he did it?"

Claire astonished herself then. "No, I don't."

At that point there was a knock on the door. "Mark," Adam Deane said.

"Come in."

Deane came in and said, "I'm sorry, but I have to report to you that Malcolm Richardson is missing."

13

efore Mark or Claire could reply, Deane glanced at Claire, "I just called your apartment to see if he could be there—since you had him stay before—but your son says he isn't. And he didn't think he had been the night before."

"No," Claire said. "He wasn't."

"When did you last see him?" Mark asked.

"Last night. He wasn't well and was throwing up so I put him in the sick room and told the nurse to look in on him this morning. She called me an hour ago and said he's disappeared."

Claire asked, "Did anyone see him between the time he went to the sick room and this morning?"

"Not that I can find out. Of course I've asked his roommate and the boys in his class."

There was a silence.

"How has he been of late?" Mark said. "He was upset, of course, over his mother's death and finding her body. And, after all, that was only two days ago, although so much seems to have happened since. But did it seem to get worse?" Mark turned to Claire. "How was he with you?"

"He was quiet. The only time he seemed, well excited, was right after he'd found his mother and was upstairs in the room with Adam and the nurse. Then he sort of clung to me and said over and over again that he didn't want to spend the night there and could he come home with me?"

"Well, of course," Adam said, "one doesn't really know how he may have felt either at the school or at your apartment. He could have been terribly disturbed, but you mightn't necessarily have known it."

Claire had the feeling that Adam, in casting around for an explanation for Malcolm's disappearance, was trying to put a little of the responsibility on her for acceding to Malcolm's desire to go home with her. She couldn't blame him, because what he said was true: who could know what was churning around under the surface in the little boy?

"I have a feeling," Mark said, "that Claire would have known it. She is a therapist after all, and she has brought up a couple of children."

"Well, other than the fact that he was understandably distressed over his mother's death and over finding her, he seemed to me to be otherwise perfectly normal, and if he had just stayed would probably have settled down."

"But he didn't stay," Mark pointed out, "and something has happened, so let's try to figure out what it is. You say you've talked to the boys."

"Yes, they're as puzzled as I am."

"His father?" Mark asked.

"He said he would not be home from abroad until the spring break, as I reported to you, but then we got a call saying he would be back for a quick trip this week and wanted to see Malcolm."

"Did you tell Malcolm this?"

"No, this news just came in this morning, and I haven't had a chance to tell him." Adam swung around to Claire. "Is there anything—any light you think you could shed on this?"

Claire tried to ignore the almost accusatory note in his voice. "I think I told you, or maybe I didn't, that I had the feeling that Malcolm was afraid of something."

"But what on earth would he be afraid of?"

There was another silence, then Mark said, "Of failing, perhaps. Was he in any danger of that?"

"No, his school marks were quite reasonable . . . It's true, of course, that they have not been as good of late, but I put that down mostly to his added responsibility in the choir. The fact that he might have to take over if another boy's voice broke. At least two of the boys are on the brink of that."

"Timothy," Claire said; then reminded, "I know you have much more on your mind, but I wonder if you were able to clear up the mystery of Timothy's pen."

"What was that?" Mark asked.

Claire felt rather than saw Adam's stiffening. "I'm delighted to be able to report that Timothy has reassured me about that. He was not responsible for that theft, nor for anything else that has been missing. And he was upset that anyone should think he would be." Adam turned to Mark. "Claire said her secretary had had her pen stolen, a pen very like one that Claire saw in Timothy's pocket. I'm glad to report—as you heard—that he had nothing to do with it."

"Thank you for asking," Claire said.

Adam looked at Mark. "Do you think I should notify the police about Malcolm?"

"I think so," Mark said. "He's a child, and any missing child has to be reported immediately." He went on. "I realize he might well walk in after having given you the fright of your life, but if something is wrong, I wouldn't be able to face his father if we didn't do everything possible."

Claire picked up the handbag she'd put on Mark's chair.

"You don't need me for this. Let me know if there's anything I can do," she said.

Joanna was sitting at her desk when Claire walked in. "Guess what?" she said, before Claire had had a chance to say anything. "I have my pen back."

Claire stopped and turned. "Where was it?"

"It must have rolled under some papers, because I could have sworn I looked in my top desk drawer not once but a dozen times. But there it was when I opened the drawer to get a pencil. I guess it rolled behind the envelopes I had there."

Claire walked over to her desk. "What envelopes?"

"These. Ordinary small envelopes with the letterhead on them." Joanna looked a little puzzled at Claire's question, but yanked open the drawer and waved at a serried rank of the envelopes.

"And the envelopes have been there all along?"

"Yes, they've always been there."

Claire asked slowly, "Isn't it odd that you didn't come across the pen before, then, if it was just behind them?"

"No. And anyway, I'm not going to look a gift pen in the mouth. I'm so glad it's back. I'm afraid Jimmy was beginning to think I didn't value it."

"Let me see it," Claire said.

Joanna put it in her hand. "I'm going to keep my eyes glued to it for as long as it is away from my grasp," she said playfully.

Claire turned the pen over. When Joanna was describing it, turquoise with black lines, she made it sound odd. Yet the pen was interesting and unusual. The black lines made shapes of various kinds and repeated themselves in a pattern all over the pen. Claire turned it over to read some words in small print: "Made in Germany."

"Does it write all right?" she asked.

"It sure does." Joanna squiggled on a piece of note paper. "See?"

Claire took the paper and stared at it. The lines drawn by the pen, a felt tip, were neither thick nor thin, but they were thicker than those from the usual ballpoint or even felt point and the black seemed blacker, more opaque. As she looked at it Claire remembered again the drawing that had fallen onto the marble floor of the chancel during the Eucharist on Sunday, and which had been picked up by—by whom?

It was one of the seminarians, of that Claire was reasonably sure. They had two at St. Anselm's. Both attended seminary and on Sunday did many of the jobs that fell to the clergy but also could be done by lay people. Unfortunately, though in no way related, the seminarians were not unalike, especially when viewed from the back in identical black cassocks and white surplices. Both were young men, both were of medium height, both had brown hair worn rather long, and both were of ordinary build. From the front their faces were quite different. But she hadn't seen them from the front.

Because they were at school during the day, she would have to wait to see them until this evening when they would be on hand for Vespers. When they were here, where did they hang out, so to speak?

Claire heard herself saying, "Take calls, Joanna, I'll be back in a couple of minutes."

I must be crazy, she thought, but a sense of urgency was gripping her. Going to the elevator, she pushed the DOWN button and waited for it to arrive. Eventually it wheezed up and she got in. She had no idea where to begin her search, but she had a vague recollection that the seminarians shared some kind of cubbyhole off the big basement room where they kept their books and other things that they didn't need down at the seminary.

Claire glanced at her watch as the elevator went down. Nine-thirty. Her conversation with Mark had taken longer than she had realized. She was reasonably sure that the homeless would be gone by now. Still, she didn't want to seem to intrude on them.

But the beds had been folded and stacked at one end of the large room and the table that was used for coffee and buns pushed against the wall. Claire could see the coffee urn was washed and the cups placed upside down ready for use again that night.

But although the area was cleared of its shelter function, there was still other activity going on. Various tables and chairs had been set up that morning and the materials for a Christmas pageant were in evidence: paste, paper, ribbons, scarves, mock robes and so on. Normally the room would have looked enormous, but with all the paraphernalia involved in Christmas shows, carol sings and other popular Advent activities it looked abnormally crowded.

Claire found herself hurrying across the room, so much so that she tried to slow down and when she seemed unable to do so, attempted to figure out what she was hurrying from. It was then she acknowledged to herself her odd feeling that she was being watched.

What rubbish, she said to herself, and despite her anxiety, smiled a little. It was the kind of thing an English friend of hers was given to saying, along with, "You must pull yourself together. . . ."

She didn't feel at all pulled together. What she felt was upset and anxious over Brett and worried over what his feeling for her—if there were any left—would be when she next saw him. She also felt bitterly ashamed of her outburst.

Don't act out! How often had she said that to clients, on the edge of blowing up in one way or the other? How remote she had often felt from their lack of control! It had been so long since she had experienced the same . . .

She turned down a short hall and found herself in the seminarians' quarters. In the room were two desks, two chairs and piles of books and papers everywhere. It was easy to see that the two people who used the room frequently studied there for class or exams between services.

Strolling over to one of the desks she hesitated, not entirely comfortable about opening drawers. While she was thinking about it she pushed some of the piles of papers and notebooks around and found what she was looking for: the service schedule on the back of which were the concertinalike lines, the whirled circles looking like a head, and the word "BANG!"

"Can I help you?"

It was Joe Martinez, looking, as he did three-quarters of the time, indignant. Claire wondered what he was ready to fight about now. "This isn't your office, is it?"

"I share it with Ned and Darren. There's a slight office shortage, you know."

"Joe," she said. "I don't know what you're so angry at me about. But let's bury whatever hatchet's between us. Before we do that, though, I do have a bone to pick with you. I wish to God you'd let me know that Jamie was with you. It would have saved me a lot of misery and headache."

"He asked me not to."

"All right. I understand that. And I understand why he felt he had to go. I just wish . . ." She found she couldn't say what she wanted to, which was, if you had just told me I wouldn't have threatened my marriage by behaving like such a shrew. But no, she thought. Blaming somebody else didn't help. Nobody made her behave that way—

"I found what I was looking for—this!" She held up the service schedule with the drawing on the back. "I noticed it lying in the middle of the chancel during the last service and saw one of the seminarians pick it up—I don't know which one. It's the same drawing that figures in the graffiti on the stairs. Have you noticed?"

"I can't say I have." He came over and stared at it with her. "I'm bound to say if I saw it in passing I'd wouldn't think too much about it. Why were you looking for it?"

"I don't think I would have either, ordinarily. But coming across it on the stairs, the same stairs where the dean's body was found, and then seeing it on the service schedule in the middle of the choir sort of forced it on my attention. It seemed as though it ought to add up to something. There was something about it that nagged at me."

"Like what?"

"I don't know. But that's the reason I came down here to

see if the seminarian had kept the paper or thrown it away. And maybe I'm looking for omens or portents or something, but the fact that whoever did pick it up, didn't throw it away just . . . well emphasized the general question mark." She expected Joe to sweep aside her reasoning, or lack of it. But he didn't. He took the paper from her and stared at it. "Who do you think drew this?"

"I can't cite you evidence, but the name that leaps to my mind is Timothy Bentham."

"You may not have evidence, but you must have a reason. Why that name and not—say, Malcolm's? Or any other boy's?"

She hesitated. If what Adam Deane had maintained about Timothy's innocence regarding the pen were true, then she had no right whatever even to imply that he was the thief. And even if he were, what would that prove or indicate about this drawing? Had it been done with the pen she'd seen in his pocket? The same pen she thought he might have stolen from Joanna? Any dark felt point could have made the same drawing. "I don't know," she said finally. "I'm aware of Timothy probably because Eric and Larry have talked about him, because they've publicly discussed whether or not he—Timothy —was going to get through Advent before his voice broke, because of the hubbub when it did break, because I have come to know Malcolm and know he's being—or was being— groomed for the succession, so to speak."

"What do you mean 'was'?"

She had spoken without thinking. She hadn't been told not to tell of Malcolm's disappearance and Joe would almost certainly sooner or later find out. "Malcolm's disappeared. I only learned it less than an hour ago. I was in Mark's office when Adam came in with the unhappy news."

"And nobody has any idea where he is?"

"No. Adam called my apartment, but Jamie assured him Malcolm wasn't there. His father's still abroad. I don't know where he'd go."

"This sort of puts a different face on things I guess." Joe paused. "Timothy was bullying Malcolm, you know."

"So that was it!"

"What do you mean?"

"I'd noticed a couple of times that Malcolm—before his mother's death—looked unhappy. I mentioned it to Larry, who, I think, agreed with me. And I told Adam, who got very stiff and protective about the school."

"Yes, he bridles worse than a new bride when anyone suggests that things aren't perfect over there. But I saw Timothy once catch hold of Malcolm's hand and twist it. It was a freakish thing that I did see him. Normally I wouldn't have because it took place in the boys' locker room outside the gym. But I'd gone in to speak to one of the St. Matthew's kids on the spur of the moment, and caught him doing it. I also heard Malcolm cry out."

"Did you report it to Adam Deane?"

"No," Joe said slowly. "I probably should have. But—"

"But what?"

"Timothy doesn't look like a disadvantaged child. In fact, he could pose for a poster entitled "WASP privilege." But the fact is, he comes from a broken home and there's some evidence of real abuse when Timothy was younger. His mother has been hospitalized more than once. And his father, in and out of family court, left home a year ago and hasn't been heard of since. I suppose the answer to your question as to why I didn't report it is there. I thought he had more than enough to contend with."

"Did you speak to Timothy about it? Why he was twisting Malcolm's hand?"

"Yes. He said Malcolm had caught a mouse and was torturing it."

"Did you check on it?"

Joe nodded. "Malcolm admitted it."

"I'll bet he was lying, Joe. Malcolm wouldn't anymore torture a mouse than . . . than Jamie would."

"Perhaps," Joe looked unhappy. "This was before

Malcolm's mother was killed and I—I suppose I was bending over backwards to give Timothy the benefit of all the doubts."

It was on the tip of Claire's tongue to point out that children should not be entirely evaluated by the sins and failings of their parents, but she'd had enough shooting from the hip for a year. Instead she said, "If Timothy had something to hold over Malcolm, he could get him to do and say whatever he wanted. He's far bigger and stronger."

"Yes. I suppose you're right. What should we do? And by the way, what do you think this drawing of Timothy's means? How's your Rorschach reading?"

"I don't know what it means."

They both stared at it.

"Does Adam Deane know about Timothy's troubled fammily background?" Claire asked.

"Of course."

"Did he tell you?"

"No, Eric Fullerton did."

"Where does his mother live?"

"In Ohio somewhere."

"How did he happen to come here, to this school?"

"That's not hard to figure out. There are auditions and parents bring their boys from all over the country. St. Anselm's Choir School is famous."

"Does he come from what could be called a privileged background?"

"If you mean money, no. He's a scholarship boy. I don't have to tell you that his voice is remarkable. He'd been singing in one of the Episcopal churches where he lived and the rector there suggested to his mother that he try for the St. Anselm's school, so she brought him."

"If he was bullying Malcolm, he could make life very miserable for him."

"Yes." Joe hesitated. "I wish we had some idea where Malcolm's gone."

"So do I."

. . .

Claire returned to her office upstairs and the rest of the morning was filled with her clients' appointments.

"Joanna," Claire called in between two of them, "see if you can get Deborah Quinn for me. She probably won't speak to me, but at least I can try."

Joanna dialed, listened for a minute or two, then put the receiver down. "Doesn't answer."

"No answering machine?"

"No, or maybe I didn't let it ring long enough. Do you want me to try again?"

"Yes. Let it ring half a dozen times."

Joanna repeated the process and this time listened longer. "There's no tape answering. Shall I keep listening or hang up."

Claire sighed. "Hang up, I guess. At least we tried." After a minute she asked, "How's the pen doing?"

"Okay, but I must have shoved it against something looking for it. The top is cracked."

Claire thought about that, but there didn't seem anything helpful to say except, "I'm sorry. Maybe Jimmy can get you another one."

"Yeah, maybe."

Joanna checked her watch and switched on the little transistor on her desk. A voice announced that in ten seconds it would be the hour.

"Is that gadget new in the office?"

"Yes. I brought it in when we started having our crime wave."

From the radio came a strident voice, "Malcolm Richardson, the son of the woman who was murdered at St. Anselm's this week, has not been seen since last night. Police are asking anyone who sees a boy resembling Malcolm please to report to this number immediately." The reporter read out a telephone number. "Malcolm is eleven years old, four-feet, eleven-inches tall, slight build, has brown hair and brown eyes."

Claire was in the middle of the next session when Joanna buzzed her. Claire picked up the phone. "Yes?" She knew Joanna was fully aware that nothing short of a major crisis justified interrupting a therapy session.

"Lieutenant O'Neill's on the phone. He says it's important."

"Excuse me," Claire said to the young man sitting there. And then into the telephone, "Yes?"

"I know you had Malcolm Richardson spending the night with you. Did he say anything—anything at all—that would give you a clue as to where he might be?"

"None, Lieutenant. You can be sure if he had I'd have told you as soon as I knew he was gone."

"Told me first, I hope. All right."

"Let me ask you something. Have you been able to figure out any reason why he should do this?"

"Other than a reaction to his mother's death and finding her body, I don't know. Have you?"

"Possibly." She thought for a moment. "I'll have to call you back about that."

"Listen Claire, this is top priority!"

"I know that. But it involves somebody else and I have a client in here now. I will call you in fifteen minutes," and she hung up. "I'm sorry about that," she said to the young man, who, unlike a previous client, seemed unfazed by the interruption.

As soon as he'd gone Claire dialed O'Neill, but he had either gone out or stepped away from his desk. She left her name and hung up. Then she stared out the window. Her next client wasn't due until after lunch.

Was there anything, anything at all, that Malcolm in his chattering said that might give her a clue as to where he might go when he ran away?

On an impulse she telephoned her apartment.

"Motley residence," Jamie said.

"Jamie, if you were eleven and you wanted to run away where would you go?"

"You mean like Malcolm." It wasn't even a question.

"Yes."

"Well, I'd say a friend's, except that he's in a boarding school and probably doesn't know anybody outside."

"That's why I'm asking you. If you were in a strange city and wanted to run away but didn't know anybody there, where would you go?"

There was a pause. "I guess the zoo."

"That's a good idea," Claire said, then added, "but you've always been an animal nut, I don't know that he is."

"According to Martha, it was him who asked to go to the Bronx Zoo."

"That's right! It was. Thanks!" She hung up. Then she tried Lieutenant O'Neill again. He was still away from his desk or out. Claire looked outside. It was a gray day, both damp and cold. Would Malcolm have gone by himself to the Bronx Zoo, that magnificent animal habitat in the north Bronx, one of the world's finest zoos? How much money would it take? If he went on the subway, only a dollar. But it was a long ride through some of the city's seamier and more desolate areas and not one that she would relish taking herself. But would that stop a little boy?

There was also the Central Park Zoo, recently rehabilitated and only a few short blocks across town.

Claire tried to buzz both Larry and Joe Martinez, and then remembered the noon service, featuring the English choir, would be starting any second. Both men would be lining up for the procession. So should she. She was supposed to read the Gospel in a part of the ceremony where she would be accompanied by two acolytes to the upper part of the center aisle. One of the seminarians would hold the New Testament open while she read it. Was there time to ask someone else to do the reading for her?

She glanced at her watch. Then she snatched her bag and her coat and made for the elevator. She reached the main floor just in time to see the procession start on its way to the church.

Devoutly hoping that her absence would be noted in time for someone else to be delegated to read the Gospel, she sped out the parish house door.

■ ■ ■

Moving as fast as she could, it took her ten minutes to reach the park and go through the gate opening onto the zoo. It was thronged, of course, by adults and children, since this was part of the Christmas break for all schools. Finding Malcolm would not be easy.

Looking carefully into the face of every child she passed, Claire made her way around the central building to the seal's pond in the middle and stood there, her eyes moving from face to face of every boy who could look remotely like Malcolm. Unfortunately, there were a lot, and she knew she shouldn't hurry. After scanning every child, and finding none of those grouped around the seal pool in any way resembling Malcolm, she walked over to the other side, decided Malcolm was not there either, and made her way into the various other buildings. Malcolm was not, as far as she could see, in any of those.

She inspected the area where two polar bears held court. Then she went to the building which housed snakes, and there she found Malcolm, staring into the huge simulated jungle where a python was moving slowly over the floor.

Slowing down, she walked up to Malcolm and said in as calm a voice as she could, "Hello, Malcolm."

He turned, took one look at her, and started to run. But she had been prepared for that and got a firm grip on his raincoat. "No, Malcolm. No more running and hiding."

His resistance seemed suddenly to collapse. "All right."

Claire put her arm around him. "How long have you been here?"

"Hours and hours."

She thought for a minute. "Have you had anything to eat?"

"No."

"Hungry?"

He nodded his head.

She stood for a moment, her arm still around the little boy. She knew the school and the police would think she ought to take Malcolm back immediately. But there was something about Malcolm's pinched, frightened face that made her decide to at least feed him first.

"All right. They have a cafeteria here. Let's go get something. I've missed lunch, too."

They repaired to the cafeteria, with Claire in something of a quandary. She felt she should call the school and O'Neill to tell them Malcolm was safe with her. But she didn't want to leave him for a moment. He still looked white and shaken, and she had no certainty that he wouldn't just take off. So she got two trays and some knives, forks and spoons and shepherded him into the cafeteria line. "Now, what would you like to eat?"

"Ice cream."

She smiled a little. "Anything first?"

"Peanut butter and jelly."

Keeping him in front of her and staying close to him, Claire took him into the line, let him choose his favorites and selected for herself coffee and a cheese sandwich. Then she looked for and found a table within sight of a pay phone.

While they were in line Claire had managed to scribble a message and a phone number on a piece of paper. When she had paid for their food and gone to their table, she stopped one of the busboys and gave him a dollar, a couple of quarters and the paper. "Would you please go to that phone, call the number on there and read that message. It's very important. When you've done that, come back to the table here and I'll give you another two dollars."

"We're not supposed to call while we're working. Not out

here. We can use one of the phones in the back if we're on a break."

Claire had been in New York too long to be that trustful. "It only counts if you use that phone. If any of your bosses gives you a hard time, send him or her over to the table here and I'll explain."

"All right," he said ungraciously.

Claire watched him closely while he dropped the quarter and punched out the number. Then she saw his lips move and he turned and stared at Malcolm. Then he hung up and came back.

"He said the kid here was missing."

"That's right. What else did he say?" Quickly she put out a hand and grasped Malcolm's wrist. "It's all right, Malcolm. Nobody's going to hurt you."

"They said they'd be here right away."

"Thanks." She handed over the other two dollars.

When he had gone she said to Malcolm, "Eat your lunch. If you don't, your ice cream will melt."

Apathetically, he picked up the sandwich. She let him eat most of it before she said in as even a voice as she could, "Why did you run away?"

He didn't say anything. Then, "I didn't feel like being in school."

"Had something—or someone—frightened you?"

"No." He said it so vehemently that Claire decided it would be less than useful to pursue that directly. She let him finish his peanut butter and jelly, then asked casually, "Are you and Timothy good friends?"

"Yes," he said, but his face looked even more frightened.

"Mr. Martinez said he saw Timothy bullying you."

"No. Anyway, it was because I had tortured a mouse." He was staring at his ice cream.

"Somehow a boy who likes zoos doesn't strike me as someone who'd torture a mouse." She stared at the ice cream, which was beginning to look very soft. "You'd better eat that before it melts completely."

"I don't want—" He looked over her shoulder. She turned around and saw Adam Deane and Lieutenant O'Neill approaching their table. Then she looked back and knew that for one moment Malcolm had considered running.

"It'll be all right, Malcolm," she said, and was angry at herself because she knew that, to a frightened boy, the words meant nothing.

"Malcolm," Adam Deane said gently, "I'm very glad to see you here. We were all very frightened."

Malcolm stared back at him, but said nothing.

"Why don't we all go back to the school," O'Neill said, "or go to the precinct if that's better, and talk."

"I don't think the precinct's a good idea," Deane said firmly. "And anyway, Malcolm has a job to do this evening, don't you, Malcolm? The annual carol service."

Claire, her eyes on Malcolm's face waited to see any indication of more reluctance or fear. But there didn't seem to be any. He looked almost resigned. "Yes," he said. "All right."

As he walked off, his arm firmly held by Adam Deane, O'Neill waited for Claire.

"Why did he run away?" he asked.

"I don't know. Joe Martinez, one of the priests, said that he was being bullied by one of the older choir boys. But, in all truth, it may have nothing to do with that. Just general depression after his mother's death and all that followed. Did Deane give you any idea of why he thought Malcolm had run away?"

O'Neill shrugged. "The thing with his mother and finding the body."

He and Claire followed the others out of the zoo, then he said suddenly, "The kid looks to me like he was scared of something."

"Yes. I think so, too, although I thought so more when I took him home. Right now he just looks numb."

"Do you have any idea—any at all—what he might be scared of, if he is—that is, if it's not just upset about his mother?"

Claire sighed. "The other boy is a kid called Timothy Bentham. Good looking, almost fourteen, quite tall for his age and well developed. His voice broke recently and Malcolm was being groomed to take over some of his solos. Whether that's still on or not I don't know. Malcolm's missed a few rehearsals and Eric Fullerton, the choir master, is a bug about the boys not missing practice."

"Why was he picking on Malcolm? Any particular reason, not that a natural bully needs a reason."

"I don't know."

"Okay, you don't know. But do you have any ideas on the subject?"

"Yes, but they're totally without proof."

"Tell me."

Claire told him what Joe Martinez had seen in the boys locker room outside the gym and Timothy's claim that he had caught Malcolm torturing a mouse.

"He doesn't look like an animal torturer to me," O'Neill said. "Not that you can tell by looking at somebody."

"No, nor to me. But when Joe asked Malcolm about it, Malcolm said yes it was true."

"Do you believe it?"

"No. I have no evidence to support this, but I'm much closer to thinking that Timothy has so frightened Malcolm that the latter will say anything he's told to. And," she went on, "there's one other thing." She told him about the drawing and the thefts, especially the theft of Joanna's pen. "Those pens come in dozens of the same editions. It's entirely possible Timothy's godmother did give him a pen exactly like the one Joanna's boyfriend gave her. Adam firmly believes Timothy's telling the truth. But if he isn't, it would explain the person who got into the office and scared me half to death."

"Show me the drawing when we get back. Do you have it?"

"Back in my office. Why are you so interested? You've got the dean's murderer, haven't you?"

"A lot of circumstantial evidence says so. But there isn't a shadow of a reason why he should have killed Lavinia Barton. Maybe I'm too fond of neat explanations, but I'm not entirely happy with our current solution to the crime."

When they got back Claire found her next client sitting in the waiting room. "I'll be with you in a minute," she said and glanced hurriedly at her watch. She was a minute and a half late. When she came out she was carrying the service schedule with the drawing on its back. "The other drawing—the one on the stairwell—is just a larger version of this. Here." And she handed it over to the lieutenant.

∎ ∎ ∎

To make up for her absence at the noon Eucharist, Claire was asked to read the First Lesson at the Carol Service, scheduled to begin at five-thirty, one of the best known and loved of St. Anselm's services. Year after year, the church was packed fully a quarter of an hour before the beginning of the service and people stood in rows in the back. All the traditional carols were sung, plus several by the choir alone. Because the service was long, the sermon was nearly always extremely short, a factor, Claire thought, that probably added to the service's popularity.

The procession, of which Claire was a part, marched in to "O Come All Ye Faithful," with verses sung in both English and Latin and a descant with the next-to-last verse. The beginning of the procession was so far ahead, Claire could not really see the choir boys until she was in the stalls, and then, because she was seated behind three rows of men and boys, could only see the faces of the half who were confronting her across the chancel.

After "O Come All Ye Faithful," they had a traditional English carol sung by the choir, then the First Lesson.

Claire squeezed past Larry and went to the lectern. As she moved out she had an immediate impression of Christmas candles and decorations. Then she was at the lectern. Just before she started reading she looked up, and stopped. About ten pews back was Brett.

An absurd happiness seized her. Common sense, to say nothing of modesty, would indicate that he had come to the service because he had once been a senior member of the vestry and always came to the Carol Service. Nevertheless, she felt a stab of joy and had to stop herself from smiling. Sounds of restlessness behind her and from the congregation made her realize she had been standing there, silent. So she hurried into her reading and when it was over went back to her choir stall. Larry gave her a searching look as she passed. "Everything all right?"

"Yes," she said happily.

She didn't know how much later it was that she became aware that Timothy was not with the choir. "Timothy's not here," she said.

"Not after his voice broke," Larry whispered back. "On the continent, in France, they'll sometimes sing alto after the voice has changed, but not in England and not here."

Claire found herself wondering what Timothy would be doing and how much he missed being the leading soprano and the center of attention.

At that point everyone stood to sing the carol "Once In Royal David's City," and Claire waited with pleasure to hear Malcolm's voice in the descant.

But when it came, beautiful as it was, she didn't recognize the voice. "Is that Malcolm?" she asked Larry. She knew Malcolm was not in the stalls across the chancel. But because, unlike Timothy, he was too small for her to see over the male choristers on her own side, she couldn't be sure whether he was there or not.

"No. I don't think he's singing this afternoon."

"Are you certain?"

As well as being rotund, Larry was quite tall, so he had no trouble in making sure. "Malcolm's not on either side. Why?"

Claire didn't feel up to explaining the entire afternoon in whispers while the rector was delivering his sermon, so she simply shook her head and whispered, "Later."

Either Mark had decided not to be brief this evening, or

something had happened, Claire thought, to her sense of time. The sermon seemed to drag on and on.

Why wasn't Malcolm there? His voice hadn't broken, so even if he had not been up to singing the solos in the old music and the descant, he surely would still be singing.

An overwhelming sense of something being very wrong gripped Claire.

Don't be so melodramatic! she scolded herself. Why must there always be something wrong? But her fear wouldn't go away. Something is happening, she thought. She tried to force her attention back to the church, the choir (but that made it worse) to the fact that Brett was out there in the congregation to Mark's seemingly endless sermon. But it was no use. Suddenly she got up, slid out of the choir stall at the end near the altar, made a brief bow of the head and hurried into the hall leading from the coffee room. Once there she stopped. Then, as though by prearrangement, she slipped down another hall, turned and opened the door marked STAIRS.

She stood for a moment with the door open, looking up towards the stairs between the third and fourth flights.

She heard a boy's voice, alto, strong. "You told your mother about me, that's why I had to kill her, just the way I'm going to kill you."

"Please, Timothy, I promise, I promise. Please don't—" And then there was a cry that tore her apart.

Picking up the skirts of her cassock she ran up the stairs, two at a time, grateful for having on the low, crepe soled moccasins she had gone to the zoo in.

As Claire turned into the next flight up, Malcolm came tumbling down towards her, his face streaming with blood. She caught him, almost falling herself. But she managed to maintain her balance and looked up.

"I knew I'd have to get you, too," Timothy said, his boy's voice sounding as ordinary as though he were saying he was going to the movies. "You guessed, didn't you? About the dean."

"What I don't know is why."

"Because he had come into the room when I was getting some money out of one of the secretaries purses. He went all over holy and said he would have to report me immediately. I said I wouldn't let him. He didn't believe me. He treated me like I was a small child—the nerve! I kept backing him down the hall to the stairs door. It was only a few feet. After that, it was easy. And Malcolm, stupid Malcolm, who had found some of the things I'd stolen, told his mother. That's why I had to get her. I watched her and watched her until she came over to the school and that stupid woman left her alone." He smiled, that same boy's angelic smile she'd seen before. "Now I'm going to get you."

Claire noticed then what he had in his hand—a heavy tape dispenser. "Is that what you killed the dean with?"

"Yes. Handy isn't it?" He hurled himself down the stairs, his hand holding the dispenser raised.

There was no way that Claire could carry the half-conscious Malcolm to safety. They were trapped. Raising her voice, she screamed as loudly as she could. Would anybody be in the parish house? Were there any custodians, secretaries, cleaners still there?

The noise jarred Timothy for a moment. Then he smiled, the same golden smile she had seen before. "That won't do any good. Nobody'll hear you."

"Oh yes, I think they will," Brett's voice said, and reaching down from the steps above Timothy he grasped the boy's fist in his hand. Timothy turned, but Brett held him easily and at that moment there was a noise below and Claire heard O'Neill's shout behind her.

"Drop it, Timothy! We know what happened back home. We understand. Now, come on down."

The golden smile vanished. "I'm not crazy!" Timothy screamed. Then, almost pathetically, he started to cry like a small boy.

Claire looked down at Malcolm, crumpled on the step at

her feet. He seemed wide awake, and while there was a slash on his head, it didn't seem particularly deep or dangerous.

. . .

"How did you find out about Timothy's past illness?" Claire asked O'Neill later, as they were all sitting in Mark's study.

"I took the drawing back and showed it to our police psychiatrist. He suggested I try and find out if Timothy had ever been treated for a psychological disorder. Deane seemed reluctant at first, but finally said he'd call the rector from the parish in Ohio. Then he called me back pretty quickly. Timothy was institutionalized more than once several years ago, but the treatments seemed to help and he did improve. But there were still those who felt his behavior might deteriorate once more, especially at puberty."

"Why didn't he tell Deane before this?"

"Timothy's mother had begged him not to. She said she was sure Timothy would be all right if he could get away from home and his abusive father."

"It's a pity two people, and, possibly, a third," Brett took hold of Claire's hand, "paid for that softness of heart—and head."

"Yes," Mark said. "It's that fine line, not always easy to find, where compassion becomes idiocy."

"Is Malcolm going to be all right," Claire asked.

"The doctor says he'll be fine. I think he already seems better knowing Timothy has been stopped, and he's looking forward to his father's arrival."

"Poor little kid," Claire said. "I hope he'll be able to sing his solos now."

"Eric plans for him to take some of the solos at the Christmas service."

Claire turned to O'Neill. "What's going to happen to Carl Quinn? He's not, after his arrest and all, the murderer."

O'Neill rubbed his head. "Yes, I'm not entirely happy about that." He glanced at Brett, "Nor about . . . well about giving every indication that we suspected you, Mr. Cunningham. I'm sorry. But we certainly weren't wrong about Quinn's sending the anonymous threatening letters, and that *is* against the law."

"After all," Brett said, "you were under great pressure, because of who the dean was."

"Pressure hardly describes it! The commissioner on the phone every day, to say nothing of the mayor and the British ambassador. However, I'm not sure pulling Quinn in was such a bad thing for him. After a couple of days in jail, a gigantic hangover and all the horrors of withdrawal, Quinn is realizing, I think, for the first time, how serious his drinking problem is. When I last saw him, he said that if he could ever clear himself of the murder he'd head for a rehab."

"I hope so, for Deborah's sake. Has Carl actually been let go?"

"Oh yes. I called the precinct from the office here."

"Then I'll get in touch with Deborah tomorrow."

There was a silence.

Brett looked at Claire. "Ready to go home?"

Her heart gave a wild skip. "Yes, I am."

. . .

When they were outside trying to hail a cab she said, "Brett. I'm sorry for being such a jealous shrew. I'm sorry for calling you a bastard. I promise never to do it again."

"And I'll try not to be such a stuffed shirt."

Claire took a breath. "I realized, after you'd left, it was Lavinia more than anything. She was such a stunner. I suppose I felt sure I couldn't compete."

"And I was so muzzled by not being able to talk about the dean and our disagreement, and why I'd been involved in the whole political thing, I couldn't seem to be reassuring about Lavinia. I was dumb about it."

"Were you in love with her?"

"When I was very young. For about a week. That's all it took for me to go fleeing in the opposite direction."

Claire looked around at the street with its lights and

wreaths and listened to the carols pouring out of every store. "It's going to feel like Christmas after all, with Jamie home. Maybe if Malcolm's father arrives in time we should invite the two of them over."

"That sounds like a good idea," Brett said. "And to complete our joy—here's a taxi."

"Now," he said, as they got in and he gave the driver their address. "Let's turn to more important matters."

He put his arm around her and pulled her to him.

The cabby—a different one this time—looked in the rear-view mirror and grinned approvingly.

ABOUT THE AUTHOR

Isabelle Holland was born in Switzerland, the daughter of an American diplomatic officer. She was educated in England and the United States and spent a number of years in publishing before turning to writing as a career. She is the author of more than a dozen suspense novels, including four earlier novels set in St. Anselm's parish, and has written a number of books for young readers. She lives in New York.

BOOK MARK

The text of this book was set in the typeface Goudy Old Style by Berryville Graphics, Berryville, Virginia.

The display was set in Carolus Roman by Boro Typographers, New York, New York.

It was printed on 50 lb Glatfelter, an acid-free paper, and bound by Berryville Graphics, Berryville, Virginia.

Designed by Anne Ling

M
HOL

7 day

Holland, Isabelle

A fatal advent

$16.95

DATE			